Hop in Then!

Hop in Then!

Ulla Bolinder

Translated from the Swedish by

Eric Swanson

in collaboration with the author

Originally published in Sweden as *Hoppa in då!*

by Anamma, Gothenburg, 1998.

© Ulla Bolinder 1998

English Translation © Eric Swanson 2016

Cover photos: DigitaltMuseum, Upplandsmuseet

Publisher: BoD – Books on Demand, Stockholm, Sverige

Print: BoD – Books on Demand, Norderstedt, Tyskland

Second edition

ISBN: 978-91-7569-502-0

As long as a person

has not felt his pains completely,

he cannot give up hope.

Arthur Janov

Wednesday, 1 January 1964

Dear Diary! No, I'm not going to start that way, because that's ridiculous. In any case, it's a new year and 1964. What could this year hold in store then? Well, that remains to be seen! That's partly what this book will be about. I haven't made any New Year's resolutions, because you can never keep them, but I have the intention to try to be more diligent in school this semester.

Yesterday, on New Year's Eve, I was with mamma and papa at Stig's and Anita's. What E-L did, other than that she went into town, I don't know, because she hasn't called yet.

Tomorrow is Saturday. My best friend and I are going out then. We usually go first to the cinema and then to Svartbäcksgatan. That's the street in Uppsala where the guys called *raggare* drive their cars up and down looking for girls. But we are not *raggarbrudar*, because we never go in big American cars. We only ride with guys in common cars. And it's so wonderful to walk there and wait for what will happen. I will probably never get tired of it. But Kicki would just as well go dancing if I wanted to. She comes with me just because she prefers to be with me. If she didn't, I would go alone, because I want nothing else than to go into town. Besides, I cannot dance.

Sunday, 5 January 1964

I have a cold, so I stayed at home yesterday evening. But E-L went out, and then she saw Håkan with a girl in Tre Liljor, she said today when she called. She saw them through the window when she passed the restaurant.

And you should have been able to figure it out, that he has been out with others the whole time. He is older than we are (he is 21 and we are 15), so it isn't strange that he is out and about. The strangest thing is rather that he wanted to meet us, I think now. He phoned and even wrote a letter to E-L. We were both interested in him, but it was E-L who was the winner. I was with his friend, Becke.

I remember how cosy I thought it was the first time we met them, when we drove in Håkan's black PV to Norrtälje where Becke lived. It was Advent and they had turned off the ceiling lights and lit living candles, and outside it was dark with snow on the street, and everything felt so moving and nice.

We had coffee and smoked, talked and listened to music. And Håkan wanted to dance, but E-L cannot dance (she believes), so he danced with me instead. He was dressed in a narrow-striped nylon shirt, which he had rolled up at the sleeves, and black pants and was very attractive, I thought. I preferred him to Becke, but I let Becke kiss me when I sat on his knee in the armchair.

(Håkan had laid hands on the bed with E-L, although it was Becke's residence.)

They gave us a lift back to Uppsala, and I wasn't home until twenty minutes before two. I'm supposed to be home at twelve if I'm not out dancing, in which case I'm allowed to be out until one. (That you can leave the dance earlier for a little hanky-panky, they evidently don't have in mind.)

In any case, I should have been home at midnight, but I didn't come until twenty minutes before two, and papa was awake and came up to me and gave me a cuff on the ear. "Aren't you supposed to be home at midnight?" he said. And actually, I am, so I didn't think it was unjustifiable that he was angry. I understood that he had been worried, and I didn't think it was wrong that I had gotten that cuff. He was sober, so it was really nothing to get hung up on.

Afterwards, I was not allowed to go out on Sunday or the next weekend either, and I had to promise not to come home that late again.

I got a letter from Örjan, the guy I was with on New Year's Eve. He wrote the following:

Hello, Eva-Lena! I heard from Göran that you had been visible in town and thought therefore to drop you some lines and explain what happened on New Year's Eve. I hope you didn't take it too seriously, because I didn't. The fact is, that I'm going out with a girl down here in Göteborg. It was perhaps wrong of me to meet you on New Year's Eve, but I don't believe you took it so seriously.

I have almost managed to stop smoking, but I do have a puff now and then. I advise you to quit while there is still time, both smoking and guys, so you aren't going astray with alcohol and other things. I don't believe so, but, but... Finally, I hope that you feel well and that you aren't annoyed with me. Greetings, Örjan.

What was he thinking? That he made such a strong impression on me that I would never be able to forget him? He didn't do that. I would rather have been with his friend, Göran, who was also with us, and whom I'm acquainted with since before. But I felt odd when I read that he was afraid that I may go astray.

I have been in love with Göran – or if I still am – but on New Year's Eve, when he was drunk and together with two girls at the same time, I thought he was disgusting. He came out to the kitchen with messy hair and his shirt outside of his pants. "Time for a new round!" he said and rubbed his hands, before he threw himself into the room with those girls again. It's bad form to be with two girls at the same time, I think. Kicki thinks so too. "Such a guy you take a dislike to," she said when I told her what he had done.

On Sunday I was out again. On my way to Svartbäcksgatan, I met a middle-aged man who took me for a whore. "How much do you want?" he said. "Fifty *kronor*?"

Is that well or poorly paid?

There weren't many cars out, and at first none stopped. Later a single guy in an Opel Rekord came and asked if I would like to ride with him. His name was Bert and he was nineteen years old. When he had driven up on Slottsbacken, he began to paw me. He had dirty fingernails and reminded me of the guy I was with the first time Kicki and I rode with some guys we didn't know, when we were disappointed because Göran and his buddy didn't want to meet us anymore. That guy was also rough and also had brown hair and sideburns.

Bert kissed very disgustingly. When I didn't let him stick his tongue into my mouth he said:

"What the hell is it? Are you prudish?"

He was to go dancing, but I didn't want to come along, so he let me out of the car in the street again.

Later a guy called Ludde stopped, and I went with him even though I didn't feel like doing that, either. He just says a lot of things that aren't true. He said that he was in love with me and had thought of me every day since the last time we met.

"But I became so jealous when I saw you ride with another guy the next evening, that I decided never to meet you again."

He's just bluffing and exaggerating.

I got a lift home from a guy in a Volvo Sport. He was

going to take part in Roslagsvalsen, the motor rally, on Saturday, he said. Between his thumb and index finger he had three black dots that mean faith, hope and charity.

Sunday, 12 January 1964

Yesterday, E-L and I were in town, but nobody stopped and asked us. We were so mad at the guys who didn't want to pick us up. On top of that, it was so cold that you could freeze your butt off. That's the disadvantage of hanging out in town. If you go dancing, and are not asked to dance, you don't have to freeze and aren't as dependent on what the boys do or do not. E-L, for example, must have someone who gives her a lift home, if she doesn't want to walk all the way (and of course she doesn't). But I can take the bus home if it isn't too late.

In any case, we were so mad at the boys who just cruised there to and fro and stared at us. If they notice that nobody picks you up, they conclude that you are nobody worth having and don't stop. It's exactly the same as when you are out dancing, that if a girl is not asked to dance from the beginning, and gets to dance most of the time, she becomes a wallflower. She receives a stamp on her that she isn't worth being asked to dance.

And that's how it is in town, as well. But then the next evening, although there are about the same boys who drive there, and although they recognize us, it can be completely different.

Yesterday evening it wasn't that many degrees below freezing outside, but you get cold when you stand and walk for several hours. E-L had her black skirt and a black, long-sleeved sweater under her coat, and I had my green skirt and rust brown cardigan with collar.

My coat was the one with the big rabbit collar, and I think it's rather nice, because it's a little styled in the middle. I have a brown coat also, but that one isn't as good. It is straight, and it's like a shawl in the same cloth that sits attached to the coat and which you can sling around your neck and up over your shoulder. Actually, it doesn't suit me, so I don't like it as well as the black one.

For the black coat I have a gray fur cap, which is in the same style as the collar, but it's so big, so I usually never use it. I don't want to have a cap. I would rather freeze. It's possible that I have a shawl sometimes, but I rarely use it at all.

Yesterday I didn't have anything on my head, and on my feet I had my black boots with high heels and with scarcely any lining and thin nylon stockings. Once I chilled one leg above the knee and a bit into my thigh, so now, when it's cold outside, it becomes red and starts to itch there.

Monday, 13 January 1964

School has begun again after the Christmas vacation. The only fun about it is that E-L and I can see each other more often again. Otherwise, I'm not especially excited. The fact is, that I'm a little lazy in terms of actual school work, even though I don't regret that I have continued to study.

When we went to the sixth grade, you had to decide if you wanted to continue in the comprehensive primary school, that was new then (it was new that you should go nine years instead of eight), or if you would like to apply for entrance into some other school, and then I applied to the girls' school, because when mamma and I discussed it with my form mistress beforehand, she recommended it.

And I was admitted to it and wound up in the same class as E-L. That's how we met and fell in love. (That was before we had begun to be interested in the opposite sex.) We talked and called, exchanged notes and wrote letters. We still do, but not as often as before. Then boys came into the picture, and that's when the seriousness of life began! No, but then we became more concentrated on them than on each other.

Yesterday we went to the movies first, to a Danish film called "The Buck in Paradise", and then we went to Svartbäcksgatan looking for boys. But there was none that stopped. I took the bus home, and E-L got a lift from a guy in a Saab, she said today.

Once Siv, who is in the same class as Kicki and me, was kicked out of a dance hall because she was drunk, and sometimes she comes to school with big hickeys on her neck, so I don't think she has any cause to look down on Kicki and me just because we walk on Svart-bäcksgatan. Today, when I met her and some other girls in the schoolyard, she said: "Hi, *raggarbruden*! Are you going to be picked up tonight?" And another time, she came up to Kicki and me and said: "What are you going to do tonight? Are you going to the movies or are you going to go out dancing?" "Going to the movies," Kicki said. "You are not going to ride in a *raggarbil* then?" Siv said.

But to be drunk and kick up a fuss so you are thrown out of a dance hall is worse than riding with guys you don't know, I think. When you go dancing you don't know the guys either, before you have danced with them. And the guy has maybe a car and drives the girl home, and then you can easily figure out what they do before she gets out. So, what's the difference? The only difference is that we don't dance with the guys first.

Saturday, 18 January 1964
Today E-L and I cut gym class and went to Café Regent and had coffee. I have become really clever in writing mamma's signature on my absence card. E-L just tells

her parents to sign for her when she has been absent from a lesson, because she has such discipline over them in that way, but I don't have it over mine, so I have to carry on falsifying.

Actually, I can't afford to come along with E-L to go for coffee as often as I do. I get 50 kronor every month, and that's supposed to be enough for stockings, coffee, cigarettes and the movies. (Not for the bus, because I have a bus pass, and they pay for it at home.) But the money isn't enough, because it costs a lot for cigarettes, and then coffee and the movies. Sometimes I go out with E-L at Tempo for lunch also, even though I can eat for free at home.

When we were at Café Regent we talked about a girl in a parallel class who is pregnant. To be pregnant at that age, isn't anything you wish for yourself. But as long as you are a virgin, you don't need to worry about it. And I intend to wait with both sex and children until I have met Mr. Right. First you are together a while, then you get engaged, then you marry, and then it can be time to start thinking about children. I wouldn't wish to be pregnant until I'm mature enough for it and feel that that's what I want. I want it to be planned.

But I will probably not wait to be intimate until after the wedding, because that would be difficult if you are in love. So you may become pregnant even though you aren't ready for it. In that case, you must try to make the best of the situation. You can, for example, go to Poland

and have an abortion. No, I wouldn't do that. But I think there should be abortion rights for everyone in Sweden as well.

Tonight I'm supposed to go with mamma and papa to visit their friends Gunnar and Viola. We will stay overnight, because they are going to have a party (and then you know what you can expect). Viola usually drinks about as much as papa and Gunnar, because she is stout and tolerates it, while mamma, who is small, drinks a lot less.

But everyone gets affected. And meanwhile, I get to lie in the room next door and listen to how they laugh and roar. They don't give a shit if I can't sleep. But I rather lie there, than sit at the table and watch them get drunk. I can't put up with the way mamma always becomes flirty and girlish when she drinks. I react physically to it and I almost feel sick.

But I don't ever say anything. I just withdraw and become like some kind of observer. I don't get involved like Anita did, for example. "Shut up!" she screamed when they became too loud at parties.

And that they later, if we are at home, have sex in the bed next to me though I'm awake, I can't stand, either. They probably think I'm asleep.

I have bought a pink, long-sleeved sweater for 22.50 *kronor* at Hennes, and I had it on when I went to town last night. With it I had my black, tight skirt and white cardigan.

Kicki was supposed to go away with her parents, so I went out alone again, and there were quite a lot who stopped. First came a single guy in a DKW, afterwards two guys in a Vedette, and then three draftees in an Opel. Finally, I rode with two guys and another girl in a Dodge.

In the fall, when Kicki and I started going out, we said that we would never ride with guys in real *raggarbilar* and never with those who have alcohol, but now I have done it, although they didn't have any alcohol. The guys were called Putte and Becke, and it was Putte who didn't have a girl. I sat in front, next to him, while Becke and the other girl half lay in the back seat. They had a record player in the car, and it was so cosy to sit there in the warmth and ride around town and listen to music. I played "Forty Days" with Cliff Richard and "Diggity Doggety" with The Streaplers and some others that I don't remember the names of.

When we had spun around town for a while, we went off to Kohagen and drove down to the waterside. I don't believe that real *raggare* are harder than common guys and throw girls off in the woods if they don't get their way, because Putte didn't get angry though I didn't even let him kiss me. But it can of course be different.

Mostly I usually let them do it, so I don't really know

why I said no to him. I think it was because of the car. He was maybe used to getting what he wanted with all the girls he picked up, and if I let him kiss me, he might think that I was with him for everything, I thought. Though now I don't believe any longer that guys in big American cars are worse than others.

He wanted to suck a hickey on my neck. When I didn't let him do it, he drew up my sweater and cardigan and sucked one below my bra instead. Then he sat up and lit a cigarette.

"What do you think of the Pearl then?" he said.

"The Pearl?"

"Yes, the car! What do you think of it?"

"Well, it's nice, I suppose. Is it yours?"

"We own it together."

But it wasn't because he had a certain type of car I had come along, if that's what he thought.

While he smoked, he stared at me without saying anything.

"What is it?" I said.

"Do you know you are sweet?"'

"No."

"Nobody has told you before?"

"Well, yes."

"Well, then you know!"

Then he asked me if I had a photo he could have.

"What are you going to do with it?"

"Look at it and remember how sweet you were."

And I had one in my wallet which he got.

"And write your name and phone number on it," he said and put the picture with the backside up against the dashboard.

But it was enough with my name, I thought, because I didn't know if I wanted him to call. But when he asked me where I lived I told him, because he would find that out anyway when they gave me a lift home.

A little later he wanted to know how many guys I have laid.

"It doesn't matter," I said.

"Yes, I want to know."

"Why?"

"Because. Is it more than twenty?"

"No."

"More than ten then?"

"No."

"More than five?"

"Stop now."

"More than five, that is!"

"I didn't say that."

"How many then?"

He was so badgering. It was none of his business, I thought. Finally, I became almost angry and stopped answering.

In the back they had started rubbing and groaning so it could be heard over the music. Putte stared at me as to see if I understood what they were doing, but I pretended not to get it.

Then we went out. We walked down to the lake and

out on the ice. The moon shined through the clouds and brightened the snow, and everything was so cosy. Up on the road the Dodge stood black and silent with fogged up windows.

"My little Swiss nut!" Putte said and lifted me up and held me above him. He must have been really strong to be able to do that.

Then he let me down and pressed his lips against mine before I could stop him.

Monday, 20 January 1964
Saturday night E-L rode with two boys and a girl in a Dodge. A Dodge is more like a real raggarbil, _and we said before that we would never ride in such cars, but she thought it was cosy. The guy she was with was called Putte, and he wanted to see her again yesterday evening and was going to come and pick her up at the bus station. But she regretted that she had agreed to it and got off the bus earlier and went to the movies with me instead._

After the movie, we rode with two guys in an Opel. Unfortunately, they didn't come up to our expectations, so after a while we hopped out again. When we passed Nybron later, we saw Sivan and Kerstin there, in the duffel coat gang. Actually, they probably have a rather boring time, and their appearance is boring as well, with their duffel coats and parkas.

I also have a duffel coat, and I wear it to school some-

times but never when I go out in the evenings, because it's unlined and sticks to my clothing when I walk.

In the gang on Nybron there is no big difference between the sexes with regard to clothing. Not about length of hair, either, because the guys often have such half long Beatles hair. Our boys have hair more like Elvis or short.

Then a boy called Greger came with his mate and asked if we wanted to ride with them. I didn't want to, because I thought that Gunnar, or what the hell he was called, was so disgusting. I said to E-L that she had to ride with them herself in that case.

The first time we met them, we both wanted Greger, but he chose E-L, and I got Gunnar. We switched seats so that she went with Greger in the back and I was in the front seat with Gunnar. I wasn't interested in him at all and didn't want him to get closer to me. But I could see that E-L liked Greger, so for her sake I didn't reject Gunnar immediately.

And when we sat there, he suddenly pulled down his fly and threw himself over me. I had no time to react before I was half way beneath him and felt his… between my legs. I was so disgusted that I just heaved him off, and then I saw his pink, loathsome… He was a pig, that's what I thought! But on pigs you scarcely see it, so it was more like on a bull. (It wasn't like on a horse anyway, because it was something long and skinny.)

Ooh, I thought it was so disgusting! Or if it just felt that way because I didn't like him. I don't know. In any

It was wonderful to ride in the Dodge, but I didn't want to see Putte again as we had decided, so I got out a bus stop before, when the bus arrived in town. Then Kicki and I went to the movies. We saw Putte and Becke later, but fortunately they didn't stop.

The first guys we rode with, dropped us off at Fyristorg, and when we went across Nybron later, we saw Sivan and Kerstin there, hanging about with the Mods. It was obvious that they saw us, but they pretended not to recognize us, and we didn't greet them, either. A long-haired guy in a parka held his arm around Sivan, and when we went by he kissed her. It was fortunate that they saw us *there*, anyway, and not on Svartbäcksgatan. But they probably never go there.

On Drottninggatan a guy named Greger and his buddy stopped. Kicki didn't want to go with them, but I really liked Greger and didn't know what to do when they asked us, and she said that I could ride with them myself if I wanted to. And Greger badgered me. But at last I decided not to do it, because I thought it would be lousy to her.

It was fun to walk in the street and notice how all the guys stared, but nobody else stopped, and finally I said to Kicki that she could go home, because I thought it might go better if I were alone.

But nobody stopped later, either. I had to wait for over an hour before somebody came. Finally, some of the guys started to hoot and grin when they drove by and saw that I still remained there. I was mad as hell when a guy in a gray PV at last stopped and asked if I would like to go with him. He looked to be about twenty-five years old, and I don't like to ride with guys that old, but he could give me a lift home anyway, I thought, and hopped in.

From Svartbäcksgatan he drove to Stora Torget – Drottninggatan – Ågatan – Munkgatan and Sjukhusvägen and on to Studenternas. There he turned into a parking lot and stopped.

"Do you smoke?" he said and took out a pack of John Silvers and smacked some cigarettes out against the steering wheel and offered them. I took one, and he lit it and pulled out the ash tray.

It's rather difficult to smoke cigarettes without a filter, I think. The paper gets moist and the tobacco falls out. You have to compress your lips round the end of the cigarette and try to suck in smoke.

"What's your name?" he said.

"Eva-Lena."

"How old are you, then?"

"Guess."

"Seventeen, eighteen."

"No, I'm fifteen."

"Fifteen? I thought you were older."

His name was Alvar and he was a concrete worker.

"Can one have a kiss, then?" he said and put his arm around my shoulders.

His mouth tasted sour. I don't know what it was. And his tongue felt hard and disgusting.

After a while he unbuttoned my coat and tried to get closer, but it didn't work because the shift stick was in the way. Then he said that we should move to the back seat instead. I didn't want to, because I didn't know exactly what he had in mind, but finally I went along with it. And then, when we sat there, he pulled up my skirt and took out his thing and placed me over it so that it was between my thighs. I was almost shocked when I felt it, because I hadn't seen him taking it out.

"You are so fucking fine", he said and started to lift and push me up and down.

I thought he was making a fool of himself and said that I didn't want to do it, but he didn't care.

"I'm not going to be rough to you," he said. "I promise that I won't be rough!"

And after a while:

"I've got to get it! It can be done quickly. And I won't play without it."

Without a rubber, he meant. He had stuck his hands under my jumper and held them over my breasts.

"Soon I can't resist any longer!" he said.

But he had to, because I wasn't going to let him do anything more. I wouldn't have gone along with anything at all if I had known in advance how excited he would be.

When we sat in the front seat again, and he had started driving, I asked him how old he was.

"I'm twenty-eight," he said.

So, he was almost twice as old as I am. I was crazy to ride with him and let him carry on with me! But I hadn't expected him to be that excited. How could he be? Can they be turned on as easily as ever? He didn't seem to be ashamed of himself either, though he behaved so foolishly. And how could he believe that I would want to do it with him? After all, he was old and ugly.

Tuesday, 21 January 1964

It says in the newspaper that there is possibly a connection between smoking and lung cancer. In Uppsala 47.8 % of men and 28 % of women are cigarette smokers.

And papa smokes, as well as Stig. But not mamma and not Anita. Actually, I shouldn't have started, either. It was in connection with that E-L and I began to go out that I did it. Then we shared a little pack of Newports a week, because then we didn't smoke on weekdays. Now we do it both in school and when we go out for coffee, as well as on the weekends. But not at home.

Mamma and papa are aware that I smoke, and they haven't forbidden me to do it, but at least papa thinks I'm too young. And nobody wants to get sick. But if you smoke as little as E-L and I do, there is no great risk.

Right now, I'm listening to "Kvällstoppen", the radio program that ranks the week's most popular songs from worst to best. In eleventh place there is a newcomer called "Go Back to Daddy", and in tenth place is "Bossa Nova Baby" with Elvis. "Five Hundred Miles Away from Home" with Bobby Bare has gone up from seventeenth to ninth place, and "Be My Baby" with The Ronettes is still on the eighth. We'll see which one comes on first place. Last week it was "She Loves You" with The Beatles.

Today we got our math tests back, and I had seven correct answers out of twelve. I did better than E-L, because she had just three. I think that seven out of twelve is well done for being me.

Before that, when Holmberg was busy going through the absence certificates, he started to laugh and said: "Ha, ha, this one here makes me think about those at home!" Because somebody had written something that reminded him of his wife nursing their new-born son.

Ooh, I don't like him! Bearded and thin haired with such ugly steel framed glasses that he pushes up. (He grabs his nose with his thumb and long finger and pushes them up with his pointing finger.) I don't understand E-L's special liking for him at all, but I guess that she has a weakness for his style, that if you have a problem, come and talk with me.

But at first, during the first year, I thought he seemed good. I remember once when we had geography, that he sat on a school desk instead of in the teacher's desk, and I thought it looked so relaxed and cool.

But later I liked him less and less. I have such mixed feelings about him. On the one hand, I think he is funny, on the other, I think he is a bad teacher. He is too in-dulgent. When you have such a teacher, you must have discipline yourself, and if you don't, things might go to hell. But you are unable to think: Well, I'll ignore the teacher and study myself. I'll disregard him! You are not able to do that. And you would preferably have teachers who do their job.

Kicki and I were going to see "West Side Story", which recently has begun at Fågel Blå, but then we didn't, and I regret that, because if we had, it wouldn't have been the way it was later.

In the beginning, nothing special happened. At first we rode with two blockheads who just said "keep on talking, damn it" the whole time, and then with a couple of draftees who invited us to coffee out at Svista. It was later, when Kicki had gone home and I rode with three guys and a girl in a Chrysler, that it happened. The girl was together with the guy who drove and sat in front with a guy on each side, and I sat in the back with the third guy called Kent.

At first, we rode around and played records. They had "Oh, Carol", "Great Balls of Fire", and "Lucille". Then the guy who didn't have a girl was supposed to go to a buddy in Stabby, and when we were on our way there, we crashed. It was at the intersection of Sysslomansgatan and Järnbrogatan. I don't know for sure whose fault it was, because I didn't see how it happened. I only felt the jolt and heard the smash before the car stood still, and a silence came over everything.

"But what the hell!" Kent said and straightened himself up in the back seat.

We had collided with a Volvo PV. One of the front fenders and a bit of the door on the driver's side had been dented, so we must have hit it from the side. The guy in the Volvo came up to us, and Kent and the two others climbed out and inspected the Chrysler while the girl and I remained in the car. I didn't know if I should stay or go away to Svartbäcksgatan again and try to find someone else who could drive me home, but before I had decided what to do, Kent came back and threw himself into the car.

"Damn, it's cold!" he said and rubbed his hands.

"How is the car?" I said. "Is it possible to drive?"

"Yes, we'll drive you home. When the cops are done, we'll pop off."

It hadn't occurred to me that the police might come. The rear window in the Chrysler had fogged up, and I hadn't noticed the police car that had stopped behind us in the street. I became nervous when Kent started talking about them and I saw that they were there. But by then it was too late to leave, and it wasn't long before the door was opened and a policeman in a black leather jacket stuck his head in the car and asked for our names and addresses. I felt odd the whole time while he was there. It felt like I had a breathless, empty room inside me, and that feeling didn't disappear until he had left again. Then I felt disappointed.

Kent had a cold and fever. When we sat in the car at the BP gas station later and waited for a buddy of theirs to come with tools and spare parts for the car, he froze so much that he shivered with cold. He lay with his head on my lap and tried to sleep. I would rather have set off, but there were almost no cars left in town, and because they had said that they would drive me home as soon as they had fixed the car, I stayed. It was frigging cold to sit there, because it was over an hour before their buddy came, and then it took another hour to fix the car.

When Kent and I were alone for a while, he began to paw me. It seemed like he thought he was going to get to lay me, and when I resisted him he got angry and tried to force me. I don't know why I didn't leave then. I think it was because I felt sorry for him, and I didn't think that anybody else would come and pick me up if I went back to Svartbäcksgatan.

I'm so afraid that the police are going to call, so that mom and pop will find out what I'm up to when I'm out. Why didn't I leave right after the collision as I had almost decided? Then I would never have had to be involved. But I didn't think that the cops would come.

Monday, 27 January 1964

First, we were at the movies, and then we went to Svart-bäcksgatan, as usual. When we want to smoke or comb our hair, we go down to Radiohörnan and place ourselves in the entrance, because there you can go a little behind to get protection from the wind, at the same time as you have a view over the street.

E-L always backcombs her hair much harder than I do. First, she lifts some hair and scratches it together with her comb to a tangled skein, then she combs some hair over it, so that it looks flat on the surface, and if she has hair spray with her, she sprays so that it will be stiff and lie still.

And that's what she was doing when a guy in a car stopped. Or guy – I thought he looked about 40 years old, and I thought immediately that he was of no interest to us. He was by himself, also, so what had he thought?

Later it turned out that it was Alvar, with whom E-L had ridden a previous evening. I don't understand that she wanted to, but she can't be too choosy when she needs to be driven home. If she will manage to get home, she has to take what is offered.

And he wasn't 40 but 28 years old. But there must be something wrong with a guy who is almost 30 and who drives around picking up 15-year-old girls. At that age, you should have found other interests, you would think.

The evening when E-L let him drive her home, nobody else was available, so she rode with him, even though she noticed that he was old. And at first there was nothing special, but then he stopped the car and proposed that they should move to the back seat, and when they sat there, he did about the same thing to her that Greger's mate did to me, with the difference that she was sitting on his knee. He took it out and got himself excited and asked her if she wanted to lay him, or rather, sit on top of him in the car.

We rode with two guys in a Simca, and they were not too bad, actually. They said, among other things, that we didn't look like we belonged to Svartbäcksgatan. Many have said that, and I take it as a complement, because it's nice to be perceived as a good girl even though you walk there. You want to imagine that you look like you have some style, and I don't think that you can see by our appearance that we are raggarbrudar. *The other girls on Svartbäcksgatan look more that way, I think. In the way they are dressed, for example, because they use more makeup and wear shorter and tighter skirts and more high heels.*

And they are probably different in their behaviour, as well. I guess that they go further than we do (not measured in meters, but with the boys, I mean). I believe that of all the girls who walk on Svartbäcksgatan, E-L and I are probably the only ones who still are virgins.

This morning it was Holmberg, our form master and teacher in mathematics and geography, who stood at the gate, checking the morning prayers cards. I don't like it when it is his turn to stand there, because I get so nervous when I'm about to pass him. At the same time, I always hope it will be him.

In math lesson he told a funny story again. Everybody laughed except me. His darling Agneta was the one who giggled the most. I wanted him to notice that I kept serious, but he didn't. He never notices anything.

Previously, I fantasized about him, that he would come and talk with me and try to find out what was wrong, but I don't do that anymore. It's never going to be the way I want it, anyway.

Saturday, 1 February 1964

Rolle, one of the boys from last Sunday, called E-L yesterday and wanted to see her this evening. They were to go to the movies. But now E-L has changed her mind, because she didn't like him very much. She's going to tell him when he comes that she doesn't want to. Afterwards she and I will go out instead. Otherwise, I had intended to go dancing tonight or stay at home.

Rolle's friend Simon was not especially handsome, but he made an impression on me because he had volunteered to be a United Nations soldier on Cyprus. I think that's admirable. It's unstable down there, so it certainly isn't risk free staying there. And I thought we could have become pen pals if we had continued to meet before he left. But never mind! There are plenty of fish in the sea!

One day, Inger asked E-L how she gets home when she has been out. "I ride with someone," E-L said. "Yeah, it's convenient to have many acquaintances!" Inger replied. But she knows that E-L doesn't know all the boys she rides with, so she was just putting it on.

And Solan, I have understood, thinks we are terrible who do what we do. She goes out with me for dancing, but she would never take part in our activities in town (these horrible things!). Ooh, how could anyone want to do things like that? she seems to think. But it isn't nearly as bad as some people think. Why does everyone believe it is so bad? E-L and I have been doing this for… let's see… almost five months, and it hasn't hurt us at all!

On Saturday I was supposed to meet a guy named Rolle in town. When I got off the bus, he wasn't there yet, so I stood under a tree and waited.

"What are you waiting for?" I suddenly heard a voice say, and when I turned around I saw Putte there.

"A guy," I said.

"What fucking guy?"

"Nobody that you know, anyway."

Then he just stared at me.

"What is it?" I said.

"Why didn't you come the time we were supposed to meet?"

"I missed the bus."

"Sure!"

"You don't believe me?"

"Hell, no!"

"That's what happened, anyway."

"I saw you in town later!"

"Yes, and I saw you too.

"And then there were two of you!"

"Yeah, and so what?"

I didn't want to admit that I had lied to him and pretended that I didn't understand what he meant. Besides, I could very well have met Kicki when I went there later. That he saw us together, didn't necessarily mean that we had decided in advance to meet. But he thought so.

"Ride with us tonight," he said.

"No, I can't."

"What the hell are you going to do then?"

"I'll meet someone, as I said before."

"What's his name?"

"That's none of your business."

"It isn't?"

"His name is Rolle, if you really have to know!"

"Rolle Nordin? Is he the one you are waiting for?"

"I don't know his last name."

I didn't want to say more, but he kept on asking.

"A small, black-haired bastard… Is he the one you are going to meet?"

"Maybe."

"He's not fucking more than seventeen years old!"

"So what?"

"Blow him off and ride with me instead!"

"No, I won't."

"Then I'll get hold of you in town."

"Really? And how will that happen, do you mean?"

"I'll get some guys together in a car and we'll come out and get you."

"Yeah, you can always try it!"

"You don't believe I can?"

"No, I don't."

I got so tired of standing there talking back to him. Finally, I went away from him and turned my back to him. Then he said in a louder voice:

"You look like shit! How do you dare go out like this?"

I didn't want to say more, but I couldn't lay off.

"What do you mean, like this?"

"With that fucking nose!"

But there is nothing wrong with my nose.

"Why do you have to be so mean?" I said.

"Because I don't want you to love me."

"I don't!"

"Yes, you do, and you want to ride with me tonight!"

I wished that Rolle would come so that I could go.

"Is he not coming?" Putte said. "Is he not coming for his little darling?"

"Stop it now!" I said.

"You've been taken in, godammit!"

But Rolle did come. Putte had his back to him, but he noticed that I looked in that direction and turned around.

"Come on!" he said to Rolle and clenched his fists.

"What the fuck is this all about?" Rolle said and stopped.

"Come and get your bird, godammit!"

And then he jumped forward and aimed a punch at Rolle's face.

"I knew this bird long before you!" he said.

"So what?" Rolle said and looked uneasy.

But there was no fight, because Putte laid off. He probably didn't think it would be worth fighting with Rolle.

"I'll come and pick you up!" he said to me and left.

When I had told Rolle that I didn't want to go to the movies, he said that he would fetch a buddy who had a car and come and pick up Kicki and me in town later on. But we didn't wait for that. We rode with two guys in a PV 544.

Last night we went with three guys in a Ford. They were totally screwy. The guy driving, rolled down his side window and yelled at an elderly man that he thought turned round a corner too slowly:

"Are you driving on brake fluid, or what?"

And to another, who didn't get started fast enough at a stop light:

"Drive, you fucking idiot, or are you waiting for the light pole to turn green also!"

The third guy also wanted to have a girl, and when we drove by one, who was probably not a *raggarbrud*, one of the others said:

"There you have a little cutie! Let's pick her up!"

"No, that one is below the age of consent."

"Oh, what the hell? The fresher the meat, the better!"

We started to drive next to her, and the guys tried to get her to stop, but she just kept on walking without paying any attention to them. She looked dead scared.

Then they started talking about once when they had been in Karlskoga, and about the sex orgies that had taken place there. Some guys had put a naked girl on a hood, and then all of them had screwed her by turns, while another guy had walked around and collected money from the onlookers.

And there had been fist fights and uproar. One guy had been so badly beaten that blood had been spurting from him, and his face had looked like minced meat afterwards.

Finally, all the cars had driven in motorcade through town with inflated rubbers fastened to the radio antennas. They came from Stockholm and belonged to a gang that was called The Road Devils, they said, but I don't know if it was true.

Thursday, 6 February 1964

We have so much German for tomorrow that I get tired just thinking about it. First a reading in Drei Männer im Schnee, *with 25 vocabulary words included, and then a written exercise from the workbook. I wish we had Möllan still with us, because she was a good teacher. ("Guten Morgen, Mädchen! Guten Morgen Fräulein Möller. Setzen Sie sich bitte!")*

Yes, she was good! Nilsson is so dry and boring. You almost fall asleep during his lessons and don't learn anything. But he is kind, anyway.

Yesterday when we had German, I was asked to recite all the dative case prepositions, because we are supposed to know them by heart. And I know them (aus, bei, mit, nach, seit, von, zu), but when the teacher asks a question and I know the answer and would like to answer, I become so tense, and my heart starts beating faster and I'm afraid that my throat will turn raucous, so I won't be able to talk. It isn't so bad for short answers, but if you need, for example, to read a text and then translate it, it's very problematic. I'm afraid all the time that it will become difficult to speak. Sometimes, I don't raise my hand even though I know the answer because I can't rely on my voice. But I want to show that I'm able, so other times I raise my hand on every question to force myself over that threshold that makes me avoid it otherwise.

We got written lesson test in history. I had not done my homework and handed in a blank paper. I have never done that before.

The girls in class who usually go out dancing on Saturday nights, talked about going to Hemvärnsgården in Almunge to watch Hep Stars or to Månkarbo to listen to Ola & The Janglers.

But Kicki and I won't do that. We are going to town to wait for some guys to stop and pick us up. We aren't ashamed, because you don't have to be worse than those who go dancing just because you walk on Svartbäcksgatan. But we usually say that we are going to the movies if anyone asks what we intend to do.

Monday, 10 February 1964
On Saturday evening I went home early. I took a walk, and then a boy in a Volvo Amazon stopped and asked me if he could give me a ride home. Yes, of course he could, if he was so keen on it!

So, I hopped in. But, of course, he wanted to be rewarded for his efforts also, so when we got home, I didn't think I would ever get out of the car. Actually, I became a little irritated with him.

I have a thick winter skirt, discretely patterned in black and green, and that's the one I had on. It's a bit flared and has the lining sewn on the inside, and it has pockets that go in through the seams. And when he discovered those pockets, he stuck his hand down in one of them, and they are deep, so he reached long in and down between my legs and started digging. He was so blunt, to say the least, and he didn't want to let go. When I tried to get his hand off me he forced back, and suddenly my skirt came apart. It split at the seam, and I got so angry with him that he had to carry on like that. I regretted that I had let him drive me. If only I had climbed out of the car as soon as he had stopped! But you think that you should give them something as thanks for the lift. If you ride with someone, you can't give a flat refusal to every-thing, because then it's no point in going with him. And after all, that's what I want.

Kicki went home early, and I rode with a guy named Hasse in a Morris. He stopped at the square in front of Gunnar's and pulled up my bra and began to fondle my breasts. He let my sweater be down over his hands, and touched and kissed me so I became… There isn't anyone who has taken off my bra before, and nobody who has touched me like he did, so that's probably why I have never felt anything. But it was rather dis-gusting to kiss him, because he had bad breath.

We drove to his home for coffee. He lived in a room on Vaksalagatan. When we got there, he made coffee and placed cups and saucers on the table. Then he lit a candle, put on a record and turned off the ceiling light.

He had mostly old songs, like "Duke of Earl", "From a Jack to a King", "Murder She Says", "Lesson One", "Blueberry Hill" and "Be-bop-a-Lula".

When we had had coffee and smoked, he led me to the bed and pulled me down on it. I didn't know how far I should let him go, but I let him take off my sweater and bra and unbutton my skirt. He didn't take anything off himself.

It was cosy to lie there and listen to the music and feel his hands. When cars drove by outside on the street, light from the headlights came through the window and glided by on the wall. You feel so free when you can go home with whoever you want and nobody knows where you are or what you are doing. I wish the evenings when I'm out would never end.

After a while he got up to change records, and when he was coming back to bed he began loosening his belt. Then I sat up and put on my bra and sweater and said I had to go.

"What a pity," he said.

But I don't think that he really thought so, because he didn't try to persuade me to stay.

Then two guys in a Vauxhall drove me home.

Tuesday, 11 February 1964
"I Want to Hold Your Hand" with The Beatles came in first this week, also, and "Glad All Över" (no, what am

I writing?) "Glad All Over" with The Dave Clark Five came in second. In third place is "Hippy, Hippy, Shakes" with The Swinging Blue Jeans.

That one E-L likes. She likes foreign and rock'n'roll songs the best, while I value Swedish and more peaceful songs as well.

This morning I overslept and missed morning prayers. And morning prayers that I think are so fun! That's one of the best things I know about! We gather in the assembly hall and sing a psalm, then a teacher comes forward and says some well-chosen words (something half religious most often), and then we sing another psalm. It only takes about fifteen minutes, and that's simply not enough time, I think. It should be at least an hour!

No, joking aside, I don't really enjoy it. I get so upset with this, that I must go to morning prayers just because I live in town, while E-L and all the others, who live in the country, can get out of it. They all have a morning prayers card that they show to the teacher who stands at the gate. But if I come too late I get written up, and then it counts against me when it's reckoned with all my other remarks. If the worst comes to the worst, it can affect my behaviour grade. But it won't go that far, I hope.

When I was working on my English lesson, pop came into my room, placed himself by the window, and began to stare out into the darkness.

"On Saturday I hope you will stay at home," he said.

It feels disgusting when he comes into my room. It gives me the creeps and a feeling of discomfort. I become stiff as a poker and just sit there waiting for him to leave again. I don't want to listen to him, and I don't want to talk to him. I just want him to disappear.

"No, I'm going out," I said.

Why can't he just let me be?

"Don't you understand that it makes us sad when you carry on like this? Don't you understand that you force us to take strong measures when you don't want to do as we say?"

"You can't stop me going out," I said.

Because he can't, no matter what he does!

"Now you listen to what I am telling you! From now on I want you to take our feelings into account also, and not just think about your own amusements!"

He is really stupid to believe that I will care about what *he* wants, when he doesn't care about what *I* want!

"What is it, that attracts you so much? What is so urgent and difficult to abstain from?"

That's none of your damned business! I wanted to shout. Get out of here and leave me alone!

But I never dare to show him how angry I am with him. I'm so cowardly. I just sat there and tried to read my book and not listen to him. But I couldn't avoid hearing.

"You sit there in some car and have a 'good time', as

I understand it. But you should know, Eva-Lena, that neither I nor your mother aren't happy about this."

I don't give a shit! And mom has never said anything.

"Is it so boring to be at home? Is it so boring to be with us?"

It was enough to make you puke. I'm out two evenings a week and he thinks that is too much. But I will *never* do as he says!

"It's that Kicki who attracts you, I understand! But from now on, I expect you to say no thanks to her and show us that you are a proper and decent girl who can be a source of joy to us!"

He just wants me to fit in with his image of how a perfect family should look like. He doesn't care about how it feels, he just wants everything to look nice and good at the surface. But I don't give a shit about his damned image!

"You can go now!" I said. "And I'll *never* change my mind!"

Because I haven't done anything wrong. If he thinks that I am going to sit at home for the rest of my life watching TV every evening just because he wants me to, he is mistaken! I will never again do anything that will make him happy.

Kicki and I went to a café and had coffee before we began walking on Svartbäcksgatan. She had bought a new single in Fyris Radio. It was "Beautiful Dreamer" with John Leyton, and she had it with her in her purse in case we would meet some guys who had a record player in their car.

I love John Leyton's voice. When I hear him sing I thrill. "Nobody thrills me like you do!"

First, we rode with a couple of guys from Alunda, but nothing happened because we didn't go along with changing places. The guy driving was so childish. He smoked a pipe, and when he began to clean it he said:

"This hole is almost like on an old person."

And the other one started talking about when he had crashed his car, and carried on about it so you almost felt sick. He had crashed into a bridge railing and had sat trapped in the car wreck for two hours before they had managed to get him free. By then he had had blood and puke all over his body, he said. It was so disgusting. But judging from his way of telling it, it had been great.

Then we went with a couple of other guys to an apartment in Sivia. Kicki got the cutest one, and I didn't feel like being with the other one, but I wound up with him in the bedroom, which had a double bed. It was actually his brother's apartment, and he was married, so that's why they had a double bed.

He kissed very disgustingly. Fortunately, he didn't want to do much, and after a while he went to sleep. Then I got up and stood by the window and smoked. It was so cosy to stand there in the dark overlooking the street with all houses and lights and cars. I would love to live in the city and have about the same apartment as the one we were in. Then nobody could interfere with what I am doing.

Monday, 17 February 1964

On Saturday and yesterday we were out. Last night we rode with two guys in a Volvo Amazon. When we had changed places, I sat in front with the driver, and I didn't have anything against it, because I preferred him to the other one. And he was uncommon in the way that he talked a lot. He seemed to have reflected on things and talked a little about music and what love is and asked questions. We sat in the car and discussed, and everything felt so cosy in some way. He wanted to have my phone number and said he would call, and I actually believe he will.

As I lay on my bed listening to "Pop '64", there was a guy who called and asked for me, but pop didn't let me talk with him. He is so damned nasty!

"Why didn't you call me?" I said. "Why didn't I get to talk to him?"

"He didn't sound pleasant."

"But if the phone call was to me, you should have called me!"

"He didn't sound pleasant, and he wasn't sober."

That's none of his business! He has nothing to do with that!

"What did you say to him?" I said.

"I let him know what I think about young rascals like him, who call and try to make themselves cocky!"

But the guy didn't call *pop*. It was somebody who wanted to talk to *me*! And he probably got angry when pop didn't let him do it.

"What kind of scamps are you associating with, Eva-Lena? What are these 'adventures' you are having at night?" he said.

It's none of his business! Nothing about me is any of his business! And he could be a scamp himself!

He doesn't want me to go out and meet guys and have fun. He begrudges me that. But he can't stop me! The nastier he is, the less I will care about what he says. The only thing I need him for is to get food, money, and a place to live, and he has to give it to me no matter what I do.

Friday, 21 February 1964

Last night I woke up when papa came home and had been drinking. He moved around swearing and muttering to himself. "No, now damn it, they are going to get it!" And then he got into one of the kitchen drawers and took out a knife and said that he was going to "stab all those bastards to death."

Mamma was also awake, and we lay on tenterhooks in

the dark and heard how he staggered around and bumped into furniture and swore. But he never came in to us, and after a while he dropped off on the sofa in the living room.

Once when Anita was little, and papa had made a scene and acted dumb, she ran away from home. She hid in a cellar in a neighbor's house and stayed there until someone came and found her.

For my own part, I have never said or done anything to show that I'm opposed to his behaviour. I have just endured it and been sad. I was sad when he scolded Anita and hit her. But it was mamma's fault also, because if she thought that Anita had been naughty during the day, she wanted papa to deal with her when he came home, and then he gave her a beating.

When I stood in front of Strandberg's and waited for Kicki, Putte came by.

"What are you waiting for?" he said.

"For my pal."

"So you aren't waiting for Rolle, then?"

"No."

I looked at the cars sliding around the square, and Putte lit a cigarette without offering me one.

"Have you been seeing the creep lately?" he said.

"The creep?"

"Yes, the creep!"

"I don't know anybody who is called like that."
"I saw you in his car."
"When?"
"One evening."
"What kind of car does he have then?"
"A Morris."
"Oh, you mean Hasse."
"Stay away from him!"
"Why should I?"
"He's hitched up and has two kids!"
"Oh, yeah? Why is he driving around town then?"
"Because he's a creep."
But I didn't care a shit about him. And I don't think he was married. I think he lived alone in that room on Vaksalagatan.

"So, what are you going to do tonight?" Putte said.
"I don't know."
"Ride in a *raggarbil*?"
"I don't know."
I didn't want to admit that he was right, because he didn't seem to like me doing it, and it was none of his business either, I thought.

Then it was silent for a while until he said:
"Come with me to my mom and have coffee."
"But I'm going to meet my pal."
"Do you want to go with me and watch the motor race on ice in Almunge tomorrow then?"
"I don't know…"
I felt sorry for him, but you can't be with somebody

just out of compassion. I tried to change the subject
and said:

"Where is the Dodge tonight then?"

Then he got angry.

"Cars are the only thing you think of!"

"No, it isn't! I just wondered."

A light green American car with long tail fins drove
by, and when he saw it he said:

"You would give everything to get to ride in that
damn carriage, wouldn't you?"

But I don't decide who to go with just because of the
car, and I told him that.

"Sure as hell you do! Cars are the only thing you care
about! A guy without a car is *nobody* to you! Ride
about in cars is the only thing you think of!"

"No, it isn't."

"Sure as hell it is!"

"You can't know that!"

"Yes, you bet I can!"

It was impossible to talk with him. When I turned
away and didn't want to say anything more, he pulled
out a notebook from his pocket and slapped it against
the flat of his hand.

"I can call any number in this and be fixed up with
a bird in no time!" he said. "So, don't you think you're
the only one!"

"I don't."

"I can fix up with whoever I want!"

"Why don't you do that, then?"

"Maybe that's not what I prefer."

I felt sorry for him, but I couldn't go along with what he wanted anyway.

"When Kicki comes I'm leaving," I said.

"Yes, shove off and cruise, godammit! Just do it! That's the only thing you care about anyway!"

"But you do it too! Why is it wrong when I do it, but not wrong when you do it?"

"Get lost!" he said.

"Yes, when Kicki comes."

But when she turned up, he was already gone.

We went with two guys in a black Volvo Amazon. Nothing special happened. If the guys are not stupid enough to skip, and not nice enough to want to ride with again, everything becomes so boring, I think. It's a waste of time to be with them then. But Kicki doesn't mind, because she doesn't have the same desire as I have, that something must happen all the time.

Wednesday, 26 February 1964

Soon "Grammofonhörnan" with Kersti Adams-Ray will start on the radio. I usually always listen to that program.

Today I at last bought a new nail varnish. I purchased colorless, because I think it's neatest with natural nails without strong color. E-L has that light pink, mother-of-pearl shining one, and that's also neat if it's carefully applied, because it's more noticeable if it's carelessly painted. And she has such destroyed cuticles, poor girl, because she constantly picks at them. She pokes out small pieces of skin and bites them loose, so it starts bleeding sometimes.

We have eyeliner on our eyes. Now I have a pen, but before I had liquid eye liner, and it became so black, so help me God! It can't be good for your eyes, either, because it's so strong. So now I have a pen. I only make a mark down to my eyelid with a little feather stitch on the sides. I seldom do anything with the downside of my eyes, and I don't use eye shadow very often, either. If I do, I use blue. Though I once had something green and glittery. It was one of those advertising samples that I got somewhere, which looked like a lipstick in a cap.

I don't highlight my eyebrows, because I already have dark eyebrows. I think it becomes too black and sooty if I highlight them. Once papa said about my eyes that he didn't understand why I must fill them in when they are already so beautiful. And secretly I agreed with him, but I do it because everyone else does it. Though I don't use that disgusting stuff you are supposed to put on your skin. No brown cream and no powder and no rouge; I just do a little makeup on my eyes and lips.

Tomorrow night Solan and I intend to go dancing at the Star. If E-L could (or would dance, because I think she would be able to do it if she wanted to), I would rather go with her, but I don't mind going with Solan either. I feel a little sorry for her, since E-L got tired of her and started being with me instead. I'm glad that E-L prefers me, but sometimes I feel sorry for Solan when E-L is mean to her. Or, she isn't exactly mean, but grumpy.

But she can be that way to everyone. Before lunch, when she is hungry, she is almost always very grumpy and sullen. It's impossible to talk with her then. I can't do it either, but I don't worry about it, because I don't take it personally.

But in those situations, I feel a little sorry for Solan, because she takes it personally when E-L takes her bad mood out on her. Solan wants for E-L and her to go to eat, but E-L perceives Solan as a burden, and then she can be very unpleasant. But I never say: "No, now you listen, Eva-Lena, if you are going to be so bloody mean and dumb, then I'll go with Solan, instead!" I never say that, because I think it depends a little on Solan as well.

Kicki intended to go dancing, but we met for a while in town first. Then a guy came up and started talking with us. It was in the newspaper that sixteen drunks were caught by the police last weekend, and he was one of them, he told us.

"Do you think that's something to brag about?" Kicki said. Then he got surly and left. Kicki doesn't like drunk guys, and I don't either, but I would never dare to say something like that to somebody who is drunk.

When Kicki had left, I bought a hot dog at Stora

Torget and went down to Radiohörnan and smoked. After a while I caught sight of a policeman who came walking on the other side of the street. I got uptight and hoped that he wouldn't see me, but the next time I looked, he was on his way across the street in my direction. My face was like petrified when he came up to me and stopped.

"Hello," he said and stared at me.

"Hello."

"Why are you standing here?"

"It doesn't matter."

"It doesn't?"

"No, I don't think so."

He had pressed pants and his black shoes shined in the reflected light of the store window.

"Isn't it so, that you are standing here waiting for a lift?"

"No, it isn't."

I don't know why I lied, because it isn't forbidden to do that.

"I have seen you here before," he said.

"Yeah?"

"You act hard and cold and try to play tough, but I don't believe that you are that way inside."

But just because you stand in a place and smoke, doesn't necessarily mean that you try to look tough.

"Do your parents know that you are hanging about here in the evenings?"

"I don't know."

"Do you think it's difficult to talk with them?"

"Maybe."

"Do you think it's easier to talk with a policeman like this?"

I didn't know what to say and blow out smoke without answering and without looking at him. But I felt that he was staring at me.

"A young girl like you, with attractive looks and a fine figure… Don't you think it's below your dignity to stand here?"

It felt unpleasant to be observed. I didn't dare to look back at him. The only thing I saw was the sabre, or what it's called, that hung against his thigh.

"What do you usually do, when you're not standing here?" he said. "Do you work?"

"No, I go to school."

"Where?"

"At the community girls' school."

"Really? Is it common for girls from that school to hang about here?"

"I have no idea."

I squashed my cigarette butt with my foot and tried to calm down, because it's ridiculous to be uptight just because someone comes up and starts talking to you.

"Listen to my advice now and walk away from here," he said. "I know what can happen to young girls who hop into cars with unknown guys. I have opened car doors sometimes and seen…"

"Everyone is not the same," I said.

"No, but the girls are not accepted if the guys don't get what they want. Go and stand at the square instead."

"Why?"

"Because it doesn't look as bad."

"But I don't care what it looks like."

And you can't stand at the square, because nobody ever stops there.

Some guys in a car that drove by stared, and one of them held up a bottle of liquor in the back window behind the cop's back.

"If you ever have a problem, you can always come and talk, but listen to a policeman's advice now and go away from here," he said.

"No, I won't."

"You are going to stay here and wait for a *raggarbil*?"

"I didn't say that."

"But that's what you are doing, isn't it?"

It was like a frigging interrogation. Why couldn't he just go and leave me alone? At the same time as I wanted him to go, I hoped that he would stay.

"We could go to the station and continue talking there," he said. "Would you like to do that? My shift ends at…"

When he stopped himself and looked at his watch, it was totally empty inside me. I thought I had misheard. Why would I come along with him to the police station? I hadn't done anything. What would we talk about there?

But he changed his mind.

"Remember my words now, and don't do anything you will regret," he said.

And that was all. As soon as he was gone, a car with two guys stopped, and the guy behind the wheel rolled down the window and moved his head, asking me to walk up to them.

"What's up?" he said and pulled out a cigarette from a pack of Princes with his lips.

"Nothing special."

"I saw a cop talking to you? What did he want then?"

"Save me from depravity."

They wanted me to go with them and I hopped in.

Watch now, you frigging cop! I thought. Watch now that I climb into a *raggarbil*!

But he wasn't there.

The guys were called Bosse and Gurra. When we had picked up Gurra's girl, Bosse came over to the back seat and put his arm around my shoulders.

"So, you need to be saved from depravity?" he said.

Sunday, 1 March 1964

The cover charge for the Star was seven kronor, so now I'm poor again. Jerry Williams and The Violents entertained. Jerry jumped up and down on the stage so sweat just splashed from him, and I thought he was so disgusting. Ooh, how disgusting I thought he was! I didn't have anything against his singing, but I didn't like his performance style at all.

Yes, and I danced, and I was nervous, as usual. I was tense in my whole body. "You are shaking!" somebody said. "Are you freezing?" "Yes, I'm so chilled," I said, even though it was red hot in there.

Ooh, it was tough! I try to work with myself not to be tense, but it just makes it worse. It's doomed to fail. It isn't until near closing time, when I begin to be in full swing, that it disappears, but then it's too late. The ones you dance with in the beginning, don't come back when they realize how tense you are. I always hope that somebody ugly and dumb, that I don't want to dance with again, will ask me to dance first, so that I can be warmed up before the interesting ones come, but it seldom turns out that way.

So, it isn't so fun all the time! It's just as tough as in school. And it's worse to go out dancing than to hang about in town, because in the dark in the cars you aren't observed so closely.

But I do like dancing, so it's a shame that I almost can't do it. I think that dancing and music is fun. Solan and I said before, that we should start dancing in Ungdoms-ringen dance club, and that's something I actually want to do, because there you can do folk dances and high jinks, and you don't have to feel the pressure to be to your advantage all the time.

Yesterday evening, when E-L was standing in front of Radiohörnan, a police officer came up to her and asked what she was doing there, she told me today when she called. He thought she should go away from there, or whatever it was.

We decided to hitch-hike to Stockholm this evening. It was her idea, because she felt that she needs to go away someplace. And it could be fun to see how it is in Stockholm. We have talked about it before, that we should go there some time.

I can't stop thinking of that policeman. Why did he change his mind? Was it because he noticed on his watch that there wasn't time for us to talk before his shift ended, or was it because he couldn't take me in without cause? I don't know.

Yesterday Kicki and I hitch-hiked to Stockholm. We got to ride with a man in a delivery van from Bladin's Painting Company the whole way. We had intended to head to Kungsgatan and watch the *raggarbilar*, but when we got there, we went into a café and had coffee instead and sat there until it began to get dark.

Then we hitch-hiked home again. It took two hours to get to Märsta, and when we got there we were stiff with cold and just went up to the first car that came along at a gas station and asked the driver if we could ride with him. It was a middle-aged man who was on his way to Uppsala.

It had snowed a little when we were outside, and after a while the smell from our hair spray and smoke from the cigarettes we had lit filled up the whole car. It was so cosy to sit there in the warmth and see the dashboard glow in the dark and listen to music from the radio while the car hissed forward on the road.

When it gets warmer outside, we intend to hitch-hike to Stockholm again, and then we are going to walk on Kungsgatan.

Tuesday, 3 March 1964

Tonight it's "Perry Mason" on TV. I usually watch that program when I don't have anything else to do.

Yesterday Barbro said to E-L: "Do you know what the girls are saying?" (The girls in class, that is.) "No, what?" "That you and Kicki ride with guys you don't know." (Yeah right, how terrible!) "They do?" "Yes, they say that you usually walk on Svartbäcksgatan."

So obviously they talk about us in class. It's Inger and her mates, for sure, who have happened to mention that there is no bus service to E-L's home on Saturday and Sunday nights, and then the other girls have put two and two together and come up with four. (Or with sex, per-haps?)

Ooh, mamma drives me crazy! I can't stand looking at her when she sits and pulls her hair! She twists it until she gets hold of a hair strand, which she then wraps around her finger and pulls out. And it's a nervous be-haviour, so it doesn't help that I say: "Don't do like that!

Don't sit there and pull out your hair!" It only helps for
a moment, because as soon as she stops thinking of it, she
starts pulling it out again.

They are perhaps going to tear down Järnbron. If they
do, Järnbrogatan will be called St Olofsgatan instead,
and the new bridge they build will be called St Olofsbron.

Last lesson Kicki and I skipped school, and she came
along with me to look at shoes. We went to Öberg's
on Svartbäcksgatan, and a salesclerk brought me some
shoes that I tried on. There was a pair of Katja of
Sweden that I wanted, but they costed 57.75 *kronor*
and I only had 50, so I couldn't purchase them.

When we were leaving without buying anything,
the salesclerk became cross with us and said:

"Yeah, when teenagers come in here they want to
try on everything, but then nothing fits anyway!"

For that reason, we will never go to that store again.

Then we went to see a housewife film at Fågel Blå.
It was rather boring, but such movies are free, so we
decided to see it all the same. When we came out from
the cinema I said:

"Guess what I am going to do on Saturday?"

"Well, what then? Come here and walk, possibly?"

"No, I'm going to smash a shop window or set fire to
a house or strip naked on the street."

"Really?" Kicki said. "Why?"

"Because I want to."

"Yes, but then a police officer may come and arrest you."

"Well, let him come," I said. "I don't care."

Thursday, 5 March 1964

Today when E-L and I were at Tempo having coffee, we talked about what we are going to do in the summer when school is out. I'm supposed to partly stay in the country with mamma and papa, and partly work. E-L, for her part, said that she doesn't really know what she is going to do.

But if we could afford it, we would set off and go camping. We could hitch-hike through Sweden and look around. Sunbathing and swimming during the days and be on the spree in some town in the evenings. I really would like to do that sometime, because it would be bloody nice! Just to do what came naturally and not know from one day to the next what might happen. It wouldn't have to be very expensive, either, if we hitch-hiked and slept in a tent. In that case we would only have to pay for food.

But mamma and papa wouldn't be happy if I just went away. Why must you have parents who hinder you from everything? E-L presumably wouldn't care about her parent's reaction, but I, who have a little better contact with mine, probably couldn't do it. Sometimes, mamma drives me so crazy that I wish her further away, but I understand that she would worry if I just set off.

On Saturday I would have preferred being alone in town in case the cop would come again, but I couldn't tell Kicki, so it was as usual.

First we went with two idiots in a Volvo Amazon without bumpers, and then with some others in a Citroën. The cutest guy wanted to be with Kicki, and I couldn't stand the other one, so I was put in a bad mood and wanted to hop out again. Everything felt like a waste of time. When we drove around town I just sat there and kept a look-out for the policeman the whole time, even though I knew that I wouldn't see him. Why can't I forget him? I think it's ridiculous to be interested in a cop.

Last night I was out by myself. I didn't feel like going with anybody, so I just walked around. In front of Wolrath's a middle-aged man in a Morris started to edge along beside me.

"Do you want to ride?" he said through the window.

I just continued walking without taking any notice of him, but he kept on rolling the car after me.

"Stop a minute," he said.

"Why?"

"So that we can talk."

"But we don't have anything to talk about!"

"Do you want to ride?"

"What do you mean by ride?"

"Ride in my car!"

When I made a sharp turn, he stopped and put the car into reverse.

"Do you want to go to Paletten then?" he said.

"Get lost!" I shouted. "I don't want *anything*!"

Then he finally drove away. What the hell was he thinking? That I was a whore? I can't stand such disgusting old men who think that you want to be with them! I feel like I could puke just thinking of one of them starting to paw me.

I didn't see him. Once a police car went by, but he wasn't in it.

Finally, I rode with a guy who said that he once had played in a band, and he gave me a lift home.

I dreamed that I was chased by two policemen. When they almost had caught me, they stopped running so I could get away. I felt sad when I woke up.

I can't stop thinking about him. When I am in town, I can't resist looking for him, and as soon as I see a policeman I feel a thrill in my stomach.

I wonder about how they work. They can perhaps change their areas, so he won't be there anymore. I will probably never see him again.

In math lesson Holmberg told us about two girls in another class whom he had seen talking with some guys in a *raggarbil*, and then he went into a long lecture about what can happen to girls who get into bad company. When he said that about the *raggarbil*, Siv and Kerstin turned around and looked at me.

I wonder what he would say if he knew what Kicki and I usually do. Nothing, I suppose, because he only cares about girls with nice curves and big tits like Maud and Agneta.

He doesn't get anything. When he sees me dressed in a pleated terylene skirt and low-heeled shoes, he thinks that I am a pleasant little family girl who sits at home and does her homework and watches TV every evening. And he wouldn't get it if I came to school in a tight skirt and high heels, either.

Friday, 13 March 1964

When I came home from school I was rather happy, but as soon as I got sight of mamma I became surly. Sometimes I can scarcely stand looking at her. At the same time I feel guilty, because mostly she hasn't done anything special.

I have a hang up about her ways. I think she is too weak in her dealings with papa. Everything would be much better if she were stronger. Then we wouldn't have any problems with papa, because he needs someone who is strong and can help him. I hate when he drinks, but otherwise I almost like him better than mamma. That's why I feel so disappointed when he comes home drunk. If

*I didn't like him for the rest, I wouldn't care as much as
I do.*

*But it will be bloody nice when I can move away from
home! I remember when Anita left. She was seventeen
and I was nine. Papa had messed with her and been
really dumb, so the next day she left to find out if there
were any rooms for rent. Then she came home and told
us that she was going to move. Papa didn't say anything
at all and had no objections. Later, he visited her and
treated her suddenly with respect. He seemed to think
that she had guts in her by not tolerating his behaviour.*

*But before you can move you must have money, and to
have money you must have a job. So, it will take at least
two and a half years before I can get something on my
own. But I'm going to do that as soon as possible. E-L
and I will perhaps rent something together, we have said.*

Sunday, 15 March 1964

*We cruised with two guys who were called Uffe and
Kjell, and against the odds I got Uffe, who was the best
(and rather handsome). He offered me a Pall Mall, which
he had in a neat cigarette leather case with a zipper at the
bottom. (You open the pack of cigarettes in one corner
and put it in the case and close it, and then you move the
leather cap to the side exactly where the pack is opened
and smack a cigarette out.)*

After a few runs around town we went to an apart-

ment on Apelgatan. We listened to music and danced (at least Uffe and I did) and then there was a little lying on a bed also. And I had taken a fancy to him and didn't mind some petting. But I got very red and irritated on my face because of his beard stubble.

There has been a fire at the YMCA. In the newspaper it says that they suspect arson, but this has not been confirmed. On the outside it's mostly the roof that is damaged.

During lunch break, I saw two cops on Forumtorget. They walked side by side with hands behind their backs, and they had watch caps and white gloves on. The sabres, or whatever they are called, dangled as they walked along. My heart started beating faster, and I could almost not breathe when they came nearer. I don't know why I become that way. Why can't I just be as usual?

Thursday, 19 March 1964

It was in the newspaper about "A Midsummer Night's Dream" which we were invited to go and see in the assembly hall. It got good reviews, and I agree that the participating girls from our school acted well.

It seems fun with theater, but I would never be able to handle it, me with my hoarse voice and shaky hands. I'm really hindered by this. And what's the cause? When I went to elementary school, it was not a problem. It began when I came to the girls' school. Everything is the girls' schools' fault! Or if it is puberty's.

I have been to the library and borrowed some books. I loaned The Emigrants *by Vilhelm Moberg and* The Song of the Red Ruby *by Agnar Mykle. There are parts of that book that are supposed to be really interesting, I've heard, but I haven't started it yet.*

Just now, I am reading the serial story in Hemmets Veckotidning. *Mamma is the one who buys it, but I usually read it too. I also buy* Bildjournalen *sometimes, because in that magazine there is a lot for teenagers. But one* krona *here, and one* krona *there, becomes money, so I can't do it very often.*

I usually borrow books from Stig and Anita also when I visit them. They have mostly detective novels, because that's what both of them like. (Agatha Christie, Maria Lang and Stieg Trenter.) And Anita has the novel Child 312, *which I read when I was younger and thought was great. And the books about Angelique, but I'm not very keen on those. E-L reads mostly detective novels as well, and she digs novels like* 491 *and* Chance *which are about youth with problems.*

Friday, 20 March 1964
Today we had a full-day test in Swedish. When we write

for an entire or half day, we are allowed to have food and beverages with us. No, but fruit and candy and a Sunkist possibly.

I had a banana, an apple and a box of Tenor. E-L had a Nickel. Nickel is what we usually buy when we go to the movies also, because those candies last a long time.

Yes, and so you have to put something together. It's so difficult with an essay, because I never seem to get busy. E-L starts writing immediately, and I feel pressured by that also, because you can leave when you have finished writing, and therefore you want to be done as soon as possible, so that you can use the time for something more fun. (Like going to Café Regent and having coffee, for example.)

So, it is a bit trying with Swedish. It's better when it is other subjects. In foreign languages it's usually a two-part written exercise where you are required, for example, to translate from English to Swedish and then from Swedish to English and possibly to write a little bit on your own, also.

Such written exercises are ok with me. But why on earth is it so difficult for me to get started when we are supposed to write an essay? And why don't I just write a subject report instead? After all, we are almost always allowed to write a subject report also.

It's because I don't think I'm able to, I suppose. But there are those who go in for the subject reports. They study really hard before the test and do well in both

I didn't take the bus home from school today. I walked instead, and then I saw a cop car approach from the oncoming direction. It was on the outskirts of town, at the place where the sidewalks end, and I was just about to cross the road when I saw the car coming. Shit! I thought and decided to walk a little slower so that they would pass me before I went over.

There were two cops in the front seat, and the one on my side stared like hell as they drove by. I pretended not to see it and continued to walk in the usual manner, and then I stopped to cross the lane. But they had done a U-turn on the road and were on their way back. I couldn't do anything before the car had stopped and one of the cops got out, went around the car and came up to me.

"Hello, where are you going?" he said.

It was *him*.

"Home."

"And where have you been?"

"In town."

"And what did you do there?"

"Went to school and went shopping."

"What did you buy?"

"An eyebrow pencil, stockings and envelopes!"

What business of his was it what I had bought? I don't understand why he asked, either, because that could hardly interest him.

"Now I remember you," he said. "Did you follow my advice and go away from there?"

Away from Radiohörnan, he meant.

"No."

It was so frigging embarrassing. I felt that he was watching me the whole time, and I didn't know in which direction I should look.

"Do your feet hurt?" he said.

"No, why?"

"I thought you were walking a bit badly."

"I see."

And that was all. He went back and sat in the car again, and they drove away. I crossed the road, and when I had walked a short way, they had turned around again and were on their way back. He waved when they drove by, but I pretended not to see it.

I wish they hadn't come. He still didn't mean anything. He was just doing his job. But what cause had he to stop me when I was just walking in the street? And was it true that he didn't recognize me before they had stopped?

He is perhaps screwy. He may enjoy what he sees sometimes when he opens car doors. He perhaps gets excited by it and wishes he could be lying there himself with the girls he thinks he wants to save. He is maybe a frigging creep.

While walking, I fantasized about what would have happened if I had begun to run as soon as I got sight of the cop car. Would they have come running after me then? Would they have slammed on the brakes, thrown themselves out of the car and tried to get their hands on me? If I had done something criminal, perhaps, but not otherwise. I don't know. Anyway, I imagined that they did it, and when they had managed to catch me, they got hold of me and dragged me back to the patrol car. I resisted and tried to get away, but they didn't release their hold of me.

These are almost the same fantasies I used to have about Holmberg before. But I didn't imagine that he would chase me.

"491" has been released and is playing at both Skandia and Röda Kvarn now, but they have increased the age limit to eighteen years, so Kicki and I cannot see it. We thought about going to a night-time matinee instead, but nothing came of it.

Everything is so complicated. I don't know what to do. Why can't I forget that cop so that everything will be normal again? I just go around looking for him all the time, and whenever I see a cop car I feel weird. I haven't told Kicki about it, because it seems so crazy to go around thinking of a policeman. I'm ashamed of it. But it isn't the same kind of interest that I take in guys. I just wish he would come and do something so that I get to feel that *excitement*.

Last night when we were walking on Svartbäcksgatan, we met Inger and Gunilla, who are in our class.

"Well, *hi!*" Inger said and acted surprised. "We really weren't expecting to bump into *you two* here! Are you going to the movies?"

"No, we aren't," Kicki said.

And Inger knew that. They both knew why we were there and what we were going to do.

Then it was silent for a while until some guys in a car drove by and shouted something.

"That you dare walk here!" Gunilla said. "I would *never* dare walk here alone!"

"You wouldn't?"

"No, not with all these terrible *raggare* who drive here!"

Inger laughed, and they exchanged meaning looks.

"Well, have a great time!" Inger said sarcastically. We'll see you at school!"

And then they left. When they were out of earshot Kicki said:

"I would *never* dare to walk here alone! Some big, bad *raggare* could come and take me! *My God*, how terrible!"

Then we rode with two guys in a Volvo Amazon. When they asked us our names, I said Chris and Liz, because I was already regretting that we had gone with them. But they went away to Skarholmen, and when we had changed places the usual happened. His hair cream smeared me, so I got a greasy face.

"How was yours?" Kicki asked when we were back in town again.

"Messy," I said. "First he messed with me, then his hair cream made a mess all over me. How was yours?"

"Excessively interested in the lower regions."

"Oh, yeah?"

"Yes, but he wasn't getting anywhere with it."

At Sieverth's we crossed the street to catch the cars coming from behind, and then we started to walk along the street again. There were loads of people we knew out. Finally, we rode with two guys in a Ford.

Tuesday, 24 March 1964

On "Kvällstoppen" the result was like this: 1) "All My Loving" with The Beatles 2) "Surfin' Bird" with The Trashmen 3) "Bonnie B" with Jerry Lee Lewis. Up to fifteenth place from nineteenth was "Anyone Who Had a Heart" with Cilla Black. ("Anyone who had a heart would take me in his arms and love me true".)

Love is, I think, the same thing as friendship, except that you have physical intimacy also. The one I love should be my best friend, and I should be his. I want us to be so close that we understand each other almost without words. If we just look into each other's eyes, we will know everything. It would feel like at last having come home.

Regarding appearance, I don't have any special re-quirements. I'm most attracted to dark haired boys, but it's of no vital importance what they look like. Well, I must of course like *the way he looks, but I think that you do that automatically when you are in love. And if you are not in love, it doesn't matter how handsome he is, because in that case you still can't be together with him.*

Svartbäcksgatan is going to become a pedestrian street only, it says in the newspaper today.

Why do they have to destroy everything? First, it's Järnbron, which we are no longer allowed to use, and now it's Svartbäcksgatan.

Last night I dreamed that I was arrested by the police in front of Hennes. A cop car braked to a stop, and two policemen jumped out and ran up to me and grabbed me and threw me into the patrol car. When I saw them coming I didn't run, and when they took me I didn't resist, because if I had done that, I was afraid that they might have let me get away.

I was supposed to be questioned, and when we got to the police station pop was there. It felt disgusting, because what I am up to is none of his business.

Damned frigging dream.

Monday, 30 March 1964
I'm listening to "Det ska vi fira" on the radio right now.

I wonder what E-L is doing? Well, I suppose I'll find out when she (or I) calls, what she has been up to.

Yesterday and on Easter Eve we were out. Last night nothing special happened. But on Saturday we wound up in a house in Norby with two guys who had picked us up on Svartbäcksgatan. They had a Plymouth, which I guess actually belonged to one of their fathers, because such cars must be rather expensive.

When we got there, E-L disappeared with one of the guy someplace, while I went with the other one into a little room beside the kitchen. And he was mannerly *and offered me a cigarette (a Lark) instead of drawing me onto the bed immediately.*

But when we had finished our cigarettes, we did not leave there; instead we placed ourselves in a lying position on the bed and devoted ourselves to petting. Or he devoted himself, because I didn't do very much. I just lay there and let his hands go on a voyage of discovery, as it says in short stories and things like that. Oh, yes!

But they had a bloody gorgeous car, and it was cosy to ride in it. This was the first time I rode in a so-called battleship. It was exactly the kind of car that E-L and I once said that we would never cruise in, just because we thought that guys in big cars were worse than others.

But that's not the case. You can't judge a book by its cover and not a guy by his car, either.

We got picked up by two guys in a Plymouth. The one I was together with was called Sten, and we went to his home. He and I were in one of the rooms, and Kicki and the other guy were in another. When we had lain on the bed and made out for a while he jumped up and rooted around in a desk drawer and came back with some typed pages that he wanted me to read. It was a porn story. When I had finished reading, he asked me what I felt. He perhaps had thought that I would be excited, so that he would get to lay me afterwards.

But I think it's a difference between boys and girls, because I'm not turned on by porno. I can only become excited with a guy who is tender and who I really like. But I have never been that way. The only time I have felt something was when I was with Hasse, whom Putte said is married. But I didn't like him, and he wasn't especially tender, either, so it can perhaps be that way anyway, if they just do the right things and aren't too rough. I don't know.

Sten was only busy between my legs the whole time. I don't know why I accepted it, because from that he could believe that I was going to let him lay me. But I couldn't make up my mind to say no. He didn't seem especially turned on, either, so I thought that I could wait a while and see what he would do before I said something. I just lay there, until he suddenly stuck his finger inside me and I felt a twinge of pain.

"What are you *doing*?" I said and jumped up.

"Did it hurt?"

"Yes, you bet it did!"

After that I didn't want to lay down on the bed again, even though he tried to get me to. I got dressed and went out to Kicki and the other guy who were sitting in the other room, smoking. He probably hadn't got to do as much with her as Sten had got to do with me.

Pop started to complain again, that I'm out too often. But we are on Easter vacation now, and it's none of his business what I do.

"Are you going to gad about again tonight?" he said at dinner.

Then he began to complain about the potatoes.

"Cook the food yourself, then, if you aren't satisfied!" I said.

He can't even boil an egg himself, but moan and complain, he can! I get mad as hell as soon as I think of it.

But I was just as angry with mom as I was with him. Why does she just sit there holding her tongue and taking it? Why doesn't she divorce him? But she is completely dependent on him, both emotionally and financially. I will never be that way on anybody. And he has no power over me. He might have had it when I was little, when I didn't dare to make him sad, but now I don't give a shit about his reactions.

Last night when Kicki and I were out, we got picked up by three guys in an Opel Kapitän. They had a room in a basement on Bangårdsgatan that we went to. We sat there and talked and smoked, and then they gave first me, and then Kicki, a lift home. Tiger, Allan and Nisse were their names.

Sunday, 5 April 1964

Svartbäcksgatan is a pleasant street to walk on, I have to say! There isn't anything special about the street itself, but it is because of the car traffic. To go there and know that at the same time the boys are driving their rounds…

If they are in a hurry, they turn already at Skolgatan and drive up Sysslomansgatan and come quickly back, but it can also happen that they cruise all the way down to the train tracks past the BP gas station before they turn back.

Yes, and then they drive up again, past Radiohörnan, where E-L and I usually stand, and on to Stora Torget. On the way they pass a lot of stores, which are closed at that time of day, but which often have a little window light on, and everything is so bloody cosy! There is like a shimmer over that street! If anything is going to happen, it's going to happen there!

Yesterday we went to the movies first, and then we rode with two guys (Tony and Bladde) in a black Volvo PV. Tony was the one who looked the best, but E-L was the one who got him. They drove away to an apartment in Salabackar, and we entered, and we drank coffee, and we did some other things as well. E-L and Tony lay on the bed and I sat on Bladde's knee in an armchair. (Well, I often sit on knees in armchairs, I think!)

No, it wasn't anything special. I didn't like Bladde very much. He was probably kind, but that wasn't enough, because it never is. There has to be more.

I love cool spring evenings when the sky is blue, and the air is clear, and you feel a draw of yearning to just get away somewhere. It feels like the whole world is laying open and waiting for you to come. On Sunday when Kicki and I got to town it felt that way.

"Indulge yourself in having a good time with Mm… Marabou milk chocolate!" we sang, while we ate our chocolate rolls that we had bought. An old man we met glared at us and looked sour. Why is it that all the elderly think that you are disturbing and rude as soon as you raise your voice a little? Why don't they get it that you sing and roar just because you're happy? But they are perhaps envious because they aren't young themselves anymore.

To stand at the square when it's dark outside and see the rows of shiny cars slowly sliding around in the street lights' shimmer feels so wonderful. There are red and white lights from all the headlights that are lit, and the paving stones glimmer.

Then you go in between the cars that have stopped in the line and feel the warmth from the exhaust pipes on your legs while the headlights light up your coat and purse and the guys in the cars stare.

And on the other side of the square, you start walking along Svartbäcksgatan… Just thinking of it makes me long to be there. I will probably never be able to stop cruising. Because the way it feels then, I want it to feel all the time.

First, we rode with three draftees who thought we should hop in and warm ourselves up for a while. It was pleasant to get in and thaw out our toes, but guys who are here just to do their military service you can't take seriously, because you know that they will soon disappear again. Some of them surely go steady with a girl back home, as well.

Then we rode with a guy named Torgny and his buddy. We went with them also just to get warm. We got Chico from him and we gave him cigarettes. He is big and fat and the type you just talk with. I would never let him do anything if he tried. Guys don't have to be *good looking* for you to want to make out with them, but I don't like it when they are fat. And they can't have a beard or long Beatles hair. But there aren't any guys on Svartbäcksgatan with hair like that.

Then we hung about in town again. We saw the guys we rode with on Saturday, but they didn't stop, and we wouldn't have gone with them either, if they had asked us, because Kicki didn't like the guy she got very much. But Tony, who I was with, was rather handsome.

There were no more guys that stopped until Kicki had gone home and I walked alone. Then Göran and his buddy Uffe came. Göran was driving, and Uffe sat beside him, and Uffe's brother Bogart was in the back seat. Uffe leaned forward, over Göran who just sat there acting like he didn't notice me, and asked if I were going home. When I said yes, he climbed out of the car and opened the door so that I could enter the back seat. I said hello to Bogart and glanced at Göran, but he still ignored me.

"What have you been up to this evening?" Uffe said and turned his head.

"Have you earned four hundred and ninety *kronor*?" Göran said.

I don't know what I have done to him that he has to be so mean. Uffe noticed that I became sad and started to talk about Restaurant Ugglan, where they had been the previous evening. Then he asked what I had done, and I said that Kicki and I had been to the movies.

"And what did you do after that?"

He sounded teasing in his voice and not angry like Göran, but I didn't want to tell him that we had been on Svartbäcksgatan when Göran could overhear it.

"We went home," I said.

And that wasn't exactly a lie, even though it took several hours to get there. After all, we were with those two guys in the apartment also.

We went to the railway station, because they were going to pick up a girl there who needed a lift home.

Uffe and Bogart went in, while Göran and I remained in the car. I hoped that he would say something while we were alone, but he didn't. He just sat there and seemed reserved. I could see his hair, which reached his shirt collar at he back of his head, and a little of his profile.

"Have you started driving a free taxi?" I said.

Then he looked at me in the rearview mirror and said:

"Payment is made in kind instead!"

When Uffe and Bogart came back, they had a girl in shepherd's plaid pants and a black leather jacket with them. Uffe and Bogart sat in the back seat, next to me, and the girl in front, right beside Göran. Uffe had purchased a hot dog, and I got a bite from it before he ate it up. Then he put his arm behind me on the backrest. I checked in the rearview mirror if Göran saw it, but he sat there and talked with the girl beside him and didn't pay any attention to me. He could talk with *her*, so he obviously didn't think *she* was a whore, anyway.

I don't understand why he has to act the way he does. What have I done to him? The only thing I know is that I didn't let him kiss me the first and second time we met, and that I started riding with other guys when he didn't want to see me anymore. He thinks it's wrong to go with *raggare*, but when I think about what he did on New Year's Eve, when he was drunk and was together with two girls at the same time, I think that is even worse. And if he can't stand it that

I am walking on Svartbäcksgatan, he should try to figure out why I started doing it.

Tuesday, 7 April 1964
Ooh, I think that my hair is so awkward! I put it up in big curlers and comb it flat, but as soon as I come outside it begins to retract and become frizzy.

Otherwise, I'm not directly dissatisfied with my appearance. I think that I have a bit small bust (but not that I have a complex about it) and I have never liked my nose very much. It's broad, and I tend to have pimples around it. Mamma and grandma have even broader noses, so mine will probably become even coarser when I get bigger, because that's how all noses are. They grow with the years. No, not when I get bigger; when I become older, I mean, because I won't get much bigger, I suppose.

But I'm rather satisfied with my eyes, and there isn't anything wrong with my legs, except that I'm a little knock-kneed.

A guy in Prallan has died in school. He just collapsed during a gymnastics lesson, they say.

After lunch break, when I entered the classroom, Siv turned around and said: "Well, the *raggarbrud*!"

I pretended not to hear it, but I realized that many of the other girls did. Kerstin and Siv laughed and stared. I don't understand why they have to carry on like that. I wrote to Kicki about it in our notepad during class, and she wrote back:

Oh, she said that? What should we call her then? The dancing ape? But actually, there is no big difference between going out to dance and going out to cruise. When you dance you take a turn on the dance floor to music, and when you cruise you take a turn around town while you listen to records. There are only two different ways to meet the opposite sex. So I don't understand why those of us who hang around in town have to get such a bad reputation!

I think that those who don't know how it is believe that we lay all the guys we meet and that's why. Some *raggarbrudar* perhaps do that.

There will perhaps be five-day weeks in school, so that we will be free on Saturdays. Therefore, we must go longer during the other days and have a shorter summer vacation. Not many want that.

After school I bought a white blouse with flounces and pin tucks at Hennes. If it's warm outside on Walpurgis Night, I'm going to wear it then with my light green suit.

Wednesday, 15 April 1964
I hate it when papa drinks and becomes loudmouthed

and rough (as mamma says), but at the same time it seems that he knows more about life than mamma. He has said it himself, and he has been through a lot, so he gives me that feeling.

Mamma, on the contrary, has not experienced anything special. They were poor when she was little, but she lived protected with grandma, while papa was in an emotional hell with his mother. That's why I think he is the wisest.

And between the two of them, he is the one who is big and strong, and she is the one who is little and weak. When they were on their way to divorce when I was twelve, I preferred to live with papa, but that was out of the question, because he was not a person you could rely on. He was a drinker, so I knew that if they divorced, I would have to live with mamma. At the same time, I knew who papa should be married to. He should be married to somebody like me. Someone like me, and not someone like mamma, was (and is) the right one for my papa.

Sunday, 19 April 1964

Yesterday I stayed home from school because of menstruation cramps. I get them sometimes, and it's so difficult, because it's almost like having colic. I'm in a cold sweat and ready to faint and don't know how to keep on my legs.

When you are having your period, you don't have to attend gym class. I don't care very much about gymnastics, but when we have dancing I think it's fun. We have learned to dance the jenka, and we get to dance other dances as well, such as the schottis and the polka, and I think I'm pretty good at it. But I'm bad at regular gymnastics.

Soon I will watch "The Lucy Show" on TV with mama. It's an amusing program, both of us think.

Mamma and papa purchased a telly as early as 1958. Then I watched the ice hockey world championship with papa. (This year Sweden won silver in the Olympics.) After that, there was "Hyland's Corner" and various series, like "Rawhide" with Clint Eastwood and Eric Fleming, for example. ("Movin', movin', movin'…")

Papa always has a book at hand in front of the TV, so if there isn't anything he is interested in, he can read instead. He sits on the sofa with a book in front of him and looks up now and then. "Is there something? Nope."

And then he keeps on reading.

Kicki didn't come out with me, because she wasn't feeling well. She always has a bad stomach ache when she is having her period.

First, I went to see a Swedish movie with Thore Skogman and Anita Lindblom. It played at Slotts, and when I passed the movie theater street afterwards Uffe and Bogart came driving, and they stopped and asked if I wanted to go with them.

Bogart was smoking Astor cigarettes and offered me one, and it was so cosy to sit there in the front seat with Uffe, smoking and swishing through the night. Uffe asked me if I wanted to go home with him while Bogart and Göran went out dancing, and I said yes. I thought that Göran would come to the house and fetch the car, because Bogart doesn't have a driver's license, but he drove anyway, so I didn't have to meet Göran.

When Uffe and I were alone, we went into his room and turned off the lamp. A street light shone on the opposite wall, but where the bed stood it was dark. He hugged me and pressed his nose against my neck.

"You're so good!" he said. "I could eat you up!"

I like him, but I could never fall in love with him, because he isn't my type. It's a pity, I think, because he is kind. He didn't do much, either. He was almost asleep, while I lay there listening to trains and cars that went by outside. When Bogart and Göran came back with the car he was supposed to give me a lift home.

"When are they coming?" I said.

"You never can tell!"

"It can't be too late, because then pop will go mad."

"Yes, I understand that. If I had a daughter who looked like you, I wouldn't dare let her out at all!"

We lay there listening to music that he had put on.

"You think you've lost your love, well I saw her yesterday. It's you she's thinking of and she told me what to say. She says she loves you," The Beatles sang.

"You were in love with Göran, weren't you?" Uffe said.

"I don't know."

"Are you in love with anyone now?"

"I don't know."

I couldn't tell him that I'm possibly still in love with Göran, because I didn't want to make him sad. Besides, I don't really know if it's true. Maybe I'm just sad because he appears to be angry with me and seems to believe that I lay all the guys I meet. Does he believe that? I don't *know* what the hell he believes!

After "She Loves You", Uffe played "Can't Buy Me Love", which is number one on "Kvällstoppen" now, and then "I Saw Her Standing There". The longer time was getting on, the more worried I was, but Uffe just laughed.

"Take it easy, take a Toy!" he said. "If they don't come you can stay here overnight."

"No, I can't."

"If you did, I wouldn't get a wink of sleep all night."

Then he asked if I'm a virgin.

"Why do you ask?"

"I'm just wondering."

"Which would you prefer?"

"What?"

"Would you prefer that I am or that I am not?"

"That you are not."

"What do you think I am?"

"I don't think you are one."

"Why not?"

"Because it shows."

"How?"

"By your movements and such."

"But I am."

"You are?"

"Yes."

Then he hugged me and said:

"You may sleep here anyway!"

But at half past one they came. We went out into the kitchen, and just when they entered, Uffe started tucking his shirt in his pants. Bogart sat down at the table, but Göran remained standing in the doorway.

"What the hell have you gotten hold of for a fucking *raggarbrud*?" he said and glanced at Uffe.

I turned away so that he couldn't see my face. In the window, that reflected the kitchen, I saw that he lit a cigarette. Then Uffe came up to me and put his arm around my shoulders.

"Don't pay attention to him," he said.

But I did, because I don't understand why he has to say something mean every time we meet.

Saturday, 25 April 1964

There is something special about Saturdays! What, I

wonder. What can it be?

In the morning you wake up, wash yourself and dress and eat breakfast and go to school… Nothing unusual there, in other words. Then you sit in your school desk and wait until it's time to go home again. During the 25 minutes' break you go to the bakery and buy half a long-shaped wheat bun. (They know it's going to be a rush, so they have already divided up the buns and put them in bags, so that they can just toss them over the counter and receive the money.) And you just scoff that fresh wheat bun because you are so hungry and because it is so good. If you haven't bought small buns with sugar on instead, that is. That's what I do sometimes, when I think that half a long-shaped wheat bun will be too much.

Yes, and then it won't be long before school is closed for the week and you are allowed to go home. At home you listen to "Sveriges bilradio" while eating something, and then it's "Tio i topp" at three o'clock. (When you hear that mentometer rattle, you know it's Saturday, if you haven't realized it before!)

Now what is different with Saturdays gets closer, because afterwards you take a bath, wash your hair, and decide what to wear. You perhaps iron a blouse and put your hair up in curlers. And why do you do that? Yes, it's because you are going out again in the evening.

When it's time, I take the bus downtown to Stora Torget, and in front of Tempo (with those debated cake-doily walls) E-L is standing, waiting for me. I jump off the bus and go up to her, and we take each other by the arm and start walking on Svartbäcksgatan, Uppsala's cruising street number one! Mostly we stop at Radiohörnan, that is located on Svartbäcksgatan 24, but sometimes we go all the way down to the BP gas station and Stugan on Repslagaregatan before we turn back.

We walk there and feel so happy and full of expectation, because just about anything can happen! A really nice boy could turn up, and then you fall in love and begin a relationship. But just getting out and meeting boys is fun. It's fun from time to time to see what will happen just that evening.

Yes, these are just the things that make Saturdays so special!

On Saturday we rode first with two guys in a VW. As soon as we had entered the car, I smelled alcohol from the one who wasn't driving, and then I saw a heap of empty bottles on the floor. Kicki saw them too.

"Well, I'll be damned!" the guy to the right said and stared at us. "I thought broads of today only wanted to ride in Yankee cars!"

"Everybody doesn't have to be the same," Kicki said.

"No, obviously not!"

He looked like a real *raggare* with greasy, combed back hair and a duck tail, and he would have fit in a lot better in a big American car than in this little asphalt bubble. But he probably didn't have a car of his own.

They were totally screwy. When we drove around town, the guy to the right rolled down the window and stuck out his head out hollered "Yabba-dabba-doo" loudly as hell, so people on the sidewalks turned around and stared at us. And the other one said:

"Do you know what similarity it is between a gal and a fox?"

"No," we said.

"Both speed up the cock!"

They stopped behind Mjölkcentralen and wanted us to change places, but we didn't want to do that, so we pretended that we had just remembered that we were supposed to meet someone and left them.

Then we went with three guys in an Opel. The guy driving also wanted a girl, so he first asked one who he apparently already knew. She had blond, back-combed hair, and she was heavily made up with white lipstick, black mascara, long drawn eye liner, blue eye shadow, brown cream, and powder. When she bent down and looked into the car, she blew a big bubble-gum bubble which she allowed to pop and then drew back in.

"Who are these others, though?" she said.

Kicki and I hoped that she wouldn't come along, and fortunately she didn't.

"Another time, perhaps," she said and straightened herself up.

"If there is another time, that is!" the guy said at the same time as he began driving off.

"Did you know her?" Kicki said.

"Yes, who doesn't know that fucking tramp!"

I wonder why guys stop for girls they think are worthless. But perhaps they don't. I think he said like he did about her because he had been turned down. Other guys probably say the same thing about Kicki and me when we don't want to ride with them.

Friday, 1 May 1964

"Beautiful May, welcome to our countryside again!" There is something special with spring. It's a lovely season, I think! And Walpurgis Night is a nice celebration.

We went to Svartbäcksgatan, as usual. To walk there when it begins to get dark, and to see the car headlights turn on, and feel the expectant atmosphere, is bloody agreeable, I have to say!

We rode with two guys from Västerås. They had a big car (a Ford Customline), and in that car we were sitting, cruising around… It was cosy, I thought, because they had a record player and played Elvis and some other music.

Tord and Johnny were their names. Tord had a bottle of pop (Zingo, exceedingly good!) and asked if we wanted some, and we don't require pressing, so E-L took a swig first and then I did (or if it was the other way round), and then we realized that there was something more than just pop in the bottle, and we thought it was so cheeky of them to try to trick us with spirits.

We went out to the woods, but we didn't change seats (we refused to), and then back to town again and out on Svartbäcksgatan to, with renewed strength, try to find some other, and hopefully better, boys! We were a bit afraid that they would get angry and throw us out into the woods (you never can tell what the raggare in Västerås have for manners and customs!), but we were allowed to go back with them to town, and there we met two other guys who we rode with for the rest of the evening.

Yesterday, when papa began drinking, mamma set off to Stockholm. She usually does that sometimes, when she thinks it's becoming too damned difficult at home. She travels to her girlfriend, and they go dancing and have a good time while papa sits at home and is jealous. Later, when she comes back, they have a row.

Last night when I came home, papa was drunk and had got more and more excited and wanted to have a hearing with mamma. He tried to force her to tell him what she had done. I heard already out in the stairwell how he yelled and screamed. "You fucking whore!" and things like that. So then it was really cheerful to come home.

Friday, 8 May 1964

Soon I'm going to watch "Drop in" on TV, and E-L will probably do the same, if I know her at all. Tomorrow evening we are going to the movies to see "Blackboard Jungle". It was after that film "Rock Around the Clock" with Bill Haley & His Comets became number one in America and rock'n'roll had its great breakthrough.

So we are going to see that film. Then we intend to let some nice boys pick us up in their car for a drive. And then... Well, nobody knows what can happen! That's the great fascination of the raggarliv!

For tomorrow we have Swedish and religion homework. Religion is the most boring subject there is. I almost never read my religion lessons. That's dumb, actually, because Christianity knowledge is a subject that you can get a good grade in if you study properly. But I can't sit there and go on with things that I'm not a bit interested in. I don't believe in God, either (though there is no requirement to do so), but I think there is some kind of life after death. I believe that man has a kind of spirit survival, because I find it hard to imagine that there is total darkness when you die. Though I don't believe in heaven and hell.

But grandma believes in God. She is a member of the Pentecostal Church, and they can be a little like Maranatha Believers, because they also belong to the Free Church Movement. I think it's so fine with grandma, because she doesn't try to impose her religion on others.

She never talks about it, but she believes in God, and she always goes to church on Sundays.

And she pays her tithing. She pays one tenth of her retirement income to the church even though she has very little, and then she sits there and eats just cowberry jam and potatoes because she is short of money.

Once in the summer, when I stayed with some of grandma's acquaintances, I went to a Maranatha Believers meeting. Agneta and I were allowed to go when they went to a Camp Meeting. But it wasn't the well-known Målle Lindberg ("Pop-Målle" called) who was preaching, but somebody else.

At the meeting they asked if we wanted to be saved. They came up to us and asked if we wanted to surrender our lives to Jesus. "Nope," we said. We thought it was fun to sing, but we actually didn't want to be there, because we became so tired. We would rather have stayed at home, but we weren't allowed to be at home by ourselves.

Later we played revival meeting in their old wash-house. We had bibles, prayed prayers, played on combs, and sang. "Peace," we said, and "God bless you!", because that's how they greeted each other, the believers, when they met.

I dreamed that I went to some kind of a military school and had a strict man for a teacher. He was about forty years old, and he had black hair and stubble. I felt sad and put myself in a corner by a door, and he came up to me and let me lean my head against his chest. I thought it was strange that he, who was so strict and hard, could know what I wanted and needed.

And that was all. When I woke up I felt sad. Because in reality, there are no such persons.

Tuesday, 12 May 1964

Gosh, how tired I am! I just can't bring myself to write about last Saturday. We rode with some different guys (but they are all the same). First, they kiss, and their lips feel either like an octopus (wet, pulpy and flabby), or else they are dry and hard. Sometimes they press so hard that your lips get pinched against your teeth, and sometimes they drive in their tongue and move it here and there. (It can be long or short, thick or thin, so it's the same difference there, as below the waist!) Some of them are so disgusting that you almost feel sick. It's very seldom that you meet a boy who kisses well, I have to say!

Yes, and then their hands sneak in under your sweater or blouse and open your bra in the back. If they are having problems unhooking it, you never help them, because you aren't that eager yourself, but at last they manage to loosen it and begin to press and knead. Some of them have a grasping style, just like they are milking a cow, and some kiss and lick or squeeze and massage.

Later on, the turn comes to the skirt, which they, after more or less difficulties, open in the side or pull up from the bottom. They can, for example, begin a little carefully by touching a knee in an upwards direction, and then they let their hand slip in under the skirt and shove it upwards with their wrist until they have reached their destination.

And there they bump against a new barrier that must be forced. This they do either from the top, in under the elastic in the waist, or from the bottom, with their fingers through the leg opening.

Though I haven't allowed very many to go that far. I don't want to, but it does happen that they take greater liberties with you than you had imagined from the beginning.

Mother's sister Margit has been with us. She always comes when I have my birthday, because when I was new-born and mom was sick, aunt Margit was the one who took care of me, and since then she has almost regarded me as her own daughter. But I don't feel that way.

I got three charms for my silver bracelet as a present. It's a cross, an anchor, and a heart which means faith, hope, and charity. They have the same meaning as those dots some guys have between their thumb and pointing finger.

I got 100 *kronor* from mom and pop. I have bought longs at Hennes for 45 *kronor* and a Shantung lipstick for 4.75, Spray Net Regular hair spray for 9.75, and VO5 hair shampoo for 4.75 at Forum. That's a total of about 65 *kronor*, and so I have about 35 *kronor* left that I can use at the movies and to buy cigarettes.

Monday, 18 May 1964

On Whitsun Eve I went with Anita, Stig, and Anders to Skokloster and Sigtuna. We went by boat, round trip, on M/S Torsund. It's a special boat that you can sail with now during the summer.

In the evening E-L and I went out, and yesterday we saw "Fun in Acapulco" with Elvis. (Just think that he had the time and interest to come with us to the movies!) No, joking aside, he wasn't with us, but in the film. The movie wasn't especially good, but his films seldom are, when you consider the plot. Though you don't go to his movies because of the plot, but to watch him and hear him sing.

I have a picture of Elvis on the wall above my writing desk. There is something special about his appearance that I cannot explain. There is a sort of attraction that isn't only because he is good-looking. It has something to do with his charisma, because he has sex appeal.

There is also something special about his voice. It can be soft, and it can be hard (ha ha!), and it can sound sensitive as well as sexy. In "Such a Night", which I sing and dance to sometimes, it is clearly heard.

I like both his peaceful songs, such as for example "Are You Lonesome Tonight" and "Love Me Tender" (Love me tender, love me sweet, never let me go! You have made my life complete, and I love you so!"), and those in the rock style, such as "Hound Dog", "King Creole", "Jailhouse Rock" and "Blue Suede Shoes".

"Jailhouse Rock" was one of Elvis' first films, and in that film, he was still the way he is when he performs, but since then they have made him more provocative. For a while he was almost forbidden in America because they were afraid of the bad influence he would have on the youth. Once, when he was on a TV program, they only showed him from the waist up, so that nobody could see his movements with his lower body. They thought that he was too provocative and that he moved himself too sexily. A police officer who had seen him in a show said: "If he behaved like that on the street, we would arrest him immediately!"

But I do like him! I can almost see him in front of me, the way he enters the scene with tight pants and a blazer on, and with the collar of his shirt turned up so it touches his hair at the back of his head. His guitar hangs by a strap around his neck, and he goes forward and places himself with spread legs in front of the microphone while the public cheers him (or scream, as they often do, the fans), and then he strums a couple of smart chords on the guitar and begins to sing. ("Well, since my baby left me, I've found a new place to dwell, it's down at the end of Lonely Street, at Heartbreak Hotel.") If it is a rock song, he might begin to shake his legs so his pant legs flap, or he grabs the microphone stand and bends himself forward with it. Sometimes he makes a jump, so that his knees touch and he comes to a halt with one shoe tip to the floor. And his hair (which mostly is rather greasy) falls over his forehead, and sweat runs down his temples, but you don't think it's disgusting, though you would if it were someone else.

First, we were at the movies, and then we went into town. When we got out of the cinema, a Ford Consul stopped. It was Tony and two other guys. Tony sat in the back seat and didn't have a girl.

"How are you these days?" he said and looked at me.

"I'm fine," I said.

"Have you hit the bottle yet, then?"

"No."

"No? Well, that's probably just a matter of time…"

"That's what you think?"

"Yes. But you can always hope that you'll manage to stay away from it."

Guys don't like girls that drink, and I would never like to be like Ankan, for instance, who also walks on Svartbäcksgatan and who is drunk almost always. I have never been drunk, and I never want to be that way either, but it felt strange when Tony asked me about it.

"Just because some drink, doesn't mean that everyone does it," I said.

Then he assumed that it was him I meant.

"What the hell do you mean? he said. Are you referring to anyone in particular, or what?"

He didn't ask if I wanted to come along, because he probably wanted a girl that he could lay. The first time I met him, when Kicki and I were with him and his buddy in an apartment in Salabackar, I said no when he tried.

"But I can be off, and then you can go out and get yourself another girl," I said.

"Be off just because you're a decent gal? No, that's wrong, I think."

But he never picked me up again.

After geography class, Holmberg wanted to talk with me. I knew it was about the written test in math, but I got uptight anyway, when he told me to remain after the end of the lesson. I waited in my desk until the others had gone out, and when he and I were the only ones left, he asked me to step forward to the teacher's desk. I felt totally shaky, but luckily he was skimming through some papers when I was on my way up.

Then I stood there beside him and felt stupid while he checked my writing results.

"This doesn't look very good, Eva-Lena," he said.

"No, I know."

"What's the reason for it?"

"I don't know."

When he asked he raised his eyes, but I didn't dare to look back. I looked at his hands that were holding the papers.

"Is there any particular reason, or do you think it's difficult in general?"

"I don't know."

"Is it because you have problems at home that things haven't gone well?"

"No."

It was totally empty inside me, and I almost couldn't answer.

"Because in the present situation, I'm afraid that I won't be able to pass you in the spring," he said.

And that was all. Afterwards, I first felt relieved, and then disappointed. He just did his job. It's part of his job to talk in private with pupils who are doing poorly and try to find out the reasons. He didn't do it because he was interested. He asked only out of duty. If I had told him that I have problems, I would have forced him to do something against his will, and that would have felt degrading. If I had been Agneta, or one of the others he likes, there would have been a differrence, but I'm only me, and he isn't interested in me. I know that, and therefore there is no point in trying. And I don't know what I would say, either, if I should try. But I can't stop wondering what he would say or do if he knew that I am a *raggarbrud*.

On Wednesday The Streaplers were at Liljekonvaljeholmen. Barbro was there and watched them, she said today.

I've bought a marine blue nylon coat for 29.90, so now I have almost no money left. And tonight, Kicki and I are going to the movies to see "David and Lisa", and then 3.75 more will go. Then we hope to meet some nice guys to be together with for a while.

It says in my horoscope for this week that a certain tension fills the air and that I should not make any important decisions until I feel that everything is under control. It's easy for me to make new contacts, and I'm not a person who resists taking the initiative, it says. A romance can begin when I meet a person of the opposite sex who makes me feel uncertain because of his sophisticated manner.

We went with two guys in a white VW. They were called Kenneth and Affe. Kenneth had light hair and blue eyes and was very handsome. But Kicki was the one who got him.

Before I knew it, I was sitting right behind him and gazed at the back of his head and his profile. He had a checked shirt with a button-down collar and a dark blue blazer. I knew that Kicki preferred him, because the other guy wasn't much to look at, but I hoped that he would choose me.

He was studying to become a civil engineer he said when Kicki asked him. Then I came to think of Göran, because he is also going to become an engineer.

"What are you doing then?" Affe said.

"Going to school," I said.

"Where?"

"At the community girls' school."

"Oh, I see, the hen house!"

"The hen house?" Kenneth said, as if he had never heard of it before.

"Yes, girls only," Affe said.

"What program are you studying?" Kenneth said.

"Humanities."

"The six-year program?"

"No, we go for five years."

"And then you graduate in…?"

"*Normalskolekompetens.*"

I looked at his hands while he was driving. He had a signet ring with a black stone on his left ring finger, and the cuffs of his shirt were seen just enough below his blazer sleeves. He looked almost perfect.

They asked us what we had done, and when we told them that we had been at the movies, Affe said:

"Haven't you been to Klockbacken and gotten stockings then?"

"What do you mean?" I said, because I didn't get it.

"Yes, all the girls who go there tonight will get a pair of nylon stockings for free."

I didn't know what to believe, but today I saw in the news-paper that it was true.

We rode out to a newly constructed house that Affe had keys to and went into one of the apartments. The house was not finished, and there was no electricity, but a little light came in from outside. Kenneth and Kicki sat in a corner on her coat, and Affe and I went to another room, where we started to make out.

When he realized that I wasn't going to let him lay me, he took his thing out of his pants and pulled my hand to it and wanted me to hold it. It was the first time I went along with that, and I didn't know how to do. I just sat there and held it, until he put his hand over mine and began to pull up and down. After a while he let go of my hand and leaned backwards, and I kept on pulling at the same rate until he told me to go faster. Then he groaned and let it come out in a handkerchief that he pulled out. I had my green skirt with twist folds on, and when I came home I saw that a little smear from him was on it.

Sunday, 24 May 1964

I've been babysitting for my sister. On the bus home, there was a guy who sat and blurted out four-letter words, which I find it so hard to say. I don't care what others do (though I don't like it), but I cannot bring myself to utter those words. I don't say fuck and horny and I don't say cock. (It's almost hard for me to write them.) Instead of fuck I say sleep with or make love (if it's appropriate), instead of horny I say turned on, and instead of cock I say thing or below the waist. Because these other words stand for the kind of sex I don't want to have, and therefore I don't want to use them.

I met Kenneth again and rode with him.

"Are you alone tonight?" he said when I had sat in the car.

"Yes."

"You had a peculiar friend," he said.

"They say we are quite alike."

"Yes, possibly in the way you look, but not in the way you act. What a catch I have made! I thought last night."

It felt as if I wanted to come to Kicki's defense, but I didn't know what to say. And if he didn't like her, he didn't. But she liked *him*.

"Where do you go if you want to practice some petting, then?" he said as he drove uphill Carolinabacken.

"I don't know. Up to the castle, maybe."

"To the left here, you mean?"

"Yes."

But he didn't turn, and we passed Carolina.

"What did you think of Affe then?" he said.

"Nothing special."

"You let him go rather far, didn't you?"

"No, on the contrary."

I noticed that he didn't know what to believe, but I didn't explain anything.

The whole way between S1 and out past Ultuna we were silent. Then he said:

"It's so difficult to know what to say to you."

"I think it's difficult to talk to you too," I said.

He looked as perfect as he did the previous evening and felt equally unreachable, though it was me and not Kicki he was with now.

Just before Flottsundsbron he turned right into a side road and stopped. I had buttoned up my coat, and when he turned towards me he saw my silver cross that I had on a chain around my neck.

"Is it from your confirmation?" he said and lifted it.

"Yes, it's hand wrought."

Then it was silent again. He dropped the cross and pulled back my hair and stroked my cheek.

"You have pretty eyes," he said.

"That's what you said to Kicki as well," I said, because she had told me that.

"Ah, *that's* how girls talk to each other!"

He didn't hold me, and he didn't try to kiss me.

"Do you have perfume on?" he said.

"Yes, why do you ask?"

"No, I just wondered… But it's best in appropriate amounts."

Why did he say like that? I leaned my head against the window and closed my eyes so that he wouldn't notice that I was hurt. Then he began to sing.

"Close your eyes and I'll kiss you, tomorrow I'll miss you, I send all my loving to you," he sang.

When I opened my eyes again, I noticed that he was watching me.

"You are so secretive that I don't know what to do with you," he said.

He didn't say anything about wanting to see me again. When I asked how often he was in town, he said that it depended on how much he needed to study and how much he felt like going out. I think he understood that I wanted to see him again and that he felt superior to me because of that.

Anyway, I can't stop hoping that he will be out on Saturday night and pick me up. I have told Kicki that we decided to see each other again on Saturday, so that she won't come out, because if I am with her and he drives by himself, he probably won't stop. I don't like lying to her, but I need to know if he wants to see me again and why it was so difficult to talk with him.

Monday, 25 May 1964

Yesterday, when E-L went to town, she met Kenneth and rode with him. I was a bit disappointed when she told me, because I actually thought that he preferred me, since he chose me on Saturday. But it evidently didn't make any difference to him who he was with. Or he preferred E-L, because he wanted to see her again next Saturday.

And when they sat in the car he said to her: "You had a peculiar friend!" I think he could have said this to come closer to her. He perhaps believed that he could butter himself up with her by putting me down. But he put himself in a worse light with her by saying like that. He evidently didn't get that, though he was supposed to be so smart. He hadn't needed to mention me at all, unless he had some ulterior motive.

I'm a bit disappointed in E-L also, because she is going to see him again. But I would most likely have done the same thing myself, because it's always the boys who come first.

I have bought a nylon coat for 39.90 kronor. I was with mamma when I bought it, and she was the one who influenced me to choose one with a leopard pattern, even though everyone else has a blue or a brown one. I liked it at first, but now I don't think it's especially nice. Though now I'm forced to have it in any case.

I think it's so difficult with clothes. I think that I never manage to find something pretty. Partly because I don't really know what I want, and partly because I don't have much money to spend.

In any case, I have bought a pair of shoes. They are the same kind that E-L has, with narrow toes and high, sharp heels that you almost can't walk in. They are beige and lion yellow, and they have a leather bow in the front.

I needed new shoes, because my black high heels that I use in the fall and spring, are broken since I got one of the heels stuck in the foot scraper outside Tempo. You can get caught and fall and break your neck in that scraper, if you aren't careful. You need to go on your toes over it, if you aren't to get caught in one of the gaps.

In any case, my shoes match my new, charming coat, because it has a little beige in its pattern. But I wonder if I will wear it very often when I go out. And in school I never use high heeled shoes.

Sunday, 31 May 1964

Yesterday evening I stayed at home, because I didn't feel like going out by myself. I took the opportunity to play records, since mamma and papa were in the country.

We have a big radio gramophone with the radio in the front on top, and if you open a hatch in the middle, there is a turntable inside. You can put on up to ten singles or EP records at a time, and then the records drop down one by one from a suction cup. It becomes a little wobbly towards the end, so it isn't so good to put ten records on, but it works.

I have records with Cliff Richard, Paul Anka, The Beatles, and some others. Yes, and with Elvis, of course! My singles with Elvis are: "Any Way You Want Me"/"Love Me Tender", "A Fool Such as I"/"I Need Your Love Tonight", "Don't Be Cruel"/"Hound Dog", "Can't Help Falling in Love"/"Rock a Hula Baby", "Blue Christmas"/"Wooden Heart".

Mamma and papa have some traditional jazz and some records with Martin Ljung and Hasse Alfredsson, for example "Rock-Fnykis", "Ester" and "Guben i låddan".

E-L, for her part, met Kenneth, I suppose. I guess I'll get to know how it turned out when she calls.

First, I saw Kenneth's car on St Persgatan, and later a several times when he drove on Svartbäcksgatan, and he must have seen me, but he neither greeted me nor stopped. There were lots of other guys who asked if I would like to go with them, but I couldn't stop hoping for Kenneth and said no to all of them.

Then I saw that he had stopped in the corner by the police station, and I went there and tapped on his side window and asked if I could go with him.

"Certainly," he said.

I heard that he said it only to be polite, but I climbed in anyway.

"Where do you want to go then?" he said and started driving.

"Any place."

When he had to stop at a red light on Kungsgatan, he said:

"What have you been up to this evening?"

"I've been waiting for you."

"For me?"

"Yes, I saw you earlier and then I didn't want to go with anyone else."

"So, you turned them down?"

"Yes, I said no to seven guys, I think."

Then he gave me a surprised look.

"So, you are *that* popular?"

After Kungsgatan, he continued on the E4 towards Stockholm. I hoped that we would go far, but in the woods on the other side of the plain, he slowed down and stopped on the roadside. We got out there and laid down on the car blanket in a glade between the pine trees. It was windless, and the sky was very clear.

"Look how many stars there are," I said.

"Yes, they are shining for you."

"And for you."

"Yes, for you and me."

He started to undress me, and when I only had my panties and bra left, he looked at me from top to bottom and said:

"You have a fine body."

Then he tried to pull my panties off.

"Do you think you are going to get to lay me?" I said.

"I don't know…"

"Anyhow, you may not."

Then he laid down on the blanket and put his right arm over his forehead and sighed.

"Are you angry?" I said.

"No."

"What is it then?"

"I'm perhaps a little confused…"

"Why?"

"Because I can't figure you out."

While I was putting my clothes back on, he watched me without saying anything. Then he stood up and shook off the blanket. It was full of fir needles on the underside which didn't loosen.

"Why did you come to my car this evening?" he said when we sat in the front seat again.

"Because I wanted to see you."

Why else would I have done it, did he think? Because I think it's so frigging wonderful to ride in a Volkswagen?

"But you didn't want to see me, did you?" I said.

"No, I prefer to decide myself if, and when, I will meet a girl."

"Why didn't you say no when I asked you then?"

Then he was silent for a while, as if he were thinking about it, before he said:

"If a girl seems interested and willing, you certainly give it a try."

So just because I came up to his car, he thought that I meant that I wanted to lay him.

"I came up to you because I'm in love with you."

But he wasn't in love with me.

"We aren't going to see each other again, are we?" I said.

"No, I don't think so…"

What a catch you have made! I thought.

"Would you have wanted to see me again if I had not come up to you as I did tonight?"

"I don't know…"

"I knew I did wrong, but I couldn't resist."

Then I didn't know what else to say and lit a cigarette. I felt that he was watching me from the side.

"They really dig you, don't they?" he said.

"Who?"

"The guys."

"I don't know."

"Yes, I think they do."

He gave me a lift straight home. When we got there, and he had stopped the car, I couldn't go, though I knew that's what he wanted me to do.

"If you don't throw me out, you will never get rid of me," I said.

"I won't throw you out."

"Why not?"

"Because I don't think it's necessary."

But I didn't know how to be off.

"Start pawing me so that I get angry!" I said.

But he just sat there and looked superior.

"You are rather experienced, aren't you?" he said.

And when I told him that I would never be able to forget him, he said:

"You sure will. You'll soon meet some other guy. Someone who is just as much in love with you as you are with him."

"Nobody like you."

"No, but someone who is even better, possibly."

I don't remember all we said. In the end he began to

read a poem about love, as to show that he knew how I was feeling.

"Why was I born to love – to love the one I cannot have? Why was love ignited in my heart at such a young age? The one who has loved cannot forget, the one who has forgotten has never loved, the one who has forgotten but still has loved, did not know what love was."

"Are you thinking of your own experiences when you read this?" I said, because it felt that way.

"Yes, I have been burned. But one gets over it, believe me."

So he thought that I was just as much in love with him as he had been in the one who had burned him and tried to comfort me with that poem. When I realized that, I opened the door and left. And he drove away, happy to have finally gotten rid of me.

Why didn't he want to see me? Was it because I was too eager? But I don't think he would have wanted it otherwise either. I think he thought that he was better than me, and that I wasn't good enough for him. But when he realized that I was interested in him, he took for granted that I was willing and drove out to the woods and tried to lay me, so I cannot think that he was better than me.

Last night, when I was in town and went out on the bridge on Skolgatan, a police car drove by. The cops inside stared, and when I noticed it, I felt weird. I don't know why that draw comes. I would like to give in to it, but I don't dare, because I'm not sure that I could be the same as usual again afterwards.

It smelled of sludge from the river and exhaust gases from the cars in the street. Some guys in a Volvo PV blinked their lights, but they didn't stop.

Then a guy came and stood beside me at the bridge railing without saying anything. It was Putte. After a while he took my hand and started walking, and I went along with him, though I didn't know if I wanted to. We walked on Västra Strandgatan and past Magdeburg, our school. He said that he was going to sea soon and that we ought to get engaged before he left. I was so surprised that I almost didn't know what to say.

"But we hardly know each other," I said.

"I know *you*."

I felt sorry for him, because he seemed so alone and sad, but you can't get engaged to someone just out of compassion.

"It wouldn't work," I said.

"You don't want to?"

"I can't."

Then he got cross and went on without holding my hand. When we had passed Saluhallen and reached Dombron he stopped.

"Shove off then, godammit!" he said and headed towards Svartbäcksgatan.

"Yes, but I don't want you to be angry."

"You don't give a shit about that! You don't give a shit about me!"

"Yes, I do!"

"No, because the only love you know is sheet metal love!"

But just because I don't want to be with *him* doesn't have to mean that cars are the only thing I'm interested in. I can be interested in other *guys*, for example. And why must he care about what I do? Because he is in love with me and wants me to be with him only? But he isn't in love with me, and I don't get why he said that we ought to become engaged. To test how I would react, or because he wants to have someone to talk about and write to while he is at sea?

I didn't want him to be angry, but the street was full of cars and I didn't care to stand there any longer and waste time.

"I must go now," I said.

"Yes, shove off and ride with your damn cars, goddammit! Just do it! I don't give a shit!"

But I don't think it was true that he didn't care, because in that case he wouldn't have gotten so angry.

Saturday, 6 June 1964
Tonight E-L and I are going to the movies and then to Svartbäcksgatan. It's positively something special about walking there! (Cést très agréable.) I like it partly because of all the stores, cafes and cinemas, and partly because of all the cars (or the contents of the cars, rather). I'm not very at home in makes of cars, but I

recognize almost all the ones I have gone with (plus Ford Anglia, the berry picker).

Yes, they are nice to have, the cars, if you want to go someplace! And you do want that. If you didn't, you wouldn't walk on Svartbäcksgatan. In that case, you would stand on Nybron instead and talk with the Mods, or sit at home and watch TV on Saturday nights.

But we prefer to walk on Svartbäcksgatan (unless we are just sitting *there, that is). We usually sit on a bench down by Skolgatan, because from there you can observe all the boys well when they stop for a red light, and they can seize the opportunity to take a peek at us while they are waiting for the light to turn green.*

Yes, and then a car stops, and we walk up and talk with the boys inside… If they don't seem too bad, we hop in and cruise around a little, talk and smoke, before they stop somewhere and propose that we change places. But before it has gone that far, you try to figure out if you can fancy a continuation or not. Because if you can't, you must come up with a way to get out of the situation.

But it's difficult to say no. We never say directly that we don't like them; instead we look for an excuse so that they won't be hurt if we don't want to go with them anymore. We usually say that we are going to meet a mate somewhere.

Tuesday, 9 June 1964

On "Kvällstoppen" this week "My Boy Lollipop" with Millie came first, "Suspicion" with Terry Stafford second and "Don't Throw Your Love Away" with The Searchers third.

On Saturday E-L and I were at a summer house in Sunnersta with three boys. It was Tony and his friend, named Ricky (he was the one E-L was with), and then a third one, named Hasse, who I was with. First, we drove to the Murco gas station on Salabacksgatan and tanked up, and they asked us if we had any money to help with gas. But we didn't have any (we said). How much can a liter of gas cost? 75 öre, possibly, and they could very well afford that, we thought.

Tony, who was the most handsome one, didn't have a girl, and Ricky said to E-L that he (Tony, that is) had some type of venereal disease and that's why he didn't want to be with somebody. Or he wasn't allowed to, because V.D. infects through sexual activity, and he perhaps thought that there was no point in being with a girl if he couldn't lay her.

Hasse offered Merry (the fruit soda with a full-grown taste) and that he had to say something funny about of course, how he now put it. It had to do with sex in any case, because it wasn't just the taste of the soda that was full-grown but something else as well. But I wasn't interested in what was going on below his waist. And before we drove off to the summer house he said: "No, in this way there will be no children made. Let's go to the cabin!" So it wasn't very difficult to figure out what he had in mind. But the only thing I let him do was pull up my bra and kiss my breasts.

Ooh, it's so difficult to be out and come home, because I prefer not to awake mamma, but she wakes up almost every time. It's really funny to share the same room with your mamma, I have to say! Why can't she sleep in the living room with papa instead and leave me alone in the bedroom?

But I'm really good at sneaking in. I unlock the door and pad in without making a sound, and close the outer door (I hear how papa snores, so when it comes to him there is no problem), and take off my clothes in the hallway and go into the bathroom and brush my teeth gently and wash off my face.

But just as I push down the door handle and creep in to mamma, I hear: "I'm not asleep!" Instead of opening the door as soon as I come into the hall and telling me she is awake she does like that, and it irritates me just as much every time.

Now this school year has come to its end. I got lousy grades. I don't know why. They are the worst I have ever had. In chemistry I was even failed.

But Holmberg didn't fail me in mathematics after all. He could as well have done it, so that I would have gotten two grades below the pass standard. I have never been failed in any subject before. Kicki didn't do very well, either, but her grades weren't reduced as much as mine.

Tonight we're going to town, because tomorrow she is leaving for the countryside and is going to be gone until the twentieth of July.

Thursday, 11 June 1964

"The flowering time now comes, with desire and striking colors, now sweet summer approaches, when grass and grain grow."

This is the song we sang at the breaking-up. And then we got our grades, which were not especially brilliant in my case. The grade in English I was disappointed about, because I had hoped for better. I have done pretty well on some of my written exercises, but it was obviously not good enough to get a high ending grade.

I'm so absent-minded in school. I don't put a lot of effort into my school work. At the same time, I would like to do better. Previously I thought that I would continue to study after the girls' school, but things have not gone well and now I don't know anymore. I would like to be a psychologist or a nurse, but I will never be accepted in those programs with my grades. So I don't know what I will do later. Get married and have children, perhaps?

I'm in the country with mamma now. (Papa is coming

out when his vacation begins.) We are going to be here until 19 July. E-L and I went out last night instead, because we can't do it on Saturday. We went with a guy E-L had met previously some time and his mate to an apartment, and E-L disappeared with Becke into the bedroom, while the other guy (whose name was Martin) and I sat in the kitchen and listened to the radio. "Twist with The Adventurers" or what the hell it was called.

And Becke started a row with E-L. She knew even before we went with them what he is like, so in a way I think she had to blame herself for seeing him. I would never meet such a hard guy again, I have to say! But she tends to feel sorry for such types and can't say no. Before there was another one she couldn't neglect, though he almost had tried to rape her.

Now I'm going to sit down in the arbor and read. In any case, it's wonderful to be in the country! On 20 July, when we are back in town again, I will work for Stig in his firm to earn some money, so I had better enjoy this time off while it lasts.

We went with a guy named Becke and his buddy to an apartment in Tunabackar. When Becke and I got into the bedroom, he drew me down on the bed and laid himself on top of me and tried to kiss me. His breath smelled of alcohol and I didn't want him to kiss me, but when I turned away he got angry and began to tear and tug at my clothes.

"Stay with me tonight," he said.

But I didn't want to be with him if he was just going to mess with me. Why couldn't he take it a little easy?

He wanted to lay me and held me fast and tried to take my pants off. When I resisted him, he pressed me down harder in bed so that I couldn't move. I didn't think he would do anything with violence, but I didn't dare give up fighting against him, because then he might not have been able to stop himself.

It was such a hassle. I didn't manage to get loose though I resisted him as much as I could.

"Don't mess around now," he said.

"But I don't want to!"

"But you do want to do it with Putte, don't you? With him you have no objections! But he's in jail now."

"He is?"

"Yeah, your guy is in prison!"

But he isn't my guy, and I don't want to do anything with him, like Becke seemed to believe. Actually, I don't give a shit about him.

My wrists were sore where Becke squeezed them, and I became so exhausted fighting against him.

"Why can't you just let me go?" I said.

"Don't you think you are somebody!" he said.

"I don't."

"You aren't any fucking beauty."

"Have I claimed that?"

"Nobody wants to have you!"
"Well, let me go then."
"Fuck you!"
"The same to you!"
"Stay with me tonight."
"But you are just messing with me."

His face was red, and the hair on his forehead and temples was wet with sweat. I was also sweaty. At last I could get myself loose enough to cast myself down on the floor. I thought about running out to Kicki and the other guy, but I wasn't able to get up before Becke had thrown himself after me and lay on top of me again. He held my wrists tightly and put down his head and pressed his cheek against mine.

"Stay with me!" he said.

Then I screamed, and Kicki and the other guy came in. They stood in the doorway and stared at us.

"I'm leaving now, Eva-Lena," Kicki said, and I could hear from her voice that she thought that I had myself to blame because I had come along with Becke.

"Let me loose!" I said and tried to get away from him.

"You only do what *she* says! You just let *her* decide!"

But finally he let me go. I was totally shaky when I got up and sticky all over my body with sweat.

We had to walk all the way from Tunabackar and down to town. In front of Stugan we met two guys in a U-marked Ford that we went with. One of them was really good at imitating voices. He could sound like Tage Erlander, Gunnar Hedlund and Olle Björklund.

I've got a letter from Kicki. It's about Uffe and Göran, and about how it was when we first started going out. She writes:

Saturday, 13 June 1964. Howdy, partner! They are going to increase the postage from 35 to 45 *öre*, so I thought I would write while I can still afford to mail the letter. But that's not the only reason I have for writing, if you think so. I thought I would also write to see how you are doing these days. Sure, it's only two days since we met, but who knows what can happen in two days? If I know you at all, anything could happen. Tonight, for example, you will probably go to town looking for some pleasant boys again. (Correct me if I'm wrong!) But I really hope that you will catch someone better than the boy you got on Wednesday!

Just now I'm sitting outside on the lawn, listening on my transistor radio to "Sommartoppen" with Pekka Langer. Radio and TV are the only two entertainments offered out here in the country. Unfortunately, there are no pleasant boys one can meet and have fun with! (No unpleasant ones either, if you prefer the hard types!) You're not offended, I hope? But I can't understand how you could be with Becke, though you knew how he is! But you can't judge a person without proof, and you perhaps needed to find out about him through personal experience to determine if the rumors about him were true or not?

Yesterday evening, when I watched "Bonanza" with the Cartwright brothers on TV, it occurred to me that I have never asked you who you think is the most handsome, Adam or Little Joe. But you perhaps prefer Hoss? For my own part, I like Adam the best. He reminds me a little of Uffe, I think. (Though that isn't the reason I like him the best.) You do remember Uffe and Göran? Yes, of course you do, because Göran was your first great love.

Now I'm going to tell you how it happened that I became a *raggarbrud*. (That's what I am, if you didn't know!) It's because you and I met two boys called Uffe and Göran. The first time we met them we were sitting on a bench down by the river. (You know which bench I mean, don't you?) We had been at the movies, and then we went around window shopping, I recall. Then you proposed that we should go to Svartbäcksgatan. We knew it was there the *raggare* hung about, but we would just go there and look (at those strange animals!), and we sat on a bench down by Skolgatan and smoked. It was in the fall, in September.

Yes, and then two boys came and asked if they could sit with us. Göran sat beside me, and Uffe sat beside you. They lived in Knivsta, and they were going to take the train home, because they didn't have a car that evening. But they made an appointment with us for the next evening, on Sunday, and that evening we went to Fågelsången and had coffee. We were going there to drink coffee with them, and we were so nervous. My hand was shaking so much that I could scarcely lift my cup, and you couldn't hold your head still, so when you tried to drink, your teeth rattled against the cup. (I see Runk-Nisse before me now, the poor chap.) And then they offered each of us a cigarette, and we couldn't say no. I think it was Uffe who offered, and he had long Chesterfields! So instead of smoking our own with normal size, we had to sit there and inhale those cigarettes in long king size.

Yes, and then they gave us a lift home in their silver-gray Volvo that they had parked at Svandammen. Göran and you sat in the back and Uffe and I sat in front, because Uffe was driving. And he said to me that I had such beautiful, blue eyes, I recall. I fell for that. Göran didn't get to kiss you, but Uffe and I kissed, because I wasn't as *distant* as you. It wasn't the first time for me, either, as it was for you.

But after we had been out and had coffee that time and been given a lift home, nothing else happened. We went down to the railway station and looked for their car, because we knew that they had a habit of parking it there, and when we saw it we danced around for joy because they were in town.

But, where were they? At the movies, perhaps?

And so we went to Saga to meet them at the cinema exit after the film. (How we could know that they were exactly at Saga, I can't remember.)

And they came out and saw us, but they just said hello and walked on. And we got ahead of them to their car and sat down on a bench that we knew they would pass when they came by. And after a while they turned up, and Uffe said: "Are you sitting here freezing?" They understood perfectly well why we were sitting there, but we pretended that we didn't know that they were parked nearby. And they went straight to their car without asking us if we wanted to come along, or if they could give us a lift home, and we were so angry.

But we continued to go into town to look for them, and one evening, when they were in their car and just whistled by though we knew that they had seen us, we rode with two other guys. They were Dick and Lasse. And Lasse was so repulsive, you thought. But we let them kiss us, and that was the first time I've got a French kiss.

Then we started to go out regularly. We usually went to the movies first and then to Svartbäcksgatan. But we were very careful about with whom we rode. We would not go with guys in big *raggarbilar*, and we would not go with guys who had alcohol, we said. But boys in common cars were probably almost worse, we discovered when we had started to ride with the other kind as well, with the exception that they possibly drank a little less. Guys who are real *raggare* don't take anything for granted. You are not a *street-walker* just because you walk on the street, I mean, but ordinary boys more often seem to believe that. Wasn't that what Göran thought about you, for example? Yes, exactly! But that's not the case.

Yes, so it happened that I came into the *raggarliv*! Interesting, wasn't it? But now I'm not able to write any more. You can write me back, if you have time between the turns. Not the turns on the street and not the turns on a knitting, I mean, but the turns that have a special meaning when you use them in a special expression. You get what I mean, don't you? Great! See you later alligator!
Kicki

On Midsummer Eve, I rode with two guys and a girl in an Opel, and for once the guy who didn't have a girl was cute. His name was Björn and he was eighteen years old. The other two were Lasse and Lena and they were engaged.

We went to Björkvallen, where Lasse and Lena got out to dance, while Björn and I remained in the car. I thought he was a little childish, because he asked me how far I usually let guys go and if I have ever been together with older guys, and he got cross when I didn't want to kiss him. For that reason, he thought that I didn't like him. But it was just his kisses I didn't like. They were so hard and strange.

He wanted to see me again and said that he would call, but he probably won't.

Yesterday it was a guy named Rune who drove for Becke, and I went with them when Becke asked me to. I didn't think that he would mess with me like he did the last time, but as soon as I had entered the car, he started. I screamed to Rune to stop, and when he did I tried to get out.

"Drive on, damn it!" Becke said.

"No, I'm getting out here," I said and tried to open the door. But I couldn't reach the door handle before he tore my hand away from it.

"Now you keep calm!" he said and pressed me down on the seat.

"If you don't let me go I'll scream," I said.

Then he covered my mouth with his hand and said to Rune:

"Put a record on, damn it! Put "Jailhouse Rock" on and drive!"

And Rune obeyed. As soon as Becke loosened his grip I screamed, but the music was so jacked up that I couldn't be heard outside.

"Shut up!" he said and twisted my arm up on my back.

"It hurts!"

"Promise that you won't make up a fuss, then."

"But you're the one who's doing that!"

"Promise that you'll do exactly as I say."

"But I want to get out!"

"So that's the sort of girl you are!"

"What sort"

"The sort that comes along for just five minutes!"

"Yes, that's right!"

"Fuck you!"

"The same to you!"

When I finally manage to get up, I leaned towards Rune and told him once again to stop.

"Just go ahead, damn it!" Becke shouted.

"Is it he or you that decides?" I said to Rune.

"We decide things together," Becke said.

"But he's the one driving."

"Yes, and he drives the way *I* want!"

I decided to try to jump out at the next red light, but it showed green all the way, and soon we were out of town.

When we rode on the Gävle highway, Becke rolled the side window down and stuck his elbow out. It was pleasant to feel the draft, because I was so sweaty. Trees and fields glided by, and Elvis sang "Lawdy, Miss Clawdy" so it felt like the tires rolled around in time with the music. Becke held his other arm around my shoulders, but he didn't say or do anything until we were there, and Rune had stopped the car on a grass area and got out. Then Becke dragged me down on the seat and laid himself on top of me. He wanted to lay me and pulled up my dress and tried to get my panties off. I tried to fight against him, but it didn't help.

"If you don't stop I'll call Rune," I said.

"Don't kick up a fuss now."

"But I don't want to do it!"

"Don't kick up a fuss I said!"

"If you do something, it will be rape."

"Nobody will believe you."

"But there's a witness."

Though I didn't know where Rune was.

"He isn't here," Becke said and started to open his fly.

And then, just as he was about to pull his pants down, I got away. I managed to open the door and hopped out. I tried to run away, but he caught me, twisted my arm, and threw me against the car so I fell. Everything happened so quickly, and then Rune came up to me and helped me up.

"Leave off now, damn it!" he said and glared at Becke.

Then Becke went to the trunk, took out a bottle of beer, put a foot on the bumper, and began to swig from the bottle. When he had finished it, he threw it away and set the car rocking with his foot. Then he hopped in behind the steering wheel and started the engine. There were some wilted birch branches stuck in the Dodge's grill, and the front window reflected the sun, so you couldn't see into the car. I glanced at Rune to check if he would react to what Becke did, but he didn't, and Becke turned the car around on the grass and drove forward a few meters and stopped. Then he said to me through the open side window:

"Are you coming?"

So he hadn't intended to leave me there, anyway.

When Rune came up to him he got out, went around the car, and opened the door on the other side.

"Come and sit here in front," he said.

It was still warm inside the car. Becke pressed in "Heartbreak Hotel" and put his arm behind me on the backrest, and Rune beat time with his fingers against the steering wheel while he drove. It felt cosy sitting there between them in the front seat, watching the roadway disappear under the car.

When we got back to town I thought that Becke would let me go, but he didn't. Rune stopped the car, but Becke held on to me.

"Ride with us tonight," he said.

"No, I'm getting out now."

"Why?"

"Because."

But he didn't budge, so I asked Rune if I could get out on his side instead. Then he said to Becke:

"Let the chick go."

"No, she's going to ride with us tonight," Becke said.

I started staring out the window, and when Becke noticed that I was angry, he said:

"Damn it, you're really dumb!"

"So are you!"

"You are the dumbest in your entire damn class!"

"What do you know about that?"

"Everything!"

"So, you know someone in my class, then?"

"No, but in another class."

"There's nobody who knows anything about me in another class!"

I was so tired of sitting there talking back with him.

"Look at me," he said.

"Why?"

"Because I say so!"

Then I turned my face towards Rune instead.

"You only look in *his* direction!" Becke said.

"I have a right to look wherever I want."

"You are looking at him just because he's the one *driving*!"

"Sure!"

"Look at me I said!"

And he grabbed my chin and turned my head towards him.

"Give me a kiss!" he said.

"Yes, if you let me go."

"Let her be off, damn it," Rune said.

But it was a long time before he did. And outside the car he stood in front of me and started to stroke his hands roughly over my hair.

"Promise that you'll ride with us some other time," he said.

But I knew I would never do it again, so I couldn't promise.

Then I went with two guys and a girl in a dark green Volkswagen. The guy driving was called Chrille, and he was cute, but there was a girl with him, so I got the other one, who they called Klangen. He was one of those naively foolish types that I'm not interested in and with whom I know that nothing could ever happen.

I went to town again yesterday evening. First, I was at the movies and watched a film with Tony Curtis, Marilyn Monroe, and Jack Lemmon. It was played at Spegeln, and it was the first time I was at that cinema. Later, when I sat on a bench near Saga and smoked, a guy came and sat down beside me.

"What are you waiting for?" he said. "Better times?"

I had seen him and heard of him before.

"You are the guy called Sudden, aren't you?" I said.

"Everyone knows the monkey, but the monkey doesn't know anyone!" he said.

Then he asked me to blow smoke from my cigarette straight into his mouth. It's called a bum puff, he said. And when I sat there with my mouth against his, there was some whistling from a passing car and a guy shouted:

"Press hard! You're already halfway in!"

I don't know if Sudden heard it. He didn't say anything, anyway. He rested his elbows on his knees and held his head in his hands.

"Aren't you feeling well?" I said.

"That's none of your business."

"But why are you sitting like this?"

"Because I'm sick and tired and soon will be in jail."

"Why?"

"Why?" he imitated me.

"Yes, what have you done to end up in jail?"

"Driving without a heavy vehicle license."

"But you surely aren't sent to jail for that?"

Then he just stared at me without saying anything. So maybe you can. I don't know.

"I'm sick and tired of everything," he said as he looked up into the tree crown. "If I could, I would put an end to everything."

After a while he asked me if I would like to come along with him to his home, and I did, though I didn't know if I wanted to.

On the way there, Rune and Becke drove by. They hooted and Sudden raised his right arm.

"Do you know them?" I said.

"Yeah, why?"

"Because I rode with them yesterday."

"I see."

"But it was no fun, because he was violent."

"Who?"

"Becke."

"Becke-in-a-hurry?"

"Yes, if that's what he's called."

"Then he should have a beating."

He lived in a two-story house on Gamla Uppsalagatan. We sneaked up the stairs to the second floor and came into a bedroom that smelled musty and stuffy. The curtains were drawn, so at first I didn't notice a boy who was sleeping in the other bed. It was his little brother.

When we lay on Sudden's bed, and he had taken his pants off, I said that I didn't want to.

"Why not? Are you going steady?"

"No, but we don't know each other."

Then he tossed his head and snorted:

"So that's your fucking style!"

"Yes, I think you should know each other first and not the opposite."

"So first you should be together for a while, and then start sleeping together, you mean?"

"Yes."

"You have the wrong style!"

"That's not what I think."

But he pulled down my panties and laid himself on top of me between my legs. He was so strong that I couldn't hinder him. When I tried to get away, he just pressed me down harder.

When I realized that I couldn't do anything, I got scared. It was maybe true that he was tired of everything, and if he was thinking about killing himself, it probably didn't make any difference to him if he raped somebody first. But then he put on a rubber, and I thought that he wouldn't have done that, if he had decided to commit suicide.

"Don't struggle now," he said and forced me to lie still. "When this is done we'll go downtown again."

I felt how he pressed and tried to come in, but the

rubber was too dry, so it didn't work. I didn't know what to do. I didn't dare to scream, and I didn't want to beg him to stop, because that would have felt so degrading. Finally I started to cry.

"Stop weeping, damn it," he said.

"But I don't want you to!"

"If we knew each other then?"

"What do you mean?"

"Would you let me if we knew each other? I could think of being together with you for a while first, if you would rather have it that way."

"But you must also like each other."

Know that you do, I meant, but he didn't get it.

"So that's how you look at me!" he said.

"Yes, I can't know what I would feel if I knew you."

"You have the wrong style I say!"

"So you think that one can lay anybody?"

"Yes, you can."

"But I don't want to."

"Then why did Becke get to do it?"

"He didn't."

"Tell me another one!"

"But I'm telling the truth. *Nobody* gets to do it."

I thought he was even worse than Becke, though he had said that Becke would have a beating because he had tried to force me.

"Why the hell did you come along with me then?" he said and jumped up and pulled his pants on. Then he said that I could get up and dress. He was angry and just left without any concern for me. Not until then I remembered his brother who had laid there the whole time and surely had overheard everything. It was maybe because of him that Sudden hadn't done anything more with me after all.

When we came out he started out for town, and I went after him. At the railroad crossing the barriers came down and he had to stop, and then I caught up to him. I asked if he were angry, but he just turned away and went up to a car and started to talk with the guys sitting in it. Then he whistled to me and shouted:

"You can ride with these guys! They'll give you a lift home!"

I wanted to say that I didn't need any help from him to get home, but then I thought that I might as well accept it and went up to the car.

"Do you have ten *kronor*?" Sudden said.

"Why?"

"Because that's what it costs."

But why would I pay for a lift home when I can get one for free as easily as ever? I just looked at him and didn't answer.

"How the hell will it be?" he said. "We don't have all night."

"No, exactly," I said and walked away from there.

I have clipped this out of the newspaper. It's about what the *raggare* did in Öregrund during midsummer.

Violent uproar in Öregrund because of an invasion by 1000 raggare.
The *raggare* invasion the small town in Roslagen, Öregrund, suffered defies all description, reports police assistant Thorsten Helander to UNT on Sunday evening, when the huge fight was over and the police could summarize the results of the midsummer celebrations in Öregrund. 1000 *raggare* of both sexes arrived in 250 cars and caused a stir in the form of drunkenness, fist fights, and disorderly conduct. Sexual intercourse scenes took place at several places. 15 *raggare* were arrested for drunkenness, but these were only the worst of the many who qualified to be taken into police custody.

...

Most of the *raggare* stayed in Öregrund and pitched their tents. Most of them showed no concern for others but just encroached upon gardens and summer cottage plots with their tents. Fences were torn down and crushed with cars. Inside the tents there were now and then fist fights, alcohol bottles were being cast about and there were other scenes as well. In town a couple of *raggare* performed their calls of nature on a street in front of strolling pedestrians. People called the police and came up with one report after the other.

...

Several of the sexual intercourse scenes were completely public. A couple were unashamedly lying on a bridge down by Hamntorget at nine o'clock on Midsummer Day morning. Similar scenes were also happening at a party location in town.

…

Even on Midsummer Day there was a lot of unrest, but everything calmed down on Sunday. Actually, it is a good thing that midsummer 1964 is over, police assistant Helander finally says.

Tuesday, 23 June 1964

Il fait beau aujourd'hui. Il fait de soleil.

I have received a letter from E-L. On Midsummer Eve she was with a guy named Björn, and on Midsummer Day evening she rode with Becke again, dumb as she is. It was he and another guy, and they went out to Ulva, and there he threw himself over her again and tried to get to lay her. But she forced her way out of the car (and avoided a fate worse than death), and after a while he calmed down and let her go back to town with them.

The next evening, she met another guy, with whom she went home. They were lying on his bed and had taken off some of their clothes, when it turned out to be the same thing with him, that he didn't want to stop when she said no. He held her and was absolutely determined to have his way with her. Eventually, she turned on the water-works, and he weakened and let her be. (Tears are a woman's best weapon!) Yes, it was a narrow escape! Actually, it was close that she lost her virginity there.

On Midsummer Eve, when she was with that Björn at a local dance and they sat in the car in the parking lot, she saw a guy being beaten, she wrote.

Violence and fist fights I do not *like! I watch out for boys who are violent and get involved in crime. Most of the boys E-L and I meet have nothing to hide, but there are others too, and I know t I want to have a well-behaved boy and not one of those half-criminal types. I'm not interested in associating with jailbirds. But if I met a boy who had been in prison I would not judge him unheard, because it would depend on* why *he had done what he had done, also. If he had done time for car theft or something like that, so it wasn't abuse or manslaughter, and if he had quit and learned from his mistakes, I wouldn't worry very much about it. But I couldn't go steady with anyone who is* constantly *involved in crime.*

On Wednesday I was out. I rode with a guy in a Volvo PV with a transparent sunshade at the top of the front windshield. He had had a real cruiser before, he said. It was a Ford Thunderbird Cabriolet. But it had sucked so much gas that he couldn't afford to keep it.

He knew Tiger. Three years ago, Tiger was *raggarkung* in Uppsala. It had been written about him and his gang in the newspaper, and Tiger was photographed with a sign that said The Naughty Devils. The gang was actually called The Night Devils, but the company that had made the sign had misunderstood the name and painted it incorrectly.

"That's what happened when The Night Devils became naughty!" he said.

I don't know if it was true or something he just made up. I'll ask Tiger about it if I meet him again some time.

The guy was kind, but he only talked about cars and guys he knew the whole time, and it became rather boring in the long run. He didn't have any music, either. But he offered smokes and candy, so he wasn't stingy. The next evening, he was going to drive to Klockbacken and listen to Chubby Checker, and he asked if I wanted to come along. But I didn't want to see him again, and I don't like Chubby Checker, so I said no.

Boris was his name. Before I met him, I saw Göran and Uffe. I had just picked up my pocket mirror and started to paint my lips when they drove by. Uffe looked at me and smiled, but Göran acted like he didn't see me.

Saturday, 27 June 1964
Life in the country is calm and peaceful. I wander in the woods and philosophize, or I lie on the grass and read old magazines. In the evenings I also become absorbed in

them before I go to sleep.

I have my own room on the second floor and when the sun shines, it can get so hot up there that you can barely stand it. But I don't want to sleep downstairs, because it's nicer to lie by myself.

In the evenings mamma and I sit in the kitchen and play cards. We often sit up to after midnight playing, because we think it's fun. We play Japanese Whist and Black Maria sometimes. Meanwhile we eat mint candies or Dr Dryels pastilles.

Yesterday was my birthday. Now I'm 16 years old. How time flies! At this time a year ago, I had still not started going out to meet boys and was completely inexperienced with regard to the opposite sex. Now I'm one year older and have probably become a little more experienced, but the question is, if I have become any wiser? That isn't what mamma and papa think, anyway, I suspect.

I got hand cream and two pairs of nylon stockings from mamma (good to have in the fall, because a pair a week for 3.95 kronor adds up to lots of money), and from papa I got 20 kronor.

So now I am in cash again. Though I don't need almost any money out here. I possibly buy an ice cream sometimes when mamma and I go grocery shopping, or a Krokant roll for 90 öre, but no cigarettes and no magazines. No coffee and no movies either, so most of my monthly allowance from mamma I can save.

A guy called Cowboy rode in a Ford Falcon with Biran and Lärling, with whom I'm also a little acquainted. Lärling is one of those withdrawn types who always drives, never drinks, and never has a girl. "Actually, it's those quiet driving types you should go in for," Kicki said once, "because they are proper boys!"

But it's the other kind that dominate. Just now, for instance, it was Biran who asked if I would like to go with them, though it was Cowboy who wanted me. At least I think it was he, because he was the one I was with the first time I met them. And he was sitting by himself in the back seat, so I knew that I was going to get him.

They say that he has been at the psychiatric hospital because he went crazy from brooding on the over-population problem. I don't know if it's true. I think he looks a bit like Elvis, with back-combed hair and sideboards.

Now he had black, pointed shoes, black slacks, and a white, long-sleeved sweater, even though it was so warm. Biran only had a thin T-shirt and was sitting with his elbow outside the window while he gulped down a Bocken's Special beer.

The first time I met them, when I was with Cowboy and we were at an apartment somewhere, Biran had a shivering fit because of drinking. At first I didn't know what it was, but Cowboy explained it to me. So he is probably called Biran because he tipples.

When we had spun around town for a while, we went out to the country. I don't really know where we were, but there was a barn that Biran thought that Cowboy and I should go into. In the meantime, Biran and Lärling sat in the grove outside and waited for us. They had opened the car doors and played records, so while Cowboy and I were inside the barn, we heard music the whole time. There was "Roll over Beethoven" with The Beatles and "Good Golly Miss Molly" and some others that I don't know the names of.

Cowboy and I had climbed up a ladder to the loft and lay in the hay. I thought that we could tell Biran that we had been doing it, even though we hadn't, so that Biran could stop worrying about what Cowboy did or didn't do. But after a while Biran opened the barn door downstairs and came in.

"Have you mated yet?" he called up to Cowboy.

"No, I…" Cowboy began. "She's a virgin and…"

I got so irritated with him. Why did he have to report everything to that bugger?

"Screw her, damn it!" Biran said and stuck up his head above the ladder.

I don't know if Cowboy noticed that I was angry, but he told Biran to get lost. Then he started to fondle me and asked me if I were angry.

"Yes, I am," I said, "but not for the reason you think."

After a while I crept over to the ladder and Cowboy followed me. I didn't feel like telling Biran a fib anymore, and when we came down Biran smiled slyly and acted like he thought that we had done it, though I knew that he didn't believe it.

"Have you cracked the hymen now?" he said to Cowboy.

"No, she didn't want to," Cowboy said and tried to look nonchalant.

Why couldn't he have just faked it, instead? But he didn't know that I would have played along.

When we sat in the car again, on our way back to town, he ignored me. Biran pressed in "Summertime Blues" and looked unmoved, but I knew he was happy about that Cowboy was cross with me. I thought it was weak of Cowboy to allow Biran to rule over him, and he noticed that. That's why he was angry. But he could have stood up for his rights and ignored Biran. That's what I would have done, if I had been him.

When we got back to town, they were going to tank up.

"Give us a ten," Biran said and glared at me.

"Why?"

"For gas, damn it!"

I didn't want to fork out any money for gas, but it felt like I had to. He got my last bill. Then, when Cowboy got out to buy cigarettes, I gave him two *kronor* to buy me a lemonade. That was the least he could do, I thought.

And he brought a bottle back, but instead of giving it to me, he popped the cap and began gulping down the lemonade himself. At first I thought that he was just going to have a couple of sips as thanks for buying it for me, but he never stopped drinking, and finally I told him that he wasn't allowed to take any more. Then he looked at Biran, who was grinning at him over his shoulder, and continued to swig.

"It's my drink!" I shouted and tried to get the bottle from him.

"You little shrew!" he said and held the bottle out of my reach.

And then he drank it until it was empty.

When Lärling came back he and Biran changed places so that Biran was now behind the wheel. Nobody said anything. Biran drummed his fingers on the dashboard and Lärling looked out the window. Finally Cowboy glanced at me and said:

"Haven't you gone yet?"

Then I realized what they were driving at and grabbed my purse and hopped out.

"Damned idiots!" I shouted and slammed the car door at the same time as Biran made a tearing start so that the tires shrieked against the asphalt.

I was so angry that I almost started to cry. Why did they have to be so mean? I regretted giving Biran money, because it was they and not me who had wanted to go to that barn. And gasoline for ten *kronor* hadn't been consumed, so I shouldn't have given them anything!

On Linnégatan a police car had stopped, and two

policemen were approaching a drunk guy who was lying on the sidewalk. One of the cops squatted by him and grabbed his shoulder. When I saw what he did, I felt weird. It was fortunate that it wasn't a girl lying there, because I couldn't have borne to see that. If they found *me* like that, and a policeman squatted by me, I would die. I don't even dare to think about how it would feel.

Tuesday, 7 July 1964

Last Saturday E-L went with some guys who had alcohol and drank so much that she got drunk. I got a letter from her today where she writes about it.

So, what do I think of that? In the old days, when we began to go out, we decided that we would never start drinking. But now she has done it. Well, she hasn't exactly started drinking, but she has tried it, anyway, and she thought it was fun.

But it doesn't make any difference to me. I'm not going to begin. I have known since I was little that I don't want to. I may take some wine, with food sometimes, but I don't want to drink until I get drunk. It isn't certain that E-L was drunk either, though that's what she writes. By being drunk she may just mean a little dizzy. After all, this was the first time she drank.

It's so peaceful here in the country. Papa isn't drinking and there aren't any rows. In the evenings we go for long walks and watch the sunsets. It's very nice, I think.

Though I know that it won't last. As soon as we are home in town again, things will be as usual. If papa isn't the one who can't manage, it will be mamma. I'll never for- get the time when they had talked about how he must stop drinking and he quit and didn't drink a drop for half a year. Then mamma thought that things had turned out so well that she went to Systembolaget and bought a bottle of aquavit so that they could celebrate. She was so dumb! She bought alcohol, and he drank it of course, and then there was no more talk of him stopping drinking. I don't get how she could be so bloody dumb!

So I don't believe that he will ever stop. I'm just happy about the days he is sober, and that's the way he has been the entire time out here.

I have also been abstinent, because I haven't smoked a single cigarette since I came here. It's almost unbelieve-able. I haven't even missed smoking, so evidently I'm not as addicted to nicotine as I believed.

I went with three guys from Gävle in a Plymouth. Their names were Palle, Lasse and Chrille. Palle and Lasse sat in front and Chrille and I in the back seat. Palle was the cutest one, but I also liked Chrille, be-cause he was kind.

At first, we cruised the usual route Svartbäcksgatan – Stora Torget – Drottninggatan – Nybron – Sysslomansgatan – Skolgatan – Svartbäcksgatan. I don't know how they would know what streets the *raggare* usually run here. But they had perhaps been in Uppsala before.

In the back window there was a heap of single records that I started to look through. Some of them had been destroyed by the sun, but the ones that weren't buckled and that I wanted to listen to, I handed over to Lasse, and he set them on. Mostly I played "Hippy, Hippy Shakes" with The Swinging Blue Jeans. It's so wonderful to sit like that in a big *raggarbil* and see how people glare when you come cruising along the street with the music streaming out the windows.

Then we went to Skogsvallen. The Spotnicks were playing there. Chrille and I stayed in the car while Palle and Lasse went in. When they had left he got out a bottle of alcohol and asked me if I wanted some. At first I was about to decline it, but then I thought that it would be no harm in tasting it. The liquor was called Explorer and was some kind of vodka. There was a ship with a red and white striped sail on the label.

Chrille mixed vodka and lime juice in two paper cups that I held up. I was a bit afraid that I would get sick from drinking and that it would taste disgusting, but it didn't. It tasted mostly like lime. The liquor flavor wasn't very perceptible when lime was mixed in.

Chrille was so nice. When I ran out of cigarettes, he gave me a whole pack of Pacifics from a carton that he had in the car, and when I started to hang on him he didn't get cross with me. He just laughed.

It wasn't my intention to get drunk, but I was. Now I know what it feels like. You say whatever comes to your mind, and you hear and feel everything, but you don't care about it. I already know that I'm going to drink again. If the guys in the Plymouth come to town again next Saturday, perhaps they will pick me up and offer liquor one more time, but otherwise I'll go with some others who have spirits.

Kicki probably isn't going to like it that I have begun drinking, because we said that we would never do that. But now when I know what it is like to be drunk, I won't be able to resist. It was so frigging delightful. And it's so wonderful to sit in such a wide, rocking American car and swish along through the summer night while smoking, drinking and listening to music.

We went out to the bathing place at Graneberg. Palle and Lasse slipped out of their clothes and ran out on the bridge and dived in, and Chrille and I sat under a tree. After a while he pulled me down and laid himself on top of me and kissed me.

I didn't have to come home early, because mom and pop had gone to see aunt Margit and wouldn't be home until this evening. I didn't dare to tell the guys that I was at home alone, because then they would perhaps have wanted to come indoors with me. I just said that I didn't have to be home at a certain time. I hope none of the neighbors saw me when I came, and tell mom and pop. But I don't think so, because I didn't get home until four o'clock.

I have checked in the cellar to see what kind of spirits pop has down there. There is one bottle of O.P. Anderson, one bottle of Eau-de-Vie, one bottle of Apricot Brandy, one bottle of Vat 69, and one bottle of Lemon Gin. I have cribbed from a list how strong each one of them are. O.P. Anderson is 43%, Eau-de-Vie 40%, Apricot Brandy 32%, Vat 69 40%, and Lemon Gin 34%. Explorer, which I drank on Saturday, is 38%.

If I had known how wonderful it is to be drunk, I would have started drinking much earlier. But I believed that you felt ill and became sick because of liquor. That doesn't happen. Well, it might happen if you drink too much, but not otherwise.

Oh, how I long for the next time! If it isn't offered to me tomorrow, I'm going to snitch a little Vat 69 from pop and drink it next Saturday. I wish I knew how carefully he keeps track of what he holds, because if he doesn't really know, I might take a whole bottle without it being noticed. He has bought his spirits to offer on special occasions, but they are so far between, that he has probably forgotten what he has.

I might take the gin bottle. Just thinking of the spirits down there makes me wanna have it. Why don't people drink more than they do when it is so wonderful to be drunk? But it's fortunate that they don't.

I got spirits from two guys in a Ford Consul. They were going to Holmen to watch Jimmy Justice, but I didn't want to do that, so I got out on Svartbäcksgatan again.

After a while Lasse and Björn came by in their car. Lasse braked and backed up next to me, and Björn opened the back door and told me to hop in. He had a white sweater and a black jacket on and looked very cute, I thought. But he got angry when he noticed that I wasn't sober.

"She is drunk!" he said and sounded grumpy.

"No, you're just happy, aren't you?" Lasse said and glanced at me in the rearview mirror.

"Yes, that's it!" I said. "I'm just happy!"

They were going to the railway station to fetch Lena, who was supposed to come in by train.

"What have you done tonight?" Björn said.

"Nothing special."

"You were at the movies, weren't you?" Lasse said.

But I hadn't promised Björn anything, so I didn't think I needed to lie.

"No, I've been hanging about in town. What have you been doing?"

"We were at the movies," Lasse said.

"Which one?" I said and looked at Björn, who sat turned away from me staring out the window.

"I could never go steady with a chick who boozes!" he said.

"You couldn't?" Lasse said and glanced at me in the rearview mirror. "That's rather lousy spoken of you."

"Don't you ever drink?" I said to Björn.

"Never!"

But I know he does, because on Midsummer Eve they had a liquor bottle in the car, and when I asked Lasse whose it was, he said that it belonged to him and Björn.

But I didn't care that he was cross with me. I was just thinking about how wonderful everything felt.

"Say something!" Björn finally said.

"I don't know what to speak about."

"Speak about whatever you like!"

"But I think it's so difficult to talk with you."

"Likewise, as the old hag at the driving school says! You're quiet and shy, just like a little mouse."

"If you ask me, I don't think you're very talkative yourself," I said.

"But it's rather sweet, somehow," he continued. "It's better than when the chicks prattle the whole time, anyway. Skip it, maids! is what we tell them then."

"And they do?"

"Oh, yeah."

Then it was quiet again. I moved closer to him and took his hand, but he snatched it away.

"Skip it!" he said.

"Is he grumpy to you?" Lasse said over his shoulder.

It seemed like he wanted to get Björn and me together and got cross with Björn for being awkward.

But I was satisfied to just sit there and listen to the music. When "Beautiful Dreamer" was played I leaned my head against the backrest and closed my eyes. Then Björn moved closer to me and put his arm around my shoulders.

"Beautiful dreamer, open your crazy eyes, you've gotta wake up, I'm here by your side," he sang in my ear, at the same time as John Leyton sang it on the record. "Beautiful dreamer, come and don't be unkind, wake up and tell me you're gonna be mine."

Wednesday, 15 July 1964

Now I have written to E-L and told her about papa. I don't know why it suddenly felt that I could do it. I suppose it's because of what she has done. That she has been drunk, that is, (if she really was). Because partly it caused me to think about papa and spirits, and partly I want her to know why I, for my part, have decided not to drink. I want her to understand the background to it, and why I don't think she should drink either (because I hope she won't do it anymore).

When papa drinks he usually buys most of his spirits on Thursday when he is paid, and then he drinks a little on Friday evening and a little on Saturday. Sometimes he carries on all weekend. When that happens, he starts on Thursday and continues on Friday evening and all day on Saturday. Then Sunday is devoted to recovery.

When it comes to his behaviour, he alternates between being sentimental and aggressive. He isn't angry at first, but as soon as he is more than tipsy, he starts yelling and roaring. Most of it is directed at mamma, but you can't avoid overhearing everything if you are at home.

And if he has been out, you hear it when he comes home and he stands there and can't put the key in the lock, and then how he stumbles and swears. And mamma and I lie there on tenterhooks, waiting for what's coming next. Because in that situation there isn't anything to stop him from pulling the door open and roaring: "Why in hell is there no food here!" or something like that.

But I'm never really afraid, because I know that he never does anything. If it isn't so late, and he has started early and is drinking at home, it even happens that I sit with him and talk. I don't stay away out of fear. I feel sorry for him, somehow, and I can't think that it's only his fault that he does what he does.

I've been to town and purchased nail polish and hydrogen peroxide. When I got home I bleached my fringe.

Tonight, I may go to the movies to see "East of Eden" with James Dean. It has gotten five stars in *Se*, it says in the announcement. Then I will go to Svartbäcksgatan to see if I meet some guys who have spirits.

I didn't go to the movies, because the weather was so nice. Yesterday, when mom and pop had gone to bed, I sneaked into the basement and took a little Vat 69. I poured it into another bottle which I hid outside until I could go to town. It wasn't enough to get drunk by, but I wanted it anyway. I drank it while I waited for the bus.

It isn't a good idea to go to town on Wednesdays. First of all, there aren't many who are out, and secondly, there aren't many who have spirits. But it's such a long time until Saturday and Sunday and I want something to happen all the time.

I rode with a guy called Tim – not Tim Frazer – and one who was called Janne. Nothing special happened.

Björn has called. He asked if I wanted to come along with him and Lasse on Saturday, and I said yes. They are going to pick me up at the bus station. But if they don't have spirits, I don't know if I want to. Before, the guys were the most important, but now I almost don't care how they are, just that they have something to offer. I think that Lasse drinks quite often when he is not seeing Lena, and on Saturday she is not coming, so maybe he has bought some. I hope so, anyway.

When I got off the bus, the Kapitän was already there.

Lena was also there, because they were going to wave her off at the railway station. There was no point in going somewhere else before we had done it, so at first we sat in the car in the parking lot in front of the railway station and talked. Lena played "Mule Skinner Blues" and Björn sang along.

"Good morning Captain… and good morning to you, sa ha ha ha ha, ha," he sang. He could sound exactly as the guy in The Streaplers before he rises to falsetto.

Then Lasse and Lena almost had a quarrel. It started when Björn said that he thought that he had seen me in town on Wednesday.

"Really? Were you in town then?" I said.

"Yeah, sure."

"I don't believe you."

"Why not?"

"Because I didn't see you."

"Which proves that you were there!" he said and sounded like I had given myself away.

"Have I claimed something else, then?" I said.

"But I said that I might call."

"Yes, but just *maybe*, and I didn't think you would."

Then he got cross and tapped Lasse on his shoulder and said:

"Toss me the bottle, damn it!"

And Lena turned to Lasse and stared at him, at the same time as she opened the glove compartment.

"Have you bought booze?" she said.

She sounded angry, as if she didn't like it.

"Don't make a fuss now," Lasse said.

"When the cat is away the mice will play," Björn said and looked at me.

Then we drank, because I also got to taste. It was Explorer and Merry. Björn was affected as fast as I was, and when Lasse and Lena were out, we just sat there and laughed at everything. I didn't want it to end. I really liked Björn and he wasn't cross with me anymore and everything felt so delightful. Why can't it always feel the way it feels when you are drunk?

When Lasse came back he had an ice cream with him, and then Björn went in, though he was drunk, and bought one with strawberry flavor for me and one with vanilla flavor for himself.

Then we cruised around town. I hung on to Björn as he sang "Mule Skinner" and spilled Merry on his shirt. I don't remember everything we talked about. He said that he usually says to girls he meets that he will call them or come by, but then he just doesn't do it. When I asked him why, he said:

"Because I get so damn tired of them. There can be ten or twelve chicks who ring me at home and ask me if I wanna see them."

I can't be interested in guys who brag and exaggerate like that, because I think it shows how childish they are.

He wanted to lay me. I had a feeling that he would get cross if I said no, but you can't do it just because the guy won't be disappointed. And I was right, because when I said that I didn't want to, he said:

"Well, that must mean that you don't like me very much!"

"Yes, I do."

"Why don't you want to do it, then?"

"Because I don't feel like it."

"I never meet a chick again who doesn't want do it with me, because that has to mean that she doesn't like me."

"You never see them again, anyway," I said. "Or was it none of those girls who usually call you who wanted to do it with you?"

"Yes, every one of them!"

"Why don't you see them again, then?"

"Now we are talking about *you*."

"Yes, and I don't want to."

Then he started to feel sick and threw the door open and rushed into the ditch.

"Is he throwing up?" I said to Lasse.

"Yes."

"Does he do this often when he drinks?"

"Yes, he gets sick very easily."

I didn't want to see it, because it's so disgusting when somebody pukes. After a while he came back and tumbled down in the other corner of the back seat.

"Do you want me to leave?" I said.

"Yes!"

"No, we'll give you a lift home," Lasse said.

When we had got there, and I climbed out of the car, Lasse did the same. I said goodbye to Björn before I slammed the door, but he didn't answer.

"Is he grumpy?" Lasse said.

"He is cross with me."

"Don't worry about it. He gets this way sometimes. I'll talk to him."

I thought it was too bad that Lasse was together with Lena, because he was much easier to get along with than Björn. Björn was so touchy and childish. For instance, he said:

"What is love? It isn't looks or money or kindness, so what the hell is it?"

I want the guy to be older and more mature than I am, so that I don't feel superior to him. And he has to be tender and caring.

Kicki has returned from the country. Yesterday we had decided to go to see "Blue Hawaii", but then we went to Gunnar's for coffee instead, before we began to walk on Svartbäcksgatan. I showed Kicki the book that I write down all the guys in. First, I write the date, number, name and age. Then I write what kind of car he rode in and the license plate number, if I have managed to put it down, and finally I pass judgement on him from one to five for his manner and looks. One is worst and five is best. I have never met a five, but Håkan, Göran and Kenneth were fours.

It's fun that Kicki is back in town again. I told her that I want to drink now and asked her if she would come along if guys who have spirits stop and ask us.

"Yes, I can *come along*, but I don't want to drink so much that I get drunk," she said.

"Then what's the purpose of drinking?" I said.

"Well, because it perhaps tastes good."

But I don't drink because it tastes good.

We rode with two guys in a Fiat the entire evening. The guy I was with offered me lemonade and smokes, so he was generous, but he wasn't very good-looking. Before, when I was with guys I didn't like, it felt like a waste of time. I was put in a bad mood if he was ugly or screwy and wanted to get out as soon as possible and try to find someone better. But now that I know I can drink almost whenever I want, it doesn't seem so important anymore that the guy is nice.

Tuesday, 21 July 1964

E-L and I went out on Sunday. Nothing special happened.

Yesterday I started working with Stig. I get to do about the same things as last summer, like type a little, sort papers and answer the telephone.

It's fun both to work and to see Stig a little more often. I like his company. We talk and joke around (we have a special jargon that we use), and if he is in for lunch, it can happen that he offers both cakes to the coffee and cigarettes.

When Kicki and I were at Tempo we met Älgen, who I have ridden with once. He was on his way to Systembolaget and asked if there was anything we wanted. Then I said that I wanted to buy a small bottle of Explorer. I gave him money and we waited until he came with it. We went behind the wall by the toilets so that no one could see that he gave me the bottle.

We are going to drink tonight, and I am going to get drunk.

Sunday, 26 July 1964
Yesterday E-L let a guy buy a bottle of vodka for her, and she drank it during the evening. I took a little too, but it wasn't very much. We had that bottle, which E-L carried in her purse, and we had paper cups which I had brought from home, and we drank the spirits (lukewarm vodka) in a back yard, where nobody could see what we were doing.

Then we walked on Svartbäcksgatan, and E-L staggered and was drunk. She went up to cars that had stopped and flung herself over them, and I had to restrain her and try to hold her up. I wasn't sober either, but I could at least stand on my own legs. And I don't know why they were so interested, the boys, but they hooted and shouted and stopped one after the other and asked if we would like to go with them. I thought we should hop into one of the cars, but E-L just hung on them and wanted to leave as soon as there was any talk of us coming along.

And just when we were crossing Skolgatan, a police car came to the intersection, and we realized that it perhaps wasn't such a good idea to remain there and started to run. Then I dropped my purse, so I had to stop and pick it up. (I had my identification card in it, so I really needed to get it back.)

And then they took me. E-L ran away, but I didn't get anywhere, because one of the police officers held me fast. I was obliged to climb into the police car, and I had to answer questions about who I was and where I lived, and when they asked how we had got hold of spirits, I said that we had been offered it. I took it easy and thought, that now they are going to give me a lift home and drop me off by the street door, and then I'll go into the stairwell and wait until they have left, and then I'll go to find E-L in town again. I took it for granted that I would be able to do it that way.

But when we got there, they drove into the yard, and I had to remain in the patrol car with one of the policemen while the other one went in to fetch mamma. I can understand that they wanted to verify my identity, because I could have made up an address, but the way they did it made me really mad.

Yes, and then mamma came out, and they spoke with

her, and then I was allowed to go in with her. She had her pink nylon coat on and was on the verge of a breakdown. Papa had to take care of her. They went into the bathroom, and she sat in there and cried while papa tried to calm her down. I, for my part, was told to go to bed.

Then E-L called, but they didn't let me talk with her and tell her that I was at home and find out where she was. I had thought that I would go out again, because after all, it wasn't very late. When things had calmed down a bit, I would explain that I was all right and that I was not drunk, and then I would go out again, I thought.

But no, that was out of the question. I had to go to bed, while papa took care of mamma. Nobody had any time for me. Mamma was quite jittery and miserable, and of course you can understand that she got upset when the police come, ring the doorbell, and ask her if she has a daughter who is called so-and-so. She thought that there had been an accident and that I had been injured. But I was so angry because I didn't get to go out to find E-L again, and I couldn't understand why I wasn't allowed to do it.

Before we started drinking we bought ice creams and sat on a bench down by the river and checked out the situation. There were lots of cars out. We saw Lasse and Björn, Tony and Tiger, Cowboy and Biran, Bosse and Gurra. Cowboy and Biran played "Long Tall Sally" so loud that it could be heard long before they came by. Of the girls Doris and Anita, Sputnik and Maggan, Ankan and Lisbet were out.

Kicki had brought paper cups with her from home, but we didn't have any mixer, so we had to drink the liquor straight. It was almost impossible to get the first gulps down, because it was like lukewarm piss, after lying in my purse, and tasted like hell.

"Yeah, it doesn't taste good, but it will do bloody good where it's going," Kicki said.

When we drank we went into a back yard so that no one would see us, but otherwise we were out on the street and staggered and sang and waved at the guys who drove by. The guys hooted and screamed, and there were a lot of them who stopped and asked if we would like to go with them. Why would they rather pick up drunk girls than sober ones? Because they think it will be easier for them to get what they want then?

In front of Fågel Blå we met a cop, and we pulled ourselves together, so he didn't notice anything. Then I got drunker than Kicki, though we drank about the same amount. She had to go and drag me and ensure that I didn't stagger out in the street, and pull me away from cars I went up to and hung on in the line at the traffic lights.

I don't remember all that happened. I laid on the sidewalk and heard the cars that went by. It was light and dark at the same time. The ground was hard and flat with old cigarette butts and a little gravel on it.

Kicki tried to lift me. I didn't help her. She yanked and pulled my arm.

"Come on, catch hold of me, try to get up, you can't just lie here, you must bloody well understand this!"

I don't know how long I laid there. When I got up again we leaned against the railing at the river and smoked. The guys drove by and stared.

"If you can't walk you crawl!" one of them shouted from a car in which they were playing "House of the Rising Sun".

"They think we are drunk," I said. "Are you drunk?"

"A little," Kicki said.

"I never wanna get sober again. I want more now."

"But if you drink more you won't be able to walk. You can't even walk now, as it is."

"Yes, I can! I'm just playing. I'm not drunk. You know I'm not drunk! Let's go to the bridge and drink a little more."

"No, it's enough now. Now we're going to stay here until some boys come and pick us up."

"But I'm not drunk! And you don't have to drink any more if you don't want to. If you don't come with me, I'll go there myself."

"Yes, let's go, damn it! But I'll hold you up. Support yourself against me here."

And we went down to Eddaspången and across the river. It was no use having paper cups when we didn't have any mixer, so I drank straight from the bottle. I didn't care that it tasted bad. If you don't breathe before it goes down, the liquor flavor isn't very perceptible. And then it feels so wonderful. Just thinking of it makes me start longing for the next time.

"Now we are going to have fun," I said. "Now we're going out again and do a bit of entertaining!"

I felt so happy. That's how I have felt every time I have been drunk. Not the whole time, but after a while, when it has begun to work properly, and before I have begun to get sober up.

"You are bloody heavy, do you know that?" Kicki said when I hung on her. "Try to walk on your own, now!"

"Are you mad at me?" I said. Do you think I drink too much?"

"No, but try to stand up on your own legs now!"

A car with two guys stopped. During the whole evening they came, in long lines, and asked if we wanted to go with them.

"Who are you?" I said as I looked in through the window. "Do I know you? No, I don't think so."

I lay over the hood while Kicki talked with them. The sheet was warm, and the engine pounded.

When you are drunk you feel and hear more than you can see. You are as in a fog and don't care what happens. I began to slip off the car and Kicki grabbed me and held me up. She was mad at me and shoved me into a gate.

"Stand up!" she said. "You need to get hold of your-self, or we'll just hop into the next car that stops,"

But I didn't want to go with any of them.

"You can go home if you want to," I said. "I can walk here on my own."

"No, you can't. You must bloody well understand that you can't!"

A car had stopped on the street again.

"What's wrong with her?" I heard a voice say. "Is she drunk?"

"Yes, she is," Kicki said.

"Hop in then. She can't walk around like that."

I heard what they said, but I didn't see them, because everything was so blurred. Another car had stopped behind the first one, and I staggered up to it and leaned against the nearest front fender.

Cars are like strong, living animals, I think. I love cars. I especially love them when I'm drunk, because then I can't size up how the guys are. Then I just see their cars and hear the engines and sense the smell of oil and gasoline. When I hear a V8 rumble, I thrill.

But then it got so scary. We had just crossed Skol-gatan, and Kicki was holding me up so that I wouldn't slip on the gravel, when a black car appeared from be-hind, slammed on the brakes and came to a rocking stop beside us.

"The cops!" I screamed and had already turned and started to run. I didn't manage to think before I was on my way across the bridge. I thought that Kicki was coming after me, but when I turned around I saw that she wasn't there. She remained standing by the police car. They had got hold of her. One of the cops was standing on the sidewalk and held her by the arm.

At the same time a car slammed on the brakes next to me. The back door was open, and the guy in the back seat shouted for me to hop in and almost dragged me in. It all happened so quickly, and before I could see more, we had sped off with a flying start.

"They took my pal!" I said. "I thought she was running after me, but the cops took her!"

"Yes, we saw it."

"But why didn't she run? I screamed and started running, and I thought she was coming after me, but she wasn't. Why didn't she run?"

"She dropped her purse."

"She did?"

"Yes, and when she turned back to pick it up, they got hold of her."

I was totally shaky.

"It was fortunate that you came, because otherwise they might had caught me as well," I said.

The guy put his arm around me, but I couldn't calm down.

"What are they going to do now?" I said. "What are they going to do with her now?"

"They will probably drive her home."

"Aren't they going to take her to the police station?"

"Maybe."

"But if she's there, I must go and get her out!"

"That can't be done, damn it."

"But I have to get her out!"

"She's most likely home by now."

"Drive me to the police station and I'll go in and ask if she's there."

"Then you'll get caught as well, don't you get it? You are drunk, for God's sake."

"No, I can pull myself together. I must know if she's there!"

"Take it easy, now."

"But it was my fault that she got caught."

"In what way?"

"Because if she hadn't gone there dragging me, none of this would have happened. She was almost sober. I was the one who was drunk."

"Yes, you obviously are."

"So I have to get her out!"

"But she is very likely home by now."

"Drive to a phone box so I can call and check."

I thought about the bottle I had in my purse and wished that I could get it out and drink a little more, but I didn't want them to find out that I had my own spirits.

They stopped at a phone box and I got out and dialed Kicki's number. But I didn't find anything out, because as soon as I asked for her, her dad hung up on me. Did that mean that she was at home and that he had found out everything?

When we got back to Svartbäcksgatan, I said that I wanted to get out, because I was to go into a back yard and drink a little more.

"But if you go out again you might also get caught," the guy said. "We'll drive you home."

"No, I'm going out. Stop here and let me off!"

I will drink more, I thought. I'll drink until everything disappears and I don't know what is going on. Then somebody has to come.

Monday, 27 July 1964

It's strange, but neither mamma nor papa have raised the issue of what happened on Saturday again. They didn't say anything about it on Saturday, either. Mamma was maybe so overwrought that she wasn't able to do it, but papa could have said something. Though if he doesn't want to acknowledge to himself that he drinks too much, he can't say: "You ought to think twice about this, so it doesn't turn out for you as it has turned out for me."

But he could at least say that I shouldn't go around carrying on like that, or that I am too young to drink, or whatever the hell. And he is a great supporter for the idea that you should do your share, so he could have said something in line with: "As long as you live here at home and I'm the one who supports you, you will behave properly!" It's strange that he hasn't said that, because *that would be quite in his style. "As long as you live under my roof you will do as I decide!"*

But he hasn't said anything. He got angry when I came home late the time we met Håkan and Becke, because he was worried and afraid that something had happened to me, but now he didn't scold me at all. But he does have experience with spirits, so he probably noticed that I wasn't drunk and thought: Well, she certainly can't have drunk very much! He probably didn't take it very seriously.

Mamma, on the contrary, acted like I had committed the world's worst crime and had come home and said: "Now I'm going to be arrested and sent to prison for a couple of years." And that isn't the way it was! But I was probably registered with the police in any case. Actually, I think that's unjust. There I go taking care of E-L, because she is drunk, and then I am the one who is nabbed by the police and enrolled in their register!

And papa has grounded me. I'm not allowed to meet E-L. I don't dare to call her either, but I have written a letter for her to know how it turned out for me.

I didn't dare to call Kicki, but now I've got a letter, so I don't need to be worried anymore. The cops drove her home. This is what she writes:

When I saw the police car, and you shouted that we ought to run,

I started running, but I dropped my purse, and when I was going to pick it up, they caught me. One of the police officers grabbed my arm and there I stood and saw you disappear in the distance. Then I had to go with them in the patrol car, and they asked me what my name was, where I lived and what we were doing there, and then they drove me home. What your name was, they never asked me, strangely enough.

And she wrote that her parents don't want her to see me anymore. They think that I attract her to do foolish things. But if she didn't want to participate, she could say no.

When I think about how she sat there in the police car and answered questions that the cops asked, I feel weird. But I'm glad that I am not the one who was caught, because it would have been so degrading to be driven home like that. And I don't want mon and pop to know what I am doing when I am out. I wouldn't have told the cops my name or where I lived, if it had been me. But they would probably have found out in the end anyway.

Sunday evening when I walked on Svartbäcksgatan it felt like everyone knew that I had been drunk the previous evening. I believed that everyone had seen me, although I hadn't seen them. Two guys in an Opel had noticed me anyway, they said when they stopped.

"You did?" I said. "I didn't see you."

"Well, that's hardly surprising!"

"What do you mean?"

"You probably didn't see anything at all, I would think!"

I hadn't finished my bottle, because I let those guys, who saved me from the cops, give me a lift home after all, and now, when the guys in the Opel had driven off, I drank a little again, in a yard. Then I sat on a bench down by the river and smoked.

The cinema audience came out of Saga after the first performance, and it became crowded on the sidewalks and a line of cars waited at the traffic lights at the intersection. I felt so full of expectation as I waited for the liquor to kick in.

After a while I got up and left. I would have been able to walk straight if I had pulled myself together, but I didn't mind that I staggered. A car stopped, and when I came nearer I saw a guy called Dimman sitting in the back seat. He rolled down the side window and leaned out.

"Are you pissed tonight as well!" he said.

"No, I'm not pissed," I said.

"Well, you aren't sober, anyway!"

I hardly know him, but he still seemed angry with me because I was tipsy.

"A broad like you shouldn't carry on and booze like this," he said.

"A broad like me?"

"Well, all broads, then!"

But what's the difference between him doing it and me doing it? I know that guys don't like girls who drink, but at the same time they are more interested when you are drunk, so it doesn't matter what you do as long as you don't meet someone you might fall in love with.

I went with two guys in a Ford. Before they came I had gulped down the rest of the vodka, and then I sat there and held the bottle out of the car and waved and shouted to people on the streets. You can do whatever you want when sitting in a car, because nobody can stop you. Some people become afraid when they see a crammed *raggarbil* come sliding and hear the music rumbling and the *raggare* screaming and bawling, and some take offence and start complaining about today's youth, and that feels so wonderful to know. But I would never have dared to do what I did on Sunday if I hadn't been drunk.

It's already August. This summer has gone by so quickly. It's soon autumn.

Last night I went with a guy called Georgen and his buddy in a blue Opel Kapitän. They didn't have any spirits, but I rode with them anyway, because I like Georgen. We lay in the back seat and kissed and hugged while Nisse drove around and played records. They had "Dead Man's Curve" with Jan & Dean, "No Particular Place to Go" with Chuck Berry, and "You're

No Good" with The Swinging Blue Jeans.

Nisse also wanted a girl, but there wasn't anybody who wanted to go with us when he asked.

"Pick up Maggan, damn it, and you'll surely have a bang," Georgen said as we drove past her.

"I want to have a girl and not a creep," Nisse said.

"All good things come in triplets: syphilis, crabs and gonorrhea," Georgen grinned. "But there isn't anything wrong with her."

"Easy for you to say, since you have already gotten the best," Nisse said.

I noticed that Nisse liked me, but I preferred to be with Georgen, because he is cuter.

Nothing special happened. They asked me if I had a mate we could go and fetch, but Kicki wasn't allowed to go out this weekend, so I said that I had no one. Then Georgen caught sight of a girl who was walking by herself and shouted to Nisse to stop.

"Well, let's drive around and check her from the front first," Nisse said.

We went down to Stugan and turned back. Then Nisse drove slowly by the girl on the other side of the street and took a peek at her.

"Hell no!" he said and sped up.

"There was nothing wrong with her," I said.

"When you already have the best in the car, you don't want to have anybody else," Nisse said and glanced at me in the rearview mirror.

Then Georgen drew me down and kissed me.

"Are you in love now, Eva-Lena?" Nisse said.

"Yes, she is!" Georgen said.

He stuck his hands under my sweater and unhooked my bra in the back. I let him draw up my sweater and bra and kiss me on my breasts, and Nisse saw everything when he happened to glance over his shoulder.

Then Georgen took off all my clothes from the waist up and rolled down the window and waved my bra outside.

"Now I let go of it!" he said and laughed.

I threw myself forward and tried to get it, and he withdrew his arm and embraced me and kissed me again. It felt strange when my breasts were pressed against his shirt. First he kissed my lips, then my neck and shoulders. When he stopped, I saw Nisse's eyes in the rearview mirror. I put my sweater back on, but my bra I stuffed into my purse, because it would have felt embarrassing to sit there and put it on while they were watching.

On Nybron, among all the Mods, an old dude called Nordan balanced on the bridge railing. He is a little cracked and someone that everyone knows about.

"Fucking daredevil!" Georgen said when we drove by. He had his hand under my sweater, and I felt thrills when he carried on with my breast, but I didn't show it to him, because then he might have believed that he could go further than I wanted him to.

Putte is back. I don't believe that he has been at sea. I think it was true what Becke said, that he has been in jail. Why did he lie? Did he believe that I'm an innocent little lamb who cannot bear to hear the truth? Or was he ashamed of himself? But I don't give a shit what he does.

I saw Georgen and Nisse, and Georgen pointed at me with his cigarette and smiled, but they didn't stop. Later, when I sat on the bench down by the river, Maggan came by and asked if we could walk together for a while.

But I wouldn't walk with anyone but Kicki on Svartbäcksgatan. The other girls are not like we are, I think, and it would feel uncomfortable to walk with someone I don't know. If I went with Maggan, for instance, she might say yes to guys that I think are repulsive and don't want to ride with, and what would I do then? So it's best not to walk with her.

Maggan took out a pack of Winners and sat down beside me on the bench and smoked. I hoped that she would leave soon, because I didn't want anyone to believe that we were together. And I thought that she disturbed by sitting there, and discouraged guys who perhaps wanted to stop and ask me to go with them.

When I was alone again, Tommy, a guy whom I've met a few times before, came by with his buddy Kent in a Valiant. All three of us sat in front and drove around and listened to music. I played "Be My Baby" with The Ronettes and another song, named "You

Never Can Tell" with Chuck Berry. When I had put it on three times in a row, Kent pressed it in a fourth time, and then I kissed him. It felt almost like I had been drinking though I hadn't.

"We saw you last Saturday," Tommy said.

"You did?" I said. "Where?"

"On the ground," Kent said and grinned.

"Oh, last Saturday," I said and felt stupid.

"Then you were really drunk," Tommy said. "Or were you just shamming?"

"No, I was drunk."

"Why?"

"Well, why do *you* get drunk?"

"I'm the one who asks questions here!" he said and tried to look strict.

"I don't know," I said. "What did you do yesterday?"

"Now she's changing the subject!" Kent said.

"We went to Holmen and danced," Tommy said.

"Who played there?"

"Jailbird Singers."

Then they talked about Ranger 7, which the Americans have taken pictures of the moon with, and about The Beatles performance at Johanneshov on Wednesday. When The Beatles sang "I Want to Be Your Man", the public had gone into ecstasy and stormed the stage so they had been forced to cancel the performance. Chairs had been tossed about and girls had fainted and the cops had stood powerless, they said.

I was playing with the knob on the glove compartment, and suddenly it opened. There was a bottle of hard liquor in it, and I took it out and pretended to drink from it.

"What the hell are you doing?" Tommy said before he realized that I hadn't screwed off the bottle cap.

"Drinking!" I said and held up the bottle so that he could see that it was closed.

"You little monkey!" he said and laughed.

"You thought I drank, didn't you?"

"Yes, you never can tell!"

"And when will you crack this?"

"Some time."

"Tonight?"

"No, not tonight."

Then I put it back in the glove compartment so that I would be spared the sight of it.

Tuesday, 4 August 1964

I stayed at home on Saturday and Sunday because papa didn't allow me to go out. If it had been E-L who was caught by the police, and if her parents had found out and said that she must stay at home, she would have been out the next evening anyway, because her papa doesn't have the same power over her that mine has over me. That's probably because she has rejected him.

But if papa says to me that I'm not allowed to go out I don't do it, because I want us to have a good relation-ship, if it's possible. I don't want to isolate myself from my parents and not have anybody who cares about me. I don't want to have it like E-L, who almost never talks with her parents and who feels almost like a lodger with them. She doesn't think she can talk with them about anything, and she has no confidence in them. Actually, I don't have any in my parents either, but I want for us to have something in common and not to live in two completely different worlds.

On "Kvällstoppen" "Long Tall Sally" with The Beatles came in first, "Tennessee Waltz" with Alma Cogan second, and "A Hard Day's Night" with The Beatles third. I like The Beatles, but their songs aren't played very often in the cars, so mostly I have to listen to them at home.

Kicki had to go with her parents to the countryside, and I went out on by myself again. When I sat on the bench down by the river, Cowboy and Biran came by and wanted me to go with them, but they didn't have any booze, so I said no. I think that Cowboy thought that didn't want to because they dumped me at the BP gas station before, but that wasn't the reason.

Then I saw Björn, Lasse and Lena in the Kapitän, Putte and Becke in the Dodge, and Tony and Ricky in an old Volvo. In another car, that Rune was driving, there was a guy who threw up through the back side window so it ran down the side of the car.

I hoped that Björn and Lasse would stop, but they

didn't. I went with two guys from Tierp, and they had liquor which I drank until I got drunk. Then I went out into town again. They were going to come here again next Saturday, and they wanted me to come along with them then, but the one I was with was only a two, so I don't know. Perhaps if they have booze.

Then Putte came by himself in the Dodge and stopped by the bench where I sat.

"Come here!" he said, and when I went up to the car he noticed that I was drunk.

"Who the hell has given you booze?" he said and glared at me.

"A guy."

"What kind of a fucking guy is it who makes a bird drunk?"

"Nobody that you know, anyway."

"Are you coming, then?"

"No, I'm not."

"If you don't hop in, I'll come out and get you."

"Yes, you can try that!"

I thought about asking him how things had been at sea, because I wanted to know if he would continue to lie, but before I could do it, he said:

"There are rumors about you in town."

"What kind of rumors?"

While talking with him, I leaned against one of the front fenders, and that made him angry.

"Don't touch the car!" he roared.

"Well, excuse me!"

"Are you getting in or not?"

"No, I've already told you!"

"So, I'm not good enough? What kind of a fucking star do you require to be satisfied?"

"None at all. I just wanna sit here."

Just then, or whenever it was, Älgen and some other guys drove by, and when they hooted Putte hooted back.

"Was he the one who took your virginity?" Putte said and glared at me again.

"Who do you mean?"

"Don't play dumb!"

"But I don't know who you mean."

"Älgen, damn it! Is he the one who took your virginity?"

"Has he said that?"

"What do you think?"

"If he has said that, he was lying."

"I surely believe him more than I believe you, damn it!"

"Well, what I have to say doesn't make any difference, then."

"So you're saying you're still a virgin?"

"Yes, that's right."

"No, you damn sure aren't! That I've found out!"

He has not, but I didn't think of it right then.

"You can be it anyway," I said.

"No, you can't. Or did you take it with a pen?"

"Sure!"

Then he went off. I started to walk up the street, and after a while a car with two guys in a Dodge Dart stopped and asked if I wanted to go with them. But the cutest guy already had a girl, so I said no.

I said no to eight offers, I think. At one point, when I stood and talked with some guys in a car, there was a line behind, and in the next car Göran was sitting. I waved when I got sight of him, but he looked away and pretended not to see me.

"Skip it then!" I shouted.

First, he was angry with me because I didn't want to kiss him, and then because I started walking on Svartbäcksgatan, and now because I drink. But what I do is none of his business. Besides, it is because of him that I began to walk on Svartbäcksgatan.

The reason why I turned down so many offers, was that I wanted to go with some guys who had spirits, before I had got sober again.

But I almost was, when I met two guys called Kåre and Roffe. They didn't have a car, but they wondered if I wanted to come with them to a place where there was a party. Roffe was very cute, but he was only fifteen years old, I found out later.

We went to a house on Ågatan. I don't know how we got there. I didn't think of it. I just walked along.

We went up a cranky staircase and came first to an attic and then to a room where there were two girls and a guy who were sitting at a table drinking Koskenkorva. They also played records, but there was no real party, as Kåre and Roffe had said. Though they offered spirits, and I got drunk. I wrote in my notebook while Roffe and Kåre were out for a while. This is how it came out:

I'm so young and you're so old, this my darling I've been told. I'm drunk. I cannot think. Oh, please stay by me Diana. Roffe has gone out. He's cute. I have gotten his picture. He has a suede jacket and a mohair scarf on. The picture was taken at an automat. We struggled for a teddy bear just for fun. I fell down from the bed. He got on top of me. Sören and Ritva brawled. They are engaged. Ritva and Yvonne live here. Ritva ran to the window thinking she would jump out, but Sören and Kåre pulled her away. Then she cried. She is depressed and is taking pills, Roffe said. She has tried to commit suicide before. When I went to the toilet, Roffe came along. He kissed me and put his chewing gum into my mouth with his tongue. I'm chewing on it now. I called Kicki, but she didn't want to talk with me. She doesn't like that I drink alcohol. Roffe isn't here. He has gone out. There is an attic outside this room. I don't know where we are. I can't remember how we got here. I'm drunk. It's so wonderful to be drunk. I never want to be sober again. When Roffe and I lay on the bed I took off my dress and bra. I don't know where he is. He's only fifteen years old. I'm older than he is. I want the guy to be the oldest. Oh, please stay by me Diana! Now I'm going to drink a little more. I never want to be sober again. My cigarette will be burned out soon. Hold me darling, hold me tight, squeeze me baby. He's only fifteen, but he has already knocked a girl up. He thought I wouldn't want to be with him if I found out about it. The girl's pop had scolded him. I don't know how I am going to get home tonight. They don't have a car. I need to go to Svartbäcksgatan again. Roffe doesn't want me to. He wants to come along with me and fix so that some buddies of his drive me home, he says. I called Kicki. She got tired of me. Now I'm drinking. I don't know what I'm writing. I'll read it tomorrow when I'm sober. Now I'm not sober. I'm drinking Koskenkorva. It's Finnish vodka, I think. Ritva is from Finland. Yvonne's guy has overturned with his car. That's why he isn't here. He got a concussion and gashes on his face. The car turned into a scrap heap. Kåre and Roffe have gone outside to fight. They went out to find some guys they have fallen out with and beat them up. They are so childish. Roffe is cute. I've got a picture from him. He got one from me too. It's the same one that I give to all the guys who ask me for a picture. I have on a black, low-cut dress, and my hair is combed to one side and hangs down over my shoulder, and I'm standing under a blooming apple tree, smiling. Everyone thinks it's a frigging good picture of me, and it is, but I don't know if it's especially like me. In the back the dress is fastened tight with safety pins, because it isn't really a dress but a black cloth that I have wrapped myself in. Why aren't they coming back? If they don't come soon, I'm leaving. The filter is burning. I turned the cigarette the wrong way when I lit it. I set fire to the tampon. Now I'm going to drink. When I've finished this, I'll be off. There are probably no cars out anymore. I hate it when it's empty in town. When everybody but me has gone home I understand that what I want doesn't exist. Then I understand that I exaggerate. For everybody else it's just a game they can quit whenever they want. Love me warm and tender dear, love me warm like the glow of the morning sun. Why can't it

It's so disgusting to wake up after being drunk and remember what you have done. You have a headache and a stomach ache and are thirsty and dry in the throat from all the cigarettes you have smoked, and you feel sick just thinking of booze. Then I regret what I have been doing and think that I will never drink again, but then I do it anyway.

A guy Roffe knows drove me home. Roffe also came along. Before I got out he asked if I wanted to go with him to the movies tonight to see "Wild Young Man" with Elvis. And I had considered seeing it, so I said yes. They have raised the ticket prices to 3.75 and 4.50 *kronor*, but he would treat, he said. But then I will not see him again, because I could never be together with – go steady with – a guy that is younger than me.

I've been to the movies with Roffe. I still think he is cute, but it's so difficult when he doesn't have a car. He got upset when I said that I needed to catch a ride home, and he wanted to come along to Svartbäcksgatan to check what guy I would go with. He thought that I should wait until somebody he knew turned up. But nobody like that came, and as long as I was together with him nobody else stopped either.

Finally, he had to give up and leave. I saw him up at the square later when the guy I rode with passed him.

On Wednesday Kicki and I met two guys called Svante and Ragnar in a red Ford Taunus, and they had spirits which they offered us. Kicki didn't drink very much, but I got rather drunk, as usual.

Kicki had snitched the key to her parent's allotment-garden cottage, because we had thought that we would go there if we met any pleasant guys, and when we had ridden around town for a while with Svante and Ragnar, we asked them if they would like to go there and have coffee.

I had been there before, so I knew it was small, with just two tiny rooms. The guy Kicki was with drove, and he had not drunk anything, but the other one was almost as drunk as I was and tumbled down on a chair at the table when we came in. His little fingernail was four centimeters long.

Nothing much happened. Svante had brought the vodka bottle in with him, and when Kicki had set out coffee cups, he poured spirits in his and asked if I also wanted some. Ragge and Kicki didn't take any, but Svante and I drank more before we got coffee.

Svante smoked Kool and offered me one. I sat on his lap and picked at his little fingernail. He worked at SGS as a slaughterman, he said, and asked what I did.

"I'm going to be a journalist."

"Yes, if you don't become an alcoholic," Kicki said.

But just because her dad is a boozer, doesn't mean that I will become one. But I probably won't become a journalist, either.

Ragnar worked at SGS too, at the intestine cleaning center. It smells so bad there, that those who work there are paid extra, he said.

Then I started feeling ill and almost thought that I would puke. Svante had to help me out. But luckily I didn't throw up. I felt better when I got out in the fresh air. But I didn't dare to drink more after that.

Sunday, 16 August 1964

Before E-L and I went into town we were at Gunnar's and had coffee, and there (in the washroom) we drank a little booze (cognac) that E-L had snatched from her papa's cellar. We weren't affected, because it was so little, but we wanted it anyway, and then out into town to look for boys!

And then HE turned up. But at first I didn't know that. Then I just knew that two guys came by in a white Saab and asked if we wanted to go with them. One was called Arne and he wasn't particularly handsome, but the other one, named Kjell, looked really nice and pleasant.

They drove off to an apartment in Eriksberg, and we went in with them. In the living room there was a record player on a shelf to the left, and there also was a sofa, which you could fold out to a bed, and a small coffee table.

And we accepted both cigarettes and vodka with lime juice, and true to her habit, E-L drank more than she could handle and got drunk. She half lay on the floor and clung to Kjell's leg and tried to get his attention, because she (as well as I) preferred him. But I realized that he didn't care about her and actually thought she was a little awkward and that it was me he was attracted to.

So when the other guy had dragged E-L away somewhere, Kjell and I started hugging and kissing. We also talked, and he asked me if I had a picture of myself that he could have. Before we parted he said that he would call me today, and I actually believe he will.

But if he wants us to go out this very evening I won't be able to, because mamma will say no. I have a cold and fever. I was a little snotty already yesterday, and I had a fever when I woke up this morning. But on Wednesday, I think, we can go to the movies or something else. If he calls, that's what I will propose.

And then you have the immediate problem of what to wear. I think I have it really bad with clothing, and I never know what to put on. I could possibly use my red twist skirt and white blouse. I can also have my white, acrylic cardigan on. But what should I have for a purse? A white purse would be most appropriate, but I don't have one. I have to take my beige-brown one.

And my poor hair! It needs to be washed and put up in curlers, and then I can sit in mamma's hair dryer. Afterwards I brush it so that it lies flat and neat, but as soon as I come outside, it becomes quite frizzy on top. And then I think that everything has gone to hell because my hair-do is ruined immediately. I usually backcomb my hair (though not as much as E-L), and then I put on hairspray to keep it in place, but it doesn't help, because if there is the least bit of humidity in the air, it frizzles all the same.

It's really strange that we always meet guys who offer us booze now, I think. We never did before. But it's fortunate, because I don't know how we would get hold of spirits otherwise. We could possibly ask someone to buy it for us, but that's so unreliable and would also be expensive in the long run. And anyhow, I have the spirits in the basement that I can take some of if I want to.

Last night we drank vodka and lime. That's what two guys in a white Saab offered us. When they saw us on Svartbäcksgatan they signaled to us to go into St Persgatan, and then they turned into it and stopped. Only one of them was cute, and he seemed to be most interested in Kicki, so at first I was going to say no, but when they asked us to come home with them for a grog I changed my mind.

They lived in Eriksberg. The cute one, called Kjell, sat next to Kicki on the sofa, and the other one, named Arne, sat beside me. We smoked and drank and listened to music. They had "It's Over" with Roy Orbison and lots of songs with Elvis, like "It's Now or Never", "Love Me Tender", "Good Luck Charm", and "Don't".

It's so wonderful to sit like that and know that you'll soon be drunk. Just thinking of it makes me wanna do it again. I will probably never be able to stop drinking.

Arne was the one who was supposed to drive later, so he didn't drink very much. Neither did Kicki and Kjell. I was the only one who got really drunk. I tried to get Kjell to choose me instead of Kicki, but it didn't work, and I didn't want to be with the other one, so I tried to set off.

It was such a hassle. Kicki talked to me and said that I couldn't go out into town when I was drunk, and Arne and Kjell held me back when I tried to slip away.

Then I started feeling ill, and they dragged me to the kitchen and gave me water. There was a glaring light there and a cold sink which I leaned my head against.

When we were about to leave, I told Kicki that I needed to wait until I had sobered up a little more before I could go home, and then she went along with me jumping out into town. While I was wiggling out of the car, Kjell said:

"If nothing else, you were the evening's entertainment!"

And Kicki said:

"Try not to do anything stupid, now!"

And then they went away. I didn't try to pull myself together anymore after that. I walked along the street, staggering and thinking how wonderful everything was. I didn't want it to end.

When you are drunk you only see the nearest things, such as the cobblestones in front of your feet where you are walking, or the wall surface if you are leaning against a house, or a cigarette butt which lies on the ground where you have fallen. You only notice details and have no general picture. There was somebody, for instance, who threw out a burning butt through a car window, and I saw how it gave out sparks when it swirled around in the air and rolled down into the gutter, but I didn't see the car it came from.

I didn't go with anyone, even though there were a lot of guys who stopped. I didn't even walk up to some of them.

"Watch out for the cops!" a guy shouted from a car.

It feels good when they warn you like that, because

then you know that they are on the same side as you
– against the cops anyway – but I wasn’t able to watch
out for any cops.

I don’t know how long I walked around. It became
sparser and sparser between the cars, and I got more
and more tired and started getting headaches. Finally,
a car with two guys stopped, and the back door opened. It was Putte and another guy.

“Come here!” Putte shouted and leaned out the door.
“We’re driving you home.”

The guy who was driving turned around and glared
at me when I had got into the car, but then he put on
a record and didn’t pay me any more attention. Putte
didn’t either, at first. He just sat there and stared out
the window.

“Are you angry?” I said and lit a cigarette. He didn’t
look at me, and when he answered he sounded angry.

“You’ve lost your style!” he said.

“Have I? Where?”

But there was no point in trying to make fun of it.

“Birds aren’t supposed to booze!” he said.

“No? So it’s only guys who can do it, you mean?”

“Don’t play dumb!”

“But that’s what you’re saying.”

Then he turned his head and stared at me.

“This isn’t the first time I’ve seen you reeling around
dead drunk in town,” he said.

“So what?”

“You’ve lost your style, I’m telling you!”

"Oh, I get it! But I may have *never* had any style! I may have been worthless the entire time, even if *you* haven't noticed."

"At least you didn't booze before."

"That's something you wouldn't know."

"Yes, I do! But I don't give a shit about what you do! Drink yourself into the gutter, if that's what you want! Just do it! I don't give a damn!"

"That doesn't seem true."

"Yes, it is!"

"Then why are you carrying on like this?"

"Because I got pissed just looking at you!"

"Why did you pick me up then?"

"Because you were so damn drunk that you couldn't even walk."

"I was not!"

"Yes, you were, and it was damn *disgusting* to see!"

"But I'm not drunk *now*."

"No, but two hours ago you were *crawling*."

"Were you in town two hours ago?"

"Yes, I was. And I saw you!"

Then I didn't know what more to say. I just laid down and put my head on his lap. I didn't care that he was angry. His legs were warm. Street lights shined in through the window and glided away over the back-rest of the front seat as the car moved. The music blared, and Elvis sang. "Don't you let me catch you messin' round that apple tree, oh yeah, ever since the world began," he sang.

Monday, 17 August 1964

Kjell rang yesterday at half past three and wanted for us to go to the movies in the evening. But I wasn't allowed to go out and told him – what was true – that I couldn't come because I was sick and had a fever. "We can perhaps see each other some other evening, instead?" I said.

But he was so anxious and absolutely determined for us to meet. It sounded like he didn't really believe that I was sick. Afterwards I had a temperature of 39.5 degrees, though I didn't have more than 38 when he called (so it might have been just as well if I had gone out).

I became so heartbroken when he didn't believe me. He must have noticed that I liked him, so why would I all of a sudden not want to meet him and even come up with a lie to avoid him? I don't understand how he could believe that! And if I were not interested, I wouldn't have suggested that we meet another evening, instead. I became so sad when I realized that he doubted me.

Afterwards I cried so much that I thought my heart would burst (as it usually is said in short stories and such things). That's why my fever went up. But now I think, that if he had such difficulties in understanding me, he wasn't the person I thought he was, and it was just as well that this came out all at once. Though I feel so clearly that I could have fallen in love with him (an he in me) if he hadn't destroyed everything like this. Because now he will probably never call again.

I was in town and met Göran. He was riding alone in his pop's Isabella, and he stopped when he saw me. I got so surprised that I didn't walk up to he car at first. I thought that perhaps I wasn't the one he had stopped for. But nobody else was there.

"Are you going home?" he said.

"Yes."

"Hop in then."

I wondered why he had changed his mind all of a sudden, because it wasn't very long ago that he pretended not to see me when I greeted him. But it was perhaps because I was drunk then.

It felt a little strange to meet him again after so long, but I know that I don't love him anymore, so I didn't feel sad. I lit a cigarette, and he glanced at me from the side and said:

"And you're still walking on Svartbäcksgatan?"

"Yes, I am."

"Why don't you go dancing instead?"

"I cannot dance."

"You could learn."

"Yes, but you aren't necessarily worse than those who go dancing just because you walk on Svartbäcksgatan."

"Well, I don't know the reason why *you* walk there, but it isn't so damn difficult to figure out why the others do it."

"And you drive there," I said.

"Yes, but not for the same reason as they do."

"Besides, it was because of you, in a way, that I began," I said.

"Yes, I know."

I didn't think of it then, but now I wonder why he said that, because I have never told him that I think so. But I have perhaps mentioned it to Uffe.

When we were going on Munkgatan I came to think of how it was in the beginning, when Kicki and I met him and Uffe. and I then said:

"Do you remember when we were at Fågelsången and had coffee?"

"Yes, those were the days!"

"It will soon be a year ago."

"It will?"

"Yes, it was in September. But God, how silly you must have thought we were!"

"Why?"

"As we were running after you and carried on. We were so childish and inexperienced."

"But you don't think you are anymore?"

"Not as much as I was then, anyway."

Because that was when Kicki and I had just started going out together.

"You were the first guy I went out with," I said.

"I was?"

"Yes."

I felt glad and wanted to talk, but he just sat there and seemed severe.

"Do you still see Uffe nowadays?" I tried.

"Yes, it happens."

"What have you done tonight, then?"

"I've been to the movies."

He didn't ask me what I had been up to, but he probably knew anyway.

He stopped on a forest road and kissed me. When he unbuttoned my skirt, I said:

"Do you know that you will be angry with me before this evening is over?"

"Why? Because I won't get what I want?"

"Yes."

"But I want to lay you."

"Why?"

"Because I feel like it."

"I see."

"Do you want to lay me?"

"No, I don't."

"But why not? Why can't I get, what everybody else gets?"

So I was right when I suspected him of believing that I have sex with all the guys I meet. And now he obviously didn't mind being one of them himself.

"There isn't anyone else who gets to do it," I said. "You probably don't believe me, but I'm actually a virgin."

"Aha. But sometime has to be the first one."

"Yes, but then I think that both should want to do it because they feel the same."

"Why don't you want it, then?"

"I don't know."

Then he said that he was in love with me. I don't get how he could think that I would swallow it.

"You are?" I said.

"Yes, but you aren't especially in love with me, I suppose?"

"No, not now. But I was before."

"You were?"

"Yes, but you were always so mean to me."

"Yes, perhaps I was…"

"Why?"

"I might have thought that you didn't like me."

"But I did."

"Why didn't you tell me, then?"

"Why didn't you tell *me* how *you* felt?"

"I don't know. Perhaps we were too young and inexperienced?"

And then he kissed me again, so I felt his wet, cold hair against my forehead.

"Obviously, you haven't gotten what I just told you," I said.

"But you would like to do it if you were in love with me?"

"I don't know."

"But human beings are also animals."

"What do you mean by that?"

"Human beings also have their physical feelings and desires."

"Yes, but not like animals that cannot think."

"One can't control one's feelings!"

"Yes, you can."

Then he sighed and rubbed his forehead.

"You're still so young," he said.

"Yes, but that's what I'll think when I get older too."

"You can't know that."

"Yes, I can. And I'm not going to do anything before I feel that I want it both in mind and body."

"You may have to wait a long time for that."

"Yes, but I can afford it."

While I buttoned my skirt, he rubbed his eyes with his thumb and middle finger and sighed again.

"No matter how long you wait, it won't make any difference," he said.

I didn't exactly feel sorry for him, but I wanted to cheer him up, because he seemed so tired and down-hearted. But I didn't know what to say.

He started the car and backed up so fast that I fell forward and nearly bumped into the dashboard.

"I'll give you a lift home," he said.

When we came out on the Norrtälje highway, we were passed by a big *raggarbil,* and then it felt like he was thinking of what I usually do again.

I'm the only one who has changed, I thought. He is the same as he was before. But now I'm not getting sad anymore because he doesn't understand.

When we got home, before I climbed out of the car, he embraced me.

"Promise you won't ever do anything that you don't want to do," he said.

Then I left, and when he was driving away I knew that I will never meet him again.

Tuesday, 18 August 1964

Last Sunday E-L was out alone and then she met Göran and rode with him. He drove out in the country some-where and said that he wanted to lay her. (Is this what he has had in mind the entire time?) But she didn't want to, and said that if it didn't feel right for her both in mind and body, she wouldn't do it. "In that case you may have to wait a long time," he said. He made use of that well-known line, that if you don't want to, then you must not care about me very much! (And if you do want to, it means that you are a woman of easy virtue and nobody worth having.)

But she didn't swallow that. She almost thought that he was a little screwy and clearly felt that she wasn't interested in him anymore. If she had met him for the first time now, he would have gotten a three and barely that, she said. So in a year, when I randomly meet Kjell again, maybe he has crashed down from his five and mean nothing at all to me? But I have my doubts about that.

Now they are playing "Tell Laura I Love Her" on the radio. It's on the fourteenth place on "Kvällstoppen".

The lyrics are so exaggerated, I think. He is burnt to death, and before he dies he… It's just too sentimental to take seriously. This is what he sings at the end: "No one knows what happened that day, how his car overturned in flames, but as they pulled him from the twisted wreck, with his dying breath they heard him say: Tell Laura I love her, tell Laura I need her, tell Laura not to cry, my love for her will never die." It's almost laughable rather than tragic.

There is another, similar song that I also think is silly. It's the one Marty Wilde sings that is called "A Teenager in Love". For example, he sings: "Well, if you want to make me cry, that won't be so hard to do. And if you should say goodbye, I'll still go on loving you. Each night I ask the stars above: Why must I be a teenager in love?"

Yes, that's a good question! I wonder how long it will be before I have gotten over Kjell? Deep down I still hope that I will hear from him again.

Thursday, 20 August 1964

Last night E-L and I set off for Stockholm. We took the train there, to be sure to arrive in time.

And then we walked on Kungsgatan. It wasn't like Svartbäcksgatan at all, because it was so wide. But two guys stopped, and we went with them to a house where one of them lived. He had a room with a private entrance to the basement. You went down a small staircase and then through a door, and that's where he had his room.

They offered vodka with lime and small ice cubes, and such drinks are treacherous, because you scarcely feel the alcohol, and think it tastes good, and I drank a little too much and got drunk. I almost can't remember what we did. In any case, my bra came off, but my breasts were very sore, because I'll soon have my period, and I didn't want him to carry on with them so much.

Then we nearly missed the last train home, but they gave us a ride to the railway station so that we made it just in time.

On the train, we first were sitting in a toilet, and I was almost as drunk as E-L, which is unusual for me, because I don't want to be. I don't like to lose control, but this time I almost did.

When we got back to Uppsala (the city of eternal youth), E-L went to Svartbäcksgatan to find someone to give her a lift home, and I took a walk home. Then I began to think about Kjell and felt sad.

When I got home I sneaked in and brushed my teeth very carefully with toothpaste and washed my face with soap and water, and then I hopped into bed beside mamma. I noticed that she wasn't asleep, so she must have felt the alcohol smell, but she didn't say anything.

She has never mentioned anything about the smell of smoke, either. Deep down I would like her to say to me that I shouldn't smoke, but she doesn't, even though she *doesn't smoke herself. But she carries on with a lot of other shit, so that's perhaps why she isn't able to admonish me. And it probably wouldn't* help, *but it would feel better if she let me know that she doesn't want me to do it.*

And it's the same with spirits. But when she notices the smell and understands what her daughter is carrying on with, she just lies there, pretending to be asleep.

Sven Ingvar's, who are going to perform in Ängby Park this evening, is rather good for a Swedish band, I think. But I prefer groups that sing in English, because then it isn't as clear if the lyrics are silly.

In my horoscope for this week it says that I could well wind up in the center of attention, and that I feel surrounded by people and happy. There is a possibility of new and exciting contacts with the opposite sex. Moderation with regard to food and drink could be well advised this week, it says.

But I'm already looking forward to the next time I'm going to drink. It's only afterwards, when I have a hangover, that it feels like I never want to do it again.

On Wednesday night I got a lift home from a guy in an Austin. It's so boring with those single guys who are out late when everybody else has gone home and who drive on Svartbäcksgatan because they still hope that something will happen. But those are mostly the kind of guys you've got to ride with when you are out late. And perhaps they think they get at least *something* if you let them kiss you as thanks for a lift. A kiss and an opportunity to drive a girl home is perhaps enough for them not to think that the entire evening has been unsuccessful. And it's fortunate that there are such guys, because otherwise you would have to *walk* home every time you haven't anyone specified to go with.

Sunday, 23 August 1964

The guy E-L was with yesterday wanted to see her again, so they will meet tonight, she said today when she called. So I will probably stay at home this evening, because I don't feel like going out alone.

Last night we were at the movies, to see "Viva Las Vegas", and then we rode with two guys in an Opel. They offered us spirits, and I drank a little, in spite of my good intentions. But I wasn't affected, like E-L. When we got back into town, she was drunk.

When we walk like that, each one of us has her role. She's the one who can't take care of herself and needs help, and I'm the one who supports her. It's something like being an actress and appearing in a show.

And I like my role, because it gives me more contact with the boys. E-L is gone from the world, and they stop and say: "She can't walk around like this, you had better come along with us, otherwise the police will soon be here." And I agree, even though I know that it isn't quite as bad as it looks. (She isn't more affected than I am, actually. It just seems that way because she relaxes more.) But okay, let's go with you! And in that case, I get the best boy (the sober one who is driving), because he is the one I have talked with first.

Yes, and we walked there, and she didn't want to go with any of the boys who stopped, as usual. I was a little worried that the police would come (I don't want to go through that again) and thought that we would be sure to get into a car as quickly as possible, but she was so obstinate.

At last Göran's friend Uffe, dressed in a dark blue military uniform, stopped and began to talk to me. E-L was hanging on the car, and he thought we ought to hop in so that she could sober up a little.

And she went along with it. She tumbled down in the back seat, and I sat in front beside Uffe. He looked good in uniform and was the same as ever. Jolly, with a twinkle in his eye, and that's what I liked about him, I recalled. He suggested that we should go with him to Ängby Park, and I would have liked to do that, but E-L didn't want to, so we got out into town again.

I had my period and felt that I needed to go somewhere and change my sanitary napkin, because it had become displaced and chafed the way it sat. Sometimes I have considered starting to use tampons instead, because it can work sometimes even if your hymen is still intact.

Because I'm so damned tired of those bloody sanitary napkins! I use Mimosept, and they have a covering net with a knot and a loop on each end to attach to the girdle. But they never sit the way they are supposed to. They either slip up in the back or up in the front or the other way round. And they are bulky to carry in your purse when you are out someplace.

In any case, I needed to change it, and in a car it isn't suitable to do it, so we walked down to the BP gas station. I walked, that is, because E-L didn't have any stability and was so disorderly. She went up and flung herself over hoods on cars and I had a proper job keeping track of her.

And the cars were waiting in a row. There were several cars that had stopped at the same time, because we had suddenly become so dreadfully popular with the boys, and two guys in a Ford Cortina looked meek and mild, I was about to say, but I mean proper, and I pushed E-L into their car and hopped in myself after her. I thought it was a relief to get in someplace where it wouldn't be the same misery as last time with the police.

But one of them had a bottle, and he sat there drinking out of it and wasn't at all like I had thought from the beginning. I didn't like him at all. No, ooh, how I disliked him! I thought he was repulsive in some way and I didn't understand how the other guy could be a friend of his, because he wasn't the same type at all. But that's often the case, that one boy is handsome and nice and the other one is ugly and screwy. And this guy was drunk. It was very much for that reason, also, that I thought he was disgusting, I think.

E-L took the bottle from him and provided for herself, but I didn't want any. She drank straight from the bottle, because she isn't that fastidious, but I don't do that, since I have some style. I don't drink from the bottle, because that's what my papa does. (He plucks the bottle out of a boot and drinks, or out of the clothes pin bag, if he has hidden it there. Sometimes mamma and I find out where his bottles are and take them away.)

But at least we got away from the street and got a lift home.

We got booze from two guys in an Opel Olympia that we rode with for a while. As soon as I felt drunk I wanted to get out into town again. Kicki had to drag me around, as usual. She thought that we should go with some other guys, but I didn't want to come along with anybody until Uffe, Göran's buddy, came by in an Amazon. When he rolled the window down and I saw that it was him, I got happy.

"It's Uffe!" I shouted. "Hi, Uffe!"

"What sorrows are you now trying to drown?" he said and smiled.

Then he talked to Kicki.

"Go with me for a while, so that she can sober up.

She can't walk around like this."

I leaned against the car and Kicki came over to me and took me by the arm.

"Now we'll go into this car for a while so that you can sober up."

"Yes, I like Uffe!" I said and waited while he climbed out and folded the front backrest forward. Kicki got to sit in front, because I laid down on the back seat.

"Is she really so damn drunk?" Uffe said.

He wanted us to go with him to Ängby Park and listen to Carli Tornehave, but I didn't feel like it, so we went back into town again after a while.

There were lots of guys who stopped. Once there was a line of cars, and when we went up to the guys who had stopped first, the guys in the car behind hooted and shouted that we should come up to them instead, and behind them, in another car, there were two more guys sitting and waiting for their turn. We could just pick and choose.

But I didn't want to go with any of them. Finally, Kicki just pushed me into a car and hopped in herself after me. One of the guys was sitting in the back seat, and he had a bottle which I took and started to drink from. At first I smoked and drank, then I climbed over to the front seat to the other guy, called Lasse. He looked better than the guy in the back, but he was rather taciturn, so at first I couldn't make him out.

They gave us a lift home. When Kicki had left, the guy in the back seat said:

"The broad had a fucking hammock! I don't like broads with hammocks."

He was totally screwy. It was fortunate that I got the other one. And he wanted to see me again and is going to meet me at the bus station tonight.

"And then we'll see to it that you stop drinking," he said.

"We will?"

"Yes, it isn't good for you to carry on like this."

But I don't think it will work. And I don't know if I want to, either.

"Do we have an agreement, then?"

"Yes," I said and thought: I can see him tomorrow, because then there aren't many who have spirits anyway, and then, when he has seen how I am when sober, he may not want to meet me anymore, and I can keep on cruising and drinking.

At home, when I was about to get out of the car, he gazed at me and stroked my cheek.

"Little troll," he said. "Go in and sleep now, and we'll see each other again tomorrow. Or tonight, rather."

And then he kissed me. He was gentle and rather handsome, but I still don't know if I want to see him again.

I was afraid that I wouldn't like Lasse when I was sober, and I almost hoped that he wouldn't come, but he did.

First, we went to the movies, to see "Who's Minding the Store?" with Jerry Lewis, and then we drove to Savoy and had coffee. He had on a white nylon shirt, gray Jersey vest, dark blue necktie, dark blue blazer, and grey terylene pants. I thought he was handsome, but I still don't know if I want to see him again. If he calls me tomorrow, as he said he would, I don't know what I'm going to say.

His name is Lars-Erik Engström and he works for Televerket. When I asked him about his interests, he said that he reads all the latest books and listens to music a lot and tries to follow all current world events.

I had put some money in the jukebox and pressed the button for "Tennessee Waltz", and when it started playing I asked him what he thought of it.

"Well, it's all right," he said. "But otherwise I prefer jazz."

I don't know what to make of him. He seems superior and shy at the same time. He sat and held my hand the whole time at the movies, and then in the car, before he drove me home, he hugged me and kissed me and gave me all kinds of pet names. Sometimes he just looked at me and drew me towards him as if he couldn't resist me. But I think he was bluffing, because how could he already be in love with me? Anyway, I'm not in love with him.

"Now we are going to help one another to get you stop drinking," he said.

I would rather go on cruising and drinking than see

him, but I couldn't tell him, because then he probably would have been sad. And when he realizes that he isn't going to get to lay me, he won't want to see me anymore, and then I can go out again.

It says in *Upsala Nya Tidning* about a watch heist that they say Älgen was in on. All the watches worth less than 250 *kronor* were thrown in Fyrisån, and now the police, or whoever it was, have fished them up again. I don't know if it's true that Älgen was in on it, but somebody said so before.

Lasse called and said that he wants to see me tomorrow evening, and we decided that he would pick me up at the bus station again. I think it's better to meet him there, rather than have him fetch me at home, because if he wouldn't come, I won't be able to get to town if the bus has already left.

I have decided to meet him tomorrow, but never again. I'm going to say that I don't feel ready to go steady and that I don't think I can stop drinking. I know that he will be sad and not understand, but I have to tell him the truth, so that he doesn't think I'm better than I am.

I met him too soon. He is big and wise, and I am little and dumb. I could just as well go out with pop, or someone else like him.

Wednesday, 26 August 1964

There was a mistake on Saturday, because I'm practically certain of, that from the beginning Lasse was more interested in me than in E-L. But if he had chosen me, E-L would have been sulky, because that's the way she always turns when she doesn't get the one she wants.

And she just helped herself, without waiting to see whom he would choose. She put her arms around him from the back seat and said that she thought he was cute.

And he fell for that. He was probably flattered. But she wouldn't have done like that if she hadn't been drunk. In that case she wouldn't have dared to do it, because she doesn't do things like that when she is sober. No, then she would have just been sitting there thinking: I hope he chooses me, I hope he chooses me." And in that case, he might not have done that. I think he either would have refrained or chosen me.

When I got to town Lasse was already there. He sat with the driver side door open and smoked and read *Expressen*. When I sat down beside him, he folded the newspaper and gazed at me.

"Hi, Star Eye," he said.

That's what he called me on Sunday too. Then he kissed me and said that he had missed me and asked me what I would like to do. I wanted to suggest that we should go to Kap and watch Alma Cogan, but I wasn't sure that he was interested in her, so I just said that I didn't know.

We went to Landings and had coffee. He took my hand and gazed into my eyes and said that he had thought of me every day.

"Don't look at me like that," I said.

"Why not? I can't resist looking at you. You are so beautiful, my little one. Don't you know that?"

"No, I'm not."

I was almost angry with him because he laid it on so thick.

"Yes, for me you are," he said.

Then we cruised around for a while before he drove me home. He stopped at the same side road as last time and started to fondle and kiss me. His hands were warm and tender, but I didn't like his kisses. I didn't like them the first or second time, either.

"What have you done to me?" he said. "I'm at my wits' end!"

And then he hugged me and said:

"You little bundle of charm! This we should celebrate by buying a bottle of booze for Saturday!"

I was so surprised that I didn't know what to say. He has said that he wants to help me stop drinking, and he almost never drinks himself, so why does he want us to do it? I didn't ask, because then he might have changed his mind. I just decided that I'll meet him one more time. If he buys the liquor, and I drink it so that I become drunk, he might not want to see me again, and then I won't have to say that I want to be free.

Then he went a little further than before, but only above my waist.

"You're so beautiful, my little one," he said and looked at my breasts. "There must be someone with a good eye for me up there, who let me meet you."

He stroked and licked one of them so I felt thrills. He was also turned on, but he still didn't go any further. Why didn't he? Did he know that I would say no if he tried for more? But just because he didn't, it was almost as if I wanted him to.

"No, now it's best if I give you a lift home before I lose my senses," he said and pulled my bra down. "May I call you on Friday?"

"Yes, of course, you may," I said.

I wanted to remind him about buying liquor, but before I did he said:

"I'll ask Leffe if he can drive on Saturday so that we can really have a booze-up!"

I don't know what I want to do after Saturday. He is gentle and nice, and he seems to like me, but it's so boring to always know beforehand what will happen when you go out. But you go into town to meet a guy who is gentle and nice and whom you can be together with. At least that's how it was before I began to drink.

I don't know what to do. If I keep on cruising and drinking everything may go to hell in the end, and I don't want that. Why can't Lasse have a big *raggarbil* and be a little more interested in spirits? And he should like the same kind of music as I like and have plenty of records in his car that I could play while we were sliding around in town.

But he doesn't like booze and partying, and he has no big car, no music, or no funny buddies. He is probably a real mother's boy.

Sunday, 30 August 1964

Last night when I was out I met a boy with whom the situation became a little problematic. I went with him in his car, and he drove to the Vaksala brick factory and parked and started to make a pass at me. I went along with him in the preliminary stage, but then I didn't want to go any further and tried to say so.

But he didn't listen. He held me fast and tried to get past my clothes, and I began to be a little worried and thought: My God, how will this end up? I was there all alone with him, so I couldn't count on getting any help.

Here everything depends on keeping cool and talking calmingly to him, I thought and tried to get my sense to control my feelings so that I wouldn't be seized by panic.

But he refused to listen and continued to pull and tear at my clothing. I was completely stuck under his body and didn't know what to do. I couldn't open the door and get out since he held me fast.

But women's cunning surpasses men's comprehension, and he didn't have much comprehension, because when I said to him that I felt uncomfortable and needed to change position, he went along with it and let go of me. I looked for the door handle, and when he loosened his grip I threw the door open and flew out.

Then I just stood outside, and he kind of woke up and said that he understood that he had gone too far and promised that he wouldn't try anything else, if I hopped into the car again. I could have hitch-hiked back to town, but I felt like I could rely on him not to try anything else, so I climbed into the car again and rode with him.

And nothing more happened. But what would I have done if he had succeeded in raping me?

Yes, first of all I would have called E-L, but then what? I would never have told mamma and papa, in any case. No, I would not! In that case they wouldn't have let me go out anymore. Papa would have gotten completely furious with the boy and with me as well for riding with him. He would have said: "From here on out you stay at home!"

And mamma would have been very upset and over-wrought. So, telling them is something that can't even be considered if the worst, in spite of everything, would happen.

And I wouldn't report it to the police, because then it would be known at home as well. And to sit there with a police officer and explain that I had jumped into a car... "Why did you do that?" "Because I didn't think it would go further than to a little kissing and hugging." You certainly can't say that! Or: "Because it usually works to say no." Undoubtedly, it is true, but they would just think I was nuts. So I wouldn't go to the police, either.

Lasse called on Friday and we decided that he and Leffe would come and pick me up at the bus station yesterday evening. I was so happy when I found out that he had bought some booze and that we were going to drink.

But don't halloo till you are out of the wood! When I got off the bus, I saw that he was alone, and when I had sat in the car he said that Leffe was unwell and couldn't drive. So we couldn't booze. I became totally hard within me when I got it.

"There's always another train", Lasse said when he noticed how disappointed I was. "Is it that important to you? My little troll, it's not the end of the world!"

But I couldn't make my disappointment disappear.

"You little fool," he gently said and hugged me. "I didn't know that it was so important to you. We can go and get the bottle if you want, and I can drive while you drink."

"No, that's not fair," I said.

"But it doesn't matter to me. I promise you. We can do it, if you just stop being sad."

"What kind did you buy?"

"Silver Rum."

"Is it good?"

"You have never drunk it?"

"No."

"Well, I thought you had drunk everything," he said and smiled. "But it's not too bad. Shall we go and get it then?"

"No, we wait until you can drink it too."

Then he turned on that gaze again.

"Do you realize what you have done now?" he said and looked moved.

"No, what?"

"You have made me the world's happiest man."

"Why?"

"You mean you don't understand? Oh, little troll! I will never, never forget what you have done tonight!"

He should have been an actor instead of a tele worker, I thought.

"Can we drink it some other time, then?"

"Certainly."

Next Saturday, I thought. I have to wait until next Saturday. Then I will not see him anymore, I have decided.

We went to the movies instead and saw a film called "Whisky Galore!" It played at Fyris, which has been reopened now. I would rather have seen another film, but when he asked me to this one, I just said yes. I don't think we have the same taste when it comes to films, either. He likes war films and Westerns and I don't. But the one we saw last night was a comedy.

Later we sat in the car and made out. This time he

pulled up my skirt and stuck his hand inside of my panties. I thought several times that I should say no, but I couldn't make up my mind to do it, and after a while he had almost gotten a finger in.

"You're so wonderful!" he whispered and began to breathe faster.

But I didn't feel anything special, and finally I took his hand away and sat up again.

Monday, 31 August 1964

A lot of new films have begun again. They change so often that you don't have time to decide to go and see a film before they have started another one. In one week (since last Monday) they have changed films both at Fågel Blå, Slotts, Saga and Grand.

E-L and I never go to war movies, and never to Westerns, either. But we could perhaps have seen "The Court Jester" with Danny Kaye if we would have gone out, because he is funny. But E-L is probably going to see Lasse again.

Last Saturday there was a roll-call at school, and today we went to school as usual. On Saturday evening E-L was going to see Lasse, so Solan and I decided to go dancing at Holmen. Family Four and Little Gerhard were performing there, and Solan likes Family Four. So we went, and both of us got to dance a lot.

E-L meets Lasse even though she would rather go out

with me and cruise. She doesn't know if she likes him, and she doesn't feel anything when he cuddles her.

Mostly I don't feel anything in that situation either, but it has happened that I have been turned on. Although never so I seriously have considered going all the way. I have never felt so attached to someone that I have wanted to do that.

Well, it could have been that way with Kjell. I would have wanted to do it with him if we had gotten time to get to know each other. Because I want to say yes to the entire person, and it's only with him I have felt that way.

Lasse came yesterday too. He had been to moto-cross in Jumkil with his pop, he said. We drove around. He thought that I should go home early and sleep just because school started today. But I don't give a shit about that. He is so boring. If he calls on Wednesday, as he said he would, I will see him one more time and tell him that there is no point in us continuing. If we can drink then, and I get drunk, I might dare to say it.

But if we are not going to drink I don't know what to do. When he said that he would call on Wednesday, and I understood that he wasn't going to come and see me then, I felt disappointed. It felt like he doesn't care about me. But he probably does, because why else would he talk so much about how wonderful he thinks I am?

I don't know what I feel for him. In the test where

you write both person's names on a paper and then strike out all letters of the same kind and reckon love, friendship and hate with the remaining letters, it was hate for him and hate for me.

But you can't believe in things like that. You have to know yourself. But when we meet I don't feel anything special, and afterwards I'm irritated by things he has said and done. It isn't until several days have gone by that I start missing him. So I don't think I'm in love with him. It's probably just that I don't want to be without the things I get from him.

"Can't you come?" I said when he asked if he could call on Wednesday, and I got what it meant.

"Well, now that school has started you need to be home and sleep so that you manage to get up in the morning."

Oh, how bloody thoughtful! I thought and made a grimace. I didn't care if he saw it, because sometimes he sounds and behaves like a frigging pop.

When we drove on Svartbäcksgatan and passed a girl called Gittan, he looked at her in a way that made me think that he knew her, and when I asked him if he did, he said:

"Yes, she's a fucking prick teaser."

"You don't say," I said.

He heard that I sounded amused and leered at me from the side and looked embarrassed.

"I helped her once when she was loaded," he said.

"I see. Do you often take care of girls in that state?"

"Yes, you must care about your fellow-beings."

"And then you found out that she was a prick teaser?"

"Yes, exactly."

I don't know why he was so embarrassed. Does he think that I believe that he hasn't met any girls before me? He has perhaps never laid a girl. Well, he must have done, since he is twenty-one years old.

Afterwards I thought that he maybe thinks that I'm a prick teaser too. He may think that way about all the girls who go along with a little but not going all the way. He probably looked embarrassed because he happened to reveal that he had tried with Gittan and had been turned down.

I wonder what he would say if he found out that he is my one hundred and fourth guy. In a year I have made out with one hundred and four guys.

But he has never asked me anything about whom I have met before. He doesn't seem interested in it. He is probably so sure that he is the only one for me that he doesn't need to worry about it. I'm perhaps the only one who is uneasy. When I think about Gittan, and that he took care of her when she was drunk, I get jealous.

Wednesday, 2 September 1964
I have been with mamma to stores to look at coats. I think it's so difficult to know which clothing style to choose. In

school some have parkas, some quilted jackets, some duffel coats, and some common coats. I already have a duffel coat and both Solan and I have parkas (but we don't write the names of pop groups and idols on them as for example Sivan and Kerstin do).

E-L wears her quilted jacket in school sometimes, but never when she goes out. On those occasions both of us wear coats and high heeled boots or shoes.

And while Solan and I wear a skirt with our parkas sometimes, Sivan and the others always have long pants. Sivan even has jeans with a fly, sometimes. I don't think that is appropriate for girls. (Not for boys either, for that matter, other than for work pants.) If Sivan has a skirt sometimes, she has a very short and tight one that comes half way up her thighs. I don't want mine that short. I think ten centimeters above my knee is just enough.

Sunday, 6 September 1964

Last night I went out alone, and then I met a boy named Gert. It was he and another boy and also a girl. I went with them, and we set off to Svista and had coffee.

The car was a 1954 Murkla (a Ford Mercury, that is). It was red with a black roof (or if it was the other way round), and inside there were white sheep skins on the front seat. And there was also a record player, of course.

Gert was 23 years old and rather tall and slender. He had blond hair, a straight nose and gray-blue eyes. Some-

times I thought he looked really good, but the next second I could perceive him as being almost ugly. I couldn't decide what to think of him.

Before we drove home, we went to the late-night matinee to see a film with Michael Landon (Little Joe in "Bonanza") called "I was a Teenage Werewolf". When we came out and sat in the car again it was so cosy, somehow. There was a certain atmosphere, which very likely was because of the car, because it felt nice to have someplace to go after the movie and not have to walk out in town.

Yes, and he wanted to see me again and is going to pick me up at seven o'clock tonight (if he doesn't break the appointment). I will wear my lion yellow lamb's-wool sweater and my brown terylene skirt that I can scarcely walk in (it's so tight and there is only a short slit in the back). But I'm not going to be walking; I'm just going to be sitting there in the car looking pretty while we drive around in town.

Lasse called on Wednesday and Friday and came on Saturday. I had hoped that we would drink, but we didn't. We went to his home and had coffee instead.

Before that, when we were driving around town, I saw Kicki on Svartbäcksgatan, and when I thought of what she was doing, I became envious and wished that I could be there too. I felt angry and thought it was

Lasse's fault that I couldn't do what I wanted.

"What is it my little one?" he said. "Are you uneasy?"

"No, I was just thinking of something."

"About what?"

That you don't keep your promises and that I don't want to see you again, I thought. But I didn't say anything.

"Do you miss being out?"

"Sometimes."

"Like now?"

"I don't know."

"But it will blow over. After you have been away from it for a while, you won't miss it anymore."

How can he know that? He doesn't understand what it is like. Nobody who hasn't done it himself knows that. I can't forget how it feels to sit in a big, American car and smoke, drink, and listen to music. The smoke and the music surround you, and the booze makes everything so wonderful… I long to get to do it again.

I know I am stupid to prefer drinking and cruising to meeting a nice and tender guy who cares about me, but I can't help it. I'm just going to see him until he breaks up, when he has realized that he isn't going to get to lay me no matter how long he waits. So probably it won't be very long before I'm out in town again.

He lives in a red two-story house. When we came in his parents sat in the living room watching TV. Lasse introduced me, and they looked at me and nodded and smiled. His dad was short and rather slender, and his mom was tall and stout.

When I got dressed up at home, I could only find one stocking that was in good condition, so I had to take one that had a ladder in it, and now I hoped that they didn't notice the tear and that the stocking had nail polish on it.

We went up to his room. There was a bed, a table, a chest of drawers, a mirror, a bookshelf, and an easy chair. While he was down fetching coffee, I looked at the books in his bookshelf. There were Manhattan series detective stories, Wild West books, and Zebra series detective stories. On the table there was a revolving ashtray and a pipe holder that carried four pipes.

I sat down in the easy chair and smoked. On the wall above the bed there was a wallpaper cover with thin wood pieces and an embroidered tapestry on which you could read: "There is no place like home."

When he came up we had coffee.

"Taste mom's buns now," he said and started to tune in a transistor radio that he had brought. I suggested that he should try to tune in Radio Luxembourg, and he smiled and said:

"That's just what I'm doing. Two minds with but one single thought!"

His mother thought I was sweet, he said.

"She did?"

"Yes, and she's right about that."

"What have you told them about me?"

"That I have met a nice and sweet girl who I like."

"Did you tell them how we met too?"

"No, I didn't."

"Why not?"

"Because I don't think it's important."

But I think it's because he is ashamed that I am a *raggarbrud* and that he doesn't want them to know that he picked me up in the street.

When we had finished our coffee, and sat there and smoked, I asked him where he kept the rum bottle.

"I've put it away."

"Where?"

"Do you want to see it?"

"Yes."

"You little fool!"

He had it in his wardrobe. When he put it on the table, I wanted to screw off the cap and start drinking right away.

"Do you want some?" he said.

"Yes please, but how about you?" I said and tried to sound indifferent.

"No, I'm driving later."

"Yes, but I can't sit here and drink all by myself?"

But he thought I could and went down to get me a glass. When he was back he poured a little rum into it and handed it over to me.

"Just don't get drunk now!" he said and smiled.

"No, I won't."

But I wished I could have done that.

What did we do then? He put the bottle back in the wardrobe and laid down on the bed, and I sat beside him and smoked and drank. I don't think he understands how it is with me and booze. He doesn't get how much I want it. Because if he did, he wouldn't give me some, so I would crave even more. At least he wouldn't do that if it's true as he said before, that he wants to help me stop drinking.

When I had finished smoking, he drew me down on the bed and kissed me. He stuck his hands under my sweater, unhooked my bra and turned me over, pulling up my sweater and moving down so that he could reach my breasts with his lips. I thought it was pleasant when he was carrying on with them, but I wished that he had stayed away from my mouth, because I don't like his kisses.

After a while he heaved himself up on an elbow and just lay there gazing at my breasts.

"For these there ought to be a sign that says Private property, no admittance!" he said. "Little Star Eye, who has created you so perfect?"

I wanted to sit up and drink more, but I didn't know if he would think that something would be spoiled if I did that, so I just lay there, and he took off my pants and stuck a finger inside me.

"You're so fine," he said. "You're really a true little woman!"

And he moved his finger and kissed me again.

Tuesday, 8 September 1964

E-L brought spirits with her to school (Apricot Brandy), and we drank it in a toilet in the main building where we usually smoke on the sly. We must be crazy! We who go to Magdeburg and all! Then you are supposed to be a bit extra well-behaved. For example, we are not allowed to smoke outside on the street, because if people see some young girls stand there puffing, they may connect them with the girls' school, and then the school gets a bad reputation. Therefore, they have set limits that we aren't allowed to smoke within. They are at Svartbäcksgatan, Järnbrogatan, Skolgatan and Sysslomansgatan. Beyond those streets, we can smoke if we absolutely have to, because there no one regards us as students at Magdeburg, they believe. But you don't have time to go that far to smoke during a break.

In any case, they are very concerned about the school's image. You can wonder what they would think if it came out that there is alcohol consumption occurring inside the school walls. If they found out, they would probably go mad and regulate us.

I met Gert again on Sunday. We didn't do anything special. We drove around and played records. I still don't really know how I feel about him, so at present I can't say very much to E-L about her seeing Lasse. (Right now, I'm doing almost the same thing myself.) Gosh, why is it so difficult to know what you feel and want?

I brought some Apricot Brandy to school, and during our long break Kicki and I went to a toilet and drank it. I don't know why we did it, because we only had about a half cup each, and by so little you are not affected. I didn't want to be, either. I did it because it's forbidden and because I want to drink.

But Lasse will call tonight and on Saturday he is coming to pick me up. Kicki thinks it's stupid of me to see him if I don't love him, but I think he would be sad if I said no, and I don't want to be without the things he gives me. No one has been as tender and considerate to me as he. Once he said that as soon as he thinks about doing something he also wonders if I would like it, and once he said that I had changed his decision to be a bachelor for the rest of his life.

I don't know why I mostly think about things I don't like, because it's the other things that take up most of our time. When we sit in the car, and he looks at me with a special expression on his face, or when he asks if I am freezing or tired or sad, I feel that he loves me.

"What is it, my little one?" he asks if I just look a bit thoughtful. "Are you sorry? Have I done something wrong?"

And once, when he happened to bump his elbow in my eye, he got totally heartbroken and said that he could never forgive himself if he harmed me.

So he cares about me, and I don't want to make him

sad. When I think about how he is, it feels almost like I'm in love with him. Sometimes I believe I am. But if I were, I think I should wanna lay him as well.

Thursday, 10 September 1964

In Swedish language and literature, we are supposed to compose and make a presentation before the class about an author. And this for someone like me, who has such difficulties with things like that! Apart from the fact that I get a frog in my throat and my voice sounds rough when I speak, my hands are shaking when I stand there and hold the papers. Others might not take much notice, but I think it's so difficult.

Why can't I be like mamma who likes to perform in front of an audience? Gosh, how she loves to read or sing or present something! That's really fun for her.

I've never told her about my difficulties with speaking in school, because she wouldn't understand it. She never understood, for example, why I didn't want to go out to the other children and dance in the courtyard when there was an after-Christmas children's party when I was little. "Why don't you go out? It's really lots of fun!" Because if I had gone out, she could also have done it. "But won't you go anyway?" But no, I didn't want to.

Afterwards they came in with a candy bag for me.

We went to Lasse's home again. I didn't want him to do what he did last time, but if you have gone along with something once, it seems silly to say no the next time, so finally I let him do it anyway. I lay there and thought about the bottle in the wardrobe and wished that he would ask me if I wanted some this time as well. But he didn't. He took off his pants and lay beside me in his underwear, and I noticed that he got randy. When he thought that I was too, he asked me if I wanted to do it. I could neither say yes nor no and didn't answer.

"Are you afraid of getting pregnant?" he said.

"Yes."

"But you don't need to be."

And then he sat up and reached for his pants. Now he's going to get a rubber, I thought. And he did. It was in a small, oblong package, which he ripped open, and when he had got it out he unfurled it and blew air in it, like in a balloon.

"It's strong," he said and bounced it against his leg. "It can take even more than this. You don't need to worry."

But I still wasn't sure. If you don't want to do it both in mind and body, you shouldn't do it at all, I have read, and with Lasse I only want it in my mind, because I love him and I don't want to disappoint him. I cannot feel in my body that I want him to come inside me. But you are supposed to feel that way. After forplay, you should be so randy that you almost can't stand it. But I don't feel that way. I don't feel anything special at all.

"Are you sad?" he said.

"Yes."

"Why?"

"Because I don't want to make you sad."

"But you don't make me sad. How can you believe a thing like that? My little fool! How can I be sad when you are here?"

"But you don't get what you want."

Then he lifted up my chin and gazed tenderly and reproachfully at me.

"What do you think of me? Do you think that's all I'm out for?"

"I don't know."

"Well, it isn't! And I can wait. It will be even more delightful when it happens."

"But I may never change my mind."

"I can wait for months, yes, even for a year."

But I don't believe that. Nobody can wait that long. And I won't want to do it in a year, either.

"My buddy waited for five months for his girl, so why shouldn't I be able to wait for you?"

"I don't know."

"Yes, I can, my little one. And waiting for you will be a real treat."

I don't know what to believe. I just know that it is my fault that he can't have a normal sex life though he is going steady. And he has a much stronger desire than I have, because he is a guy.

Why am I so selfish when he is so unselfish? I'm not worthy of him. If he had said that he doesn't believe that I really like him when I said that I didn't want to, it would have been much easier, because then I would have known that he doesn't care about me, but when it is like this, I feel guilty.

Why can't I care about him as much as he cares about me? I must learn to do that. I don't want to be egoistic and childish. I shall set myself aside and give him everything he wants, because it isn't right that he has to sacrifice himself for my sake. I will prove that I love him.

When I think about Lasse and feel that I love him, it isn't very difficult to think that I could lay him, but then, when we meet and he tries to turn me on, I'm not able to feel that I want to. I couldn't yesterday, anyway. Instead I got irritated with him and thought that everything he said sounded affected and ridiculous. It came to be that way because I didn't feel worthy of it and couldn't accept it. I didn't think it was true that I am as wonderful as he said. And it isn't, as long as I can't be unselfish. I must learn to think more about his needs than about my own if I should be worthy of his love.

In town we met Kicki and a guy named Gert, who she has started going out with. He has a Ford Mercury.

When I saw her sitting there in the car looking satisfied, I got envious. Lasse asked me what I was thinking about, but I was ashamed and didn't want to tell him.

"Is it something I have said or done?" he said.

"No, it doesn't have anything to do with you.

"What is it then?"

Right then we met the Plymouth that I went with this summer the first time I got drunk.

"I'm only thinking of somebody I know," I said.

Then he said nothing more. But it wasn't Chrille I was thinking of. I thought of how it feels to be drunk. I long to drink and be drunk again. Booze is the only thing that means as much to me as Lasse. Sometimes it seems to me that it means even *more*.

Monday, 14 September 1964

I went out with Gert on Wednesday, Friday, Saturday and Sunday. We haven't done anything special. On Friday we went to his place in Märsta, and on Saturday we rushed away to Gävle and mixed with the raggarbilar *there. Yesterday evening we cruised at home in Uppsala. Then I saw Lasse's car, but I didn't manage to see E-L, and I don't know if she saw me, either, because I forgot to ask her about it in school today.*

When Gert comes to fetch me, he drives into the yard (or backs in, rather), and then he hoots so that I can hear that he is here. It feels nice to be fetched like that, and he doesn't have just any car, either. Even mamma and papa seem a little impressed. But it is a bit problematic with him, because he wants more than I do when it comes to the physical, and I don't really know what to do about it. I like to kiss and hold him, but I don't want to do more, and he doesn't think that's enough. He has an egoistic manner, and he be- comes surly when he doesn't get what he wants. I'm the one who is supposed to adapt myself to him and not the other way round, he thinks, and that makes me feel that he doesn't care about me enough. But he may feel the same for his part, when I don't want to go along with what he wants.

On Saturday when we were on our way to Gävle, he told me a little about himself and his earlier life. When he was 16 years old he went to sea. Before that he had worked at a restaurant, so he started in that career path and worked on the boat as a mess man.

But when he returned from sea he messed up. Partly because of a burglary, and partly because of an assault. He and some military guys got into a fight at a kiosk near Svandammen.

And when he was supposed to do his military service, and was on his way to Karlskrona and the ship he was assigned to, he and his mate made a little detour and robbed a service station, or whatever it was. Then he reported to the ship and was to be an officer cadet. But before he had started, the police turned up and put a stop to it. He was arrested and convicted, and for that reason he hasn't done his military service.

Thursday, 17 September 1964

I'm staying at home instead of going to school today. I'm not sick, but I'm thinking of Kjell and feel sad.

And why do I do that? Well, it's because it ended with Gert yesterday evening. In that case, I should rather be thinking about him *you might think, but now it feels like he was only a parenthesis and that it's Kjell I have been interested in the entire time.*

I was at home with Gert yesterday, in his apartment, and he wanted me to touch him in a certain place. Not that he wanted me to give him an ejaculation perhaps, but he wanted me to touch him, and I just couldn't do it. I felt such reluctance.

We are talking about under the belt here, and he had a belt with a large buckle on it, and below the belt I just couldn't do it. With his upper body it went well, to hug him and so on, but I didn't want anything further down. We lay on his bed and ate grapes, and he felt sorry for me and wondered how my sex life would be, just because I didn't want to do it with him. But I didn't want it his *way, and he didn't understand* my *way, so he dumped me. He gave me some money to take a taxi to the train station in Märsta, and then I walked home from the railway station in Uppsala. I felt sad, but not because it was over actually, but because he had been so uncaring about my feelings. I thought it was rotten and started to think about Kjell and wished that it hadn't turned out the way it did with him.*

Saturday, 19 September 1964

I had such mixed feelings for Gert. Most of the time I felt I was in love with him, but sometimes I just thought, no way! Because he wasn't especially responsive, or how to say. He wasn't romantic anyway. I think he was one of those types who is used to slovenliness with girls in cars.

And there was nothing on the intellectual level either, so what was it, really? I suppose it was just that I was impressed with his car and flattered that he wanted to see me. If he had come by in an old Volkswagen, there might not have been anything at all.

Tonight, I intend to go dancing at the Star (or is it called Galaxy?). Les Vagabonds will be playing there. I have bought a new blouse that I will wear then, with my black skirt. It's black and white striped with a white collar and white cuffs. This will make me stylish (no, it won't!).

I always feel that I'm badly off with clothes com- pared to others. My classmates, for example, who go around in their chic dresses and neat skirts and never seem to have any problems with wearing the right thing.

And their hair mostly looks like they have just come out of the hairdressers. I usually go to the beauty salon on Bangårdsgatan to have my hair done. I try to have it as flat as possible with only some waves, so they put my hair up in big curlers.

But what good does it make to have beautiful hair if you don't have a nice face as well? And I have problems with pimples around my nose and on my chin. It makes it worse to squeeze them, but I do, and then I put on a salve that is supposed to make them disappear.

E-L is going to ask Lasse if I may buy a bottle of spirits that he already has bought for them, and then she and I will go out and drink it together. But she's the one who is going to pay for it. We intend to do it on Wednesday if Lasse doesn't want to meet her then.

It will be fun going out with her again, but for my part I could just as well do it without the spirits. I don't think it's necessary to drink. The spirits are some kind of rum, and I have heard about rum and cola, but I have never drunk it.

I asked Lasse if Kicki could buy the Silver Rum that he and I were supposed to drink before, and he went along with it. Kicki and I are going to share it, but he didn't seem suspicious. On the contrary, he probably thinks that I don't want to drink anymore now when I'm seeing him, and that's why I thought that Kicki could buy the rum from him. We will meet her at Radiohörnan tonight and hand it over to her.

We went to his place, and when we were lying almost naked on the bed he got an erection and asked if I wanted to do it. I didn't know, and I told him so, but he rolled a condom on and laid down between my legs and tried to get in.

"Promise you'll tell me if it hurts," he said.

But I didn't feel anything special, and finally he got it in and started to frig.

"Are you sure it doesn't hurt?" he said several times. "I could never forgive myself if I hurt you."

He panted and got red and sticky on his face because of sweat.

"Little woman," he whispered. "If you only knew how wonderful you are!"

I thought he was ugly and made a fool of himself. When I watched him, he began to avoid my gaze and looked like a shamefaced dog, so then I just closed my eyes until he was done. The bed creaked and squeaked so it must have been heard in the living room downstairs, where his mom and dad were watching TV, but it didn't seem to bother him. He just bumped on so his sweat ran. The door wasn't even locked, so any-body could have come in while he was carrying on.

Finally, he started bumping more rapidly. Then he groaned and collapsed and lay still.

"Have you had enough now, my little horny one?" he said and smiled.

"Yes, I have. How about you?"

"Yes, for now. But it's just as important that you have."

When he had pulled out of me, he checked to see that the rubber was intact. His semen looked like snot.

Now it's going to be like this all the time, I thought. I will never be able to say no again.

He offered me a pack of Meils that he had gotten two for the same price – 2.50 *kronor* – as for one, and we smoked.

"Are you sad?" he said.

"No, why should I be?"

"If you regret what you have done."

"No, I don't."

A little later I asked him how many girls he has laid before me.

"Why do you ask?" he said.

"Because I want to know."

"And if I don't answer?"

"Then I'll wonder why you don't want to tell."

"How many have *you* laid?"

"You know. Nobody else."

"Now the maid is lying!"

"Do you think that?"

"Yes."

"Then why do you think I wanted to wait?"

"I don't know. But now we'll sleep."

Why didn't he want to tell me how many girls he has laid? Is he ashamed of that he has laid too many or too few, or that he hasn't laid any girls at all? It wouldn't surprise me if I were his first. That's perhaps why he wasn't in such a hurry and could wait.

No, I don't know. Anyway, when I met him I was the *raggarbrud* who had made out with one hundred and three guys without going all the way.

We handed the rum over to Kicki and went to Lasse's home and had coffee. Afterwards, when we lay on his bed, he wanted to do it again. First he took off my skirt and panties, then he pulled my legs apart and started licking me down there. I felt foolish while he was going on with it and didn't know what to do. Didn't he think it was disgusting? I would have.

"You are so fine my little one," he said and changed his position so that he could stick a finger in. "Well, what's this? Is the maid possibly horny?"

I didn't know what to say, and he smiled, stood up, and dropped his pants. When he saw that I noticed his distended underwear he said:

"Well, now you see what you cause!"

Then he laid down beside me again and carried on. After a while he began to breathe faster and said:

"Oh, little troll, you're one great YES, all of you!"

And while rock 'n' roll was playing on the radio, I let him do it again. He wanted to wait for me before he let it come, but I said that he didn't need to, because I knew that nothing would happen.

"But it isn't just me who should have the pleasure of it," he said. "I think that's wrong. So now we are going to take it easy so that you can catch up."

But finally he couldn't hold it back any longer. He grunted and became red in his face and got fixed eyes when he came.

"Forgive me, forgive me!" he said and pressed his forehead against my shoulder. "It wasn't like this it was meant to be."

"It doesn't matter," I said.

"Are you sure?"

"Yes, I am."

Then he lifted his head and gazed at me with that warm and tender look he usually has sometimes.

"What did I do to be lucky enough to meet you?" he said.

"But there's nothing special about me."

"Yes, it is, my little one. You're so fine! And I promise that it will be better next time."

Then he fell asleep, while I lay there listening to Radio Luxembourg and thought about what I am going to do on Wednesday. I have a bad conscience when I think of it. Why can't I love him as much as he loves me? Why am I so hard and cold? I lie to him and use him while he loves me and trusts me. It isn't fair.

But I'm so glad that Kicki and I are going out. It has been such a long time since I was drunk, and I want to be that way again. Just thinking of spirits makes me crave drinking. I picture the bottle in front of me and imagine how it feels taking a swig and swallow, knowing that it will soon hit me. Getting that numbing feeling in my head and body is so wonderful.

Monday, 21 September 1964

Nothing special happened at the Star (no dream prince turned up), but I did get to dance a lot.

The Social Democrats won the election, though they lost a little support. All the parties lost support, except for the Communists who gained. The Conservative party lost the most, as far as you know.

Yesterday I got the spirits from E-L and Lasse in town. I've put the bottle in the storage room, and I'll fetch it when mamma and papa have gone out on Wednesday. E-L will come here before we go out, and we will sit here and drink first.

On Saturday E-L let Lasse take her virginity. I was a little surprised when she told me, because I have gotten the impression that he doesn't especially turn her on. But I suppose that she knows what she is doing. Though I doubt that she is really in love with him.

I have the cinema ads in the newspaper here, and there is a lot of films to chose between. I might see "Rebel Without a Cause", because James Dean is sweet, and I haven't seen it yet.

When Anita was younger, James Dean was her greatest idol. She has seen all his films ("East of Eden", "Rebel Without a Cause", and "The Giant"). He starred in only three films before he died in 1955 when he was 24 years old. He died in a car accident when he and a

Before we went into town we sat at Kicki's home and drank, because her parents weren't at home. She had bought Coca-Cola, which we mixed with the rum, and made ice cubes that we put in our drinks. It was so cosy to sit there and smoke and drink and listen to music, knowing that we would soon be out in town again. When we were ready to leave, we poured the cola into the rum that was left and took it with us. I had the bottle in my purse.

And then we were there. I don't know what I had expected, but it felt like I didn't belong there as much as before. I couldn't forget that I was only there temporarily and that I wouldn't continue to come and walk there. And I thought about how sad Lasse would be if he found out that I was out.

We rode with two guys in an Opel. Kicki sat in front with a guy named Jörgen and I was in the back with the other one who was called Roine. After a while he tried to kiss me. When I turned my head away he said:

"What's wrong? Why don't you want to?"

"I shouldn't have come."

"You shouldn't have come?"

"No, I shouldn't have gone out tonight."

"And what should you have done instead?"

"Sat at home and watched TV."

"Well, that sounds damn fun!"

"No, but I'm not being honest now."

"You're not?"

"No, it isn't fair to you that I'm sitting here."

Then he sighed and threw himself back against the backrest and said:

"What's his name?"

"Lasse."

"How long have you been together with him, then?"

"A month."

"A month?"

"Yes. Are you angry?"

"No, I'm sad."

"Sad? Why is that?"

"Because I like you."

"I like you too," I said.

And when I had said that, it was so strange, because then it felt as if I liked him more than I like Lasse. How could it be that way?

Kicki and I hadn't drunk anything in town, so when Roine and Jörgen came, we had sobered up a little and they didn't notice that we had been drinking. But now I took the bottle out of my purse and took a gulp.

"Do you want some?" I said to Roine when I noticed that he was watching me.

"What does your guy think about you being out like this?" he said and shook his head.

"He doesn't know."

Everything felt so awkward. How could I like him better than Lasse, though I didn't know him? Was I just imagining things or was it true?

No, it *couldn't* be true! It's probably because I'm not quite sober I'm feeling this way, I thought.

But I didn't stop drinking. I held up the bottle towards Roine and said:

"When this is finished, I'll be drunk."

"Yeah, that's for sure."

"But this will be the last time."

"That you drink?"

"Yes, I can't ever do it again. I can't ever drink, and I can't ever go out again."

"Then you will be in serfdom?"

"Yes, in serfdom."

We rode and rode, and Jim Reeves sang and sang. Kicki sat with her head against Jörgen's shoulder and sang with the music, and I smoked and drank. It's so good to smoke while drinking. Roine did nothing but watching me.

"I wanna see you again," he said.

"Yes, but that's impossible."

"Why?"

"I've already told you."

"But it will be over some time."

"No, it will never be over."

Then he threw his head back and laughed so his Adam's apple bobbed.

Thursday, 24 September 1964

E-L came, and we sat here and drank before we went into town. We mixed rum and cola that I had bought. Before Coca-Cola was banned in Sweden because it has an ingredient that they didn't think was good. But it was released in the 1950's. And if you add Magnecyl to Coca-Cola and drink it, you can be drunk, it's claimed.

But we didn't need to try such tricks, because we had access to real spirits. E-L said, that even from the first time she was drinking she knew she would do it again. She felt immediately that it appealed to her. If she had known how it feels to be drunk she would have started drinking much earlier. But she didn't think she would have begun if she hadn't been out so often by herself this summer. For example, she wouldn't have said to me, if I had been there also and we had been offered spirits: "Take some, of course you should take some!" She couldn't have said that if she hadn't tried it herself first, she said.

Yesterday evening we didn't walk especially long on Svartbäcksgatan, and E-L wasn't that slack and disorderly, either. We went with two boys in an Opel, and E-L drank more in the car, because she had the bottle with her in her purse. But I didn't take any and neither did the driver.

His name was Jörgen, and he seemed nice. I sat with him in front and played records. They had one with Jim Reeves that I especially like, and I sat and sang a little to the music. "I love you because you understand dear, every single thing I try to do." That one I sang, and I leaned my head against his shoulder, like you often do in cars when sitting next to the driver. He asked me if he could call, and I said he could, because I liked him. He was much more my style than Gert, for example, and I really hope that I will hear from him again.

Jörgen wanted to see Kicki again, so he's coming to pick her up tonight. They are going to Ängby Park to watch The Swinging Blue Jeans. I would also like to go there, but I won't see Roine. He said that he wanted to see me, and it's true that I liked him, but you can't break up with the one you are going steady with just because you meet someone else you like. It's Lasse I am together with, and he is the one I love, so I won't go out and meet others anymore.

I feel sorry for Lasse who won't get to lay me to-night. Yesterday when he called me, he said that he missed me both in mind and body, so I know that he is hoping for it. But I have my period, so it can't be done.

When Lasse came, he hugged me and said:

"This week has felt like a whole year!"

Then I started to cry.

"But what is it, my little one? Are you crying?"

Forgive me, forgive me! I thought.

He asked me what it was, but I couldn't say.

"Cry, little one, if it helps!" he said and held me tight.

Then he tried to comfort me.

"It's alright, it's alright… I'm here… I'll be here as long as you want."

Why is he so kind? I don't deserve it.

A little later, when we were on our way to his home, he said:

"So how was your week?"

"Fine."

"Yes, you were probably out on Wednesday evening and raved it up!"

He smiled when he said it, and I smiled back.

"That's right," I said.

"Ah, you admit it! Now tell me what you did, and don't try to cram me with lies!"

"I was in town cruising and drinking."

"Yes, just what I thought! And did you meet any nice guys?"

"Yes, there was one guy in particular. But perhaps you saw me when you were out yourself?"

"No, I was at home, studying."

"Math?"

"No, English."

Now he thinks that he is going to be rewarded for this week's effort, I thought. Now he thinks that he is going to lay me soon.

But he wasn't as disappointed as I had thought. I don't know if he was disappointed at all.

"You're not in shape? he said. Then you should rest and take it easy."

We played cards with his mom and dad and watched TV. Once when his dad happened to put his hand on my knee, Lasse got angry with him and said:

"Hands off!"

But it was only a friendly gesture on his dad's part.

Why does it have to be like this? Lasse was supposed to pick me up at seven o'clock, but at a quarter past six he called and said that his car had conked out and that he couldn't come.

"But can't you fix the car?" I said, because I didn't know how to stand it, if I had to stay home.

"Yes, but I can't get it done tonight."

I became totally numb by disappointment and could hardly speak. He doesn't care about me, I thought. The only reason he isn't coming is that he knows that we can't frig.

"Are you still there?" he said.

"Yes."

"Don't be sad. We'll get together on Saturday."

I wanted to say that it didn't matter, but I couldn't.

"You?" he said appealingly. "Time flies. And I'll call you on Tuesday."

"You don't have to call if you don't want to."

"But my little one! Just because I can't come this evening doesn't mean that I don't care about you!"

"It doesn't?"

I knew I was going too far, but I couldn't help it.

"What can I say so you'll understand?"

"You don't have to say anything."

"But you know I want to get together with you as much as you want to get together with me."

No, I don't, I thought.

"Promise that you won't be sad. And don't do anything stupid."

"Stupid?"

"Yes, but you do what you want…"

"No, I'm doing what *you* want."

"What do I want then?"

"Avoid me."

"But don't you understand? It isn't that I don't *want* to come, but that I can't make it."

"Right. See you on Saturday then."

"Yes, but I'll call before then. Goodbye, Star Eye! And don't be sad."

I didn't know what to do after that. The bus had already left, so I couldn't go to town, and I couldn't call Kicki, because she was out with Jörgen. There was nothing at all I could do.

Once when I asked Lasse why we can't meet more than twice a week, he said that it is because he can't afford it. But if he really wanted to see me he *could* afford it! When Kicki and Gert were together they met four times a week, and he probably didn't have more in- come than Lasse has, and Gert also had a bigger car, that sucked more gas, and an apartment of his own, and he lived farther from town. Lasse says he neither can afford it nor has the time. First, he works all day, then he is studying in the evenings, then he helps his father with bookkeeping at the family firm, then he must do repair work on his car, then he reads all new books, then he listens to music, and then he follows the world events. After all that, if he has any time to spare, he meets me. That's the order of his priority list. He is first on my list and I am last on his.

Tuesday, 29 September 1964

"Have I the Right" with The Honeycombs, which is in third place on "Kvällstoppen", is rather good, I think. ("Have I the right to kiss you, you know I'll always miss you…") "Such a Night" with Elvis remains in sixteenth place. I like that song. ("It was a night, oh, what a night it was really was such a night!")

On Saturday Jörgen and I were at Ängby Park to see The Swinging Blue Jeans perform. On Sunday we were at his place. He lives in Eriksberg (or Sommarro as it's also called) with his parents. When we came in they sat in the kitchen, and they greeted me, and I greeted them. He had his room right behind the kitchen. It was small and rather narrow. I believe it was actually a dining room that he had gotten as his room.

He could play the guitar, and he played it for me. It wasn't at all like I'm used to when I accompany someone home, like now we're going to lie down here on the bed. He just played, and then we talked and listened to his Jim Reeves records.

After a while his mother came and asked if we wanted some coffee, and then we went out to the kitchen and sat down with his parents and had it. When he gave me a lift home he asked me if he could see me again, and I said yes, of course.

Thursday, 1 October 1964

I have been with Jörgen, and he played the guitar again. (If someone wants me to fall for him, he should play something melting on the guitar!) He played, and I sang.

I think it's so cosy with song and music. I wish that we could have kept Söderberg as our music teacher, because then my singing might have come to something. When we had her, I was attentive during the lessons, but when we got Bosse instead, there was no discipline anymore. He is perhaps 25 or 26 years old, and he has no idea how to keep track of 15–16-year-old-girls. There is no order, and as soon as a teacher can't manage the classroom, the students don't care about the subject matter. The only thing we think about now, is that we can smoke before our music lesson. (We smoke in YMCA, in the washroom there, before we go in for our lesson.) So nothing will become of my singing, either, I guess. Bosse doesn't care if someone happens to have a good singing voice. He possibly notices it when we sing individually for him, but it isn't anything he gets enthusiastic about and encourages.

Why must everything be so lax in school? There is really no point in going there, when you have teachers who are so uninterested in their job that they come last to class and leave first from their lessons and in between just sit and sleep at the teacher's desk while we get to listen to some old tape recording. I'm thinking of Frasse now, because if you want to find someone who is less interested in French and teaching, you have to look really hard! How much French do I know? Je suis une jeune fille. Tu es un garçon. Je t'aime. (But that's perhaps enough, because that's what life is all about, actually.)

And Bergström who is blind and who we don't give a damn about! We sit there and do our nails and lips and eyebrows and God knows what else, during his lessons. Everyone carries on with something. Some girls change seats. It's cruel actually, because he has made a seating chart in his head and almost no one sits in her correct seat. When he asks a question, the one he mentions by name answers from a different location than he expects, or if another girl in that seat answers, he can't recognize her voice.

And some girls do each other's hair or study homework from another subject or just write notes to friends. Not to mention the girls who sit with their books open and answer all the questions. Sometimes he says: "You don't have your books open now, do you?" "Of course not!" they say, although they really have. It's so sad.

But even if he weren't blind, I believe it would be difficult to seize much interest for his lessons. He is so dry and boring. A good teacher should engage the students to feel interest in the subject, and support and encourage those who are in difficulty, so that they won't give up and quit. The teacher shouldn't neglect how things are going and leave the students to their fate if they don't manage to keep up.

When I waited for Lasse I was so nervous that my pulse was one hundred and twenty before I saw his car coming up the road. I wouldn't manage one more time that he calls and says that he cannot come. It was so difficult and took so long to get out of the petrification that I don't want to go through that again.

We went to the movies and saw a Swedish film with Christina Schollin and Jarl Kulle. I thought we would go to his place afterwards, but he drove around in the country instead, along small roads, before he stopped in the woods and started to fondle me. After a while we got out, and he pulled my skirt up and my panties off. I bent forward and held on to a tree trunk, and he grabbed me from behind and pushed it in. It felt odd to have all my clothes on, except for the panties, and to do it outside. Afterwards, he pinched the rubber together and checked that it hadn't leaked, before he took it off and put a hole in the moss with his shoe and shoved it in. Then he moved moss and dirt over it.

I wish I had something to drink. It's true that I don't want to be with any other guy than Lasse, but I wish I could get drunk sometimes. As soon as I think of spirits I want it. It never goes away. If I dared, I would take some of pop's booze in the basement. But it won't work, because I have nowhere to go. After all, I can't sit at home with mom and pop and drink.

I went out Wednesday evening. When I was waiting for the bus, a Ford Anglia drove by and stopped a little farther on. It was one of them with an inward sloping rear window.

"Are you going to town?" I heard someone call.

I thought it was a guy, but when I came up to the car, I saw that it was a middle-aged man. I don't like to go with older men, because it becomes so awkward when they try to strike up a conversation and you realize that they don't understand anything. And you don't know what they imagine, either.

"Nasty weather this evening," he said when I had sat down beside him and started up with a jerk. "But that's probably just what you can expect this time of year."

It smelled hair-lotion and wet wool in the car, and something else that I couldn't recognize.

"What are you doing this evening then?" he said.

"I don't know."

"You are going to town to enjoy yourself, of course."

"Perhaps."

There were flecks on his face from the rain on the front windshield when the light from oncoming cars shone on it.

"Well, I'm on my way home," he said. "I live in Luthagen. Perhaps you would like to come home with me and stay for a while?"

Why do all old men think that you want to be with them? How can they be so stupid? Don't they understand that you think they are ugly and disgusting?

When we got to town it was pouring down. He let me out on Kungsgatan, and from there I walked to Svartbäcksgatan. My stockings were gray spotted in the back of my legs by the dirty water that splashed up as I walked.

And then I was there again. It was so cosy with the lights from the store windows and the neon signs that reflected in the rain-washed street, and with all glistening cars that slid by along the sidewalks.

I stood in a gateway and smoked. After a while a couple of guys in a Chevy stopped, but I said no to them. Then a guy in a black car drove by and braked and backed up to me. When I looked at him he tossed his head, asking me to come closer, and I put down my umbrella and walked up to him. He had dark hair and a black leather jacket and was rather handsome.

"Hey," he said and stared at me. "What are you doing tonight?"

"Nothing special."

"Are you coming with me then?"

"Yes, I suppose so."

When I sat in the car and he had started driving, he took out a pack of Lido cigarettes and offered me one. It's so cosy to sit in a car when it's raining and watch the wind shield wipers go back and forth and listen to the sound of the tires hissing on the asphalt.

On Vårdsätravägen he stopped the car and started to paw me. I knew that I only had myself to blame because I had come along with him, but I still didn't want to let him do anything, because he was in such a hurry and so rough. Why are some guys like that, that they can't take it easy and have to go ahead straight away? They just lose when they act that way.

He tugged at my pants and tried to force my legs open. I got so tired fighting him off, and he was so hot that steam was coming from inside his leather jacket. Why couldn't he just let me be? He wouldn't be able to do anything in the car anyway.

"If you don't stop I'm going to report you to the police," I said.

"Don't fool around! You came along of your own free will."

But I still don't think they have a right to force you.

I don't know how long it went on. The rain pattered on the roof, and the windows steamed up. Finally, I slipped out of my shoes, and when he let his guard down I pushed myself free, threw the door open, and got out. I heard him shout something, but I just left without paying any attention to him. The asphalt was full of yellow leaves and the rain spattered.

Then I heard him turn the car and come after me.

"Stop all this nonsense," he said through the window. "You'll get soaking wet if you walk like this."

But I would rather be soaked than let him carry on with me. I was walking on the left side of the road, and he let the car roll beside me as slowly as I walked.

"Come and sit here in the car now," he said. "I promise not to mess with you. I don't know what got into me. It's true. I usually don't behave like this. But it was like I couldn't think any longer."

At first I didn't answer, but he just kept on trying to persuade me, and finally I said:

"Leave off! You don't care about me! You're just afraid that I'll go with somebody else and tell him what you have done!"

"But nothing happened, and nothing will happen, either, if you'll just come with me."

I froze so my teeth were chattering, and I wanted my purse and shoes, so when he had begged a little more, I did what he said and climbed into the car again.

"Damn, what an ordeal," he said and stared at me.

"Just drive!"

"Yes, I just need to take a little breather, first."

I was mad as hell and didn't want to talk with him anymore.

"You are entitled to be upset," he said. "But you were so sweet that I lost control and didn't know what I was doing. This has never happened to me before and after this evening it will never happen again. So every cloud has a silver lining, as they say."

But I don't believe that this was the first time he behaved violently. And saying that he lost control because I was sweet was just bullshit. I don't think this was the last time it happened, either.

"Do you live far from here?" he said.

"Not really. But I'm not going home yet."

"You aren't? What will you do then?"

"Why?"

"Well, it isn't any of my business. But you'll get sick if you walk around in your soaked clothing."

He said that just because he wanted to give me a lift home, so that I couldn't go to the police and report him when he had let me out. I knew that he was afraid of that and was pondering on how he could find out if that's what I was going to do. But he could just as well worry, I thought.

When we came back to town he stopped outside

Centralbadet, and I got out of the car and slammed the door.

"You aren't mad, are you?" he said through the open window when I was about to go.

"Yes, I am!"

"But you won't do anything hasty, will you?"

Then I turned around and looked at him and said:

"I'm not going to the cops, if that's what you mean. So you can sleep well tonight!"

Then I went away.

When I was back on Svartbäcksgatan, I started to freeze again and didn't know what to do.

Forgive me, Lasse, I thought. Forgive me, forgive me! I'll never do like this again. Please, forgive me!

I went into a gateway and checked in my pocket mirror how I looked. All my lipstick was gone, and my hair was wet and flat and couldn't be backcombed again. I painted my lips and lit a cigarette and stood there waiting for someone to come. My feet and knees felt like pieces of ice, and I froze so my teeth chattered.

Finally a car with a single guy stopped, and he drove me home.

The guy from Wednesday gave me a hickey on my neck, and it didn't disappear before I was supposed to meet Lasse, so I put a plaster over it and thought that I would tell him that my cat had scratched me if he would ask something about it. The bruises on my arms weren't gone, either, but if I turned off the lamp when I undressed, he might not see them, I thought.

He noticed the plaster as soon as I got in the car.

"What have you done to your neck?" he said.

"I've been scratched by the cat."

"Is it so ill-tempered?"

"No, but it got scared when I lifted it down from a tree."

Then he said nothing more. I didn't know what he thought, but I hoped that he had swallowed it.

We went to his place, as usual. When we lay on the bed and I reached for the lamp he said:

"No, keep it on. I want to see you."

At first I put my arms on his back while he lay on top of me, but then he sat up and wanted to gaze at me, and I couldn't hide them. He saw the marks and grabbed my wrists and looked first at them and then at me.

"Did the cat this too?" he said and got a severe expression on his face.

"No."

"It didn't scratch you on the neck, either, did it?"

I could neither lie nor tell the truth and didn't answer.

"Tell me now! What has really happened?"

"Nothing."

"*Nothing*? Do you think I'm *dumb*?"

"It was a guy who got angry when I didn't want to go with him."

"When did you meet him then?"

"On Wednesday."

"Did you go out on Wednesday?"

"No, I was with Kicki. But he saw me at the bus stop when I was on my way home."

"Did he drag you into his car?"

"No, but he tried."

I thought that would explain the marks on my arms and felt relieved.

"Then, how did you get the mark on your neck?"

"Just as I said. From the cat."

I was dead scared that he would pull off the plaster and see the hickey underneath, but he just bowed his head into his hands and took a deep breath.

"What's the matter?" I said.

"I don't know if I can stand this any longer."

"What?"

"That I can't rely on you."

"Yes, you can rely on me."

"No, it doesn't feel that way."

"But I couldn't help it that that guy came by and started messing with me!"

"That isn't it."

"What is it then?"

He lifted his head and looked sadly at me.

"Why did you lie?"

"What do you mean, lie?"

"Why didn't you tell me what really happened, in the first place?"

"Because I thought you would get angry."

"But don't you understand that we must be able to trust each other? You must trust me, and I need to be able to trust you."

"I'm probably too immature for you," I said.

"Yes, but it doesn't have to be that way."

"No, but it feels like you don't care about me when you rather do other things than spend time with me."

"But I've already explained that."

"You're the most important in my life, and I'm the least important in yours."

"That's not true, and you know it."

"No, I don't. I only know how it feels."

Then he was silent for a while before he said:

"Sometimes you demand so much of me."

"And you demand that I should be as mature as a twenty-one-year-old."

"Yes, that's probably wrong…"

I don't remember everything we said, but finally we made up again.

"Oh, my little Star Eye! he said and drew me close. "What were we going to do?"

I love him, and I don't want it to end. I'm never going to be stupid again. I'm going to be the way he wants me to. I'm going to be as wise as he is and never again demand too much.

Now everything is all right between us again. It may be good to fall out sometimes, because afterwards you appreciate each other more.

On Sunday we were at Fågelsången and had coffee before he gave me a lift home. He usually drives to a place in the woods, near where I live, and then we sit in the car and fondle until it's time to frig. Now when it's cold outside we can't lie on the ground, but we can do it standing up. And it's more enjoyable to do it outside than indoors in a bed, I think.

I wish I could let Lasse come home with me, because mom and pop know that I'm going steady with a guy now. But I don't dare. They wouldn't take it naturally, and I'm afraid that pop would start questioning or scolding Lasse if we went in. I can't rely on them to behave mannerly. Why do they have to be so stupid? Why can't they just be *normal*, like everyone else's parents?

Friday, 16 October 1964

When mamma and I went to bed, we knew that papa would be drunk when he came home. We lay in the dark and listened while he unlocked the outer door, and then he flung the bedroom door open and pulled off mamma's quilt and yelled something. He didn't hit her, but he was violent, and a porcelain figure that grandma has given her fell to the floor and shattered.

I knew that he wouldn't hit her, because he has never

done that, even though he has been menacing many times. It has been close a few times when she has plucked up courage and tried to put her foot down. But most of the time she just goes away and cries.

And he soon calms down again. After his outburst last night, he went to bed and fell asleep immediately. But it isn't fun at all to have a papa who comes home drunk.

I don't know what to do. On Saturday we were at Lasse's home all evening, and yesterday we went to Sigtuna and bought hot dogs. On our way back, he fondled me and put his finger in, while he was driving. I touched him too, and he got an erection. I don't know why, but when we do it in the car I get more randy than when we are at his place lying in bed and can start frigging at any time.

He stopped on a forest road and wanted me to give him a blow job. I know there are girls who don't mind doing it, but I find it disgusting. I don't think I could do it even if I were drunk. But he had run out of condoms, so we couldn't frig.

Then he said that there was something he wanted to talk with me about. I wasn't prepared for what was to come, and at first I didn't get it.

"I think it would be best if we didn't see each other anymore," he said.

He wanted us to break up. I got so frightened that I felt like I couldn't breathe.

"To never meet again?" I said.

"Yes, I think that will be the best."

I didn't understand.

"But why?"

"Because I think we are too different."

"What do you mean, different?"

"We have different values and live after different principles."

And I have also thought so, but why must we break up because of it? After all, it has been like that the entire time.

"I don't understand," I said.

"What don't you understand?"

"Why we can't stay together."

"But I've already told you."

"Don't you like me anymore?"

"Yes, you know I do. But the advantages should preferably outweigh the disadvantages… And I can't deal with your demanding of me sometimes."

"Why haven't you said anything before, then?"

"I probably thought that things might get better. But the time when I realized that you don't trust me, and that I maybe can't trust you either, it was like something fell apart."

"But I do now! I do trust you! And I promise that you can trust me too! Maybe you couldn't do it before, but now you can."

Then he embraced me and said in his usual voice:

"Little Star Eye, you are so fine! But I think I need

some time to be alone and think this through."

"But if we don't see each other I can't prove that it's true that I have changed."

But it didn't help. He pushed me away and looked pleadingly at me.

"For my sake? Just so that I get some time to think this through thoroughly?"

"But I don't understand what it is that you need to think through."

"Try to trust me now. If I say I need time, that's the way it is."

"What am I supposed to do in the meantime, then? Just wait around for you?"

"You can do whatever you want and feel completely free."

"How long will this take, then?"

"I don't know… A couple of weeks, a month…"

When he knows for sure what he wants he will call, he said, and then we can meet and decide what to do. I'm not allowed to call him in the meantime, and I'm supposed to seize the opportunity and consider this too. But what should I consider when I already know that he is the only one I want?

I know it's my own fault that it has come to this. I have been egoistic and childish and have not cared about him as much as he has cared about me. Why couldn't I understand already from the beginning how wonderful he is? Why did I need to get hung up on trifles and go out and meet other guys just because I felt unsatisfied? Why couldn't I be thankful for what I had? It serves me right that he doesn't want to see me. But I can't manage without him. I love him and want to be with him all the time. I feel so afraid when I think that he might not come back.

Monday, 19 October 1964

I've been seeing Jörgen and everything has been fine. But E-L isn't happy, because yesterday when she met Lasse he said that they should be separated for a while. He thinks that she demands too much of him, or whatever it was, and needs time to think. Meanwhile she should feel free to go out and do what she wants, he had said. So now she is probably going to start cruising and drinking again, even though she says that she won't meet any other guys until she knows how it will be with Lasse.

I must do as he said and leave him alone until he wants us to meet again. I'm not going to force myself on him. I will prove that I can be home and study and watch TV and maybe go to the movies sometimes with Kicki, but I'm not going to cruise and get drunk. I will be faithful and wait for him, and then when he contacts me and asks me what I have been doing, I won't have to lie to him like I did before.

I never want to lie to him again. It's lies and things you never share that cause problems. I will never do anything again that I can't tell him about. Because it's true that we must be able to trust each other.

Now I believe that he will come back. When we have been apart for a while, and he has got to know how empty it will be, he will call me, and then we will never be apart again.

No, it doesn't work! What if he meets someone else? What if he calls me later just to say that he wants us to end? I couldn't handle that. Dear God, do something so that he doesn't meet somebody else! He said that he wouldn't go out, but I know he will. And then he may meet a girl who is as mature as he is, and he will realize what he has missed all this time. I'm so scared. If I must stop hoping that things will be good between us again, I don't know what will happen.

How could I be so stupid that I thought I could stay at home? That's laughable.

I went to town and walked on Svartbäcksgatan. I wanted to go with somebody quickly, because I was afraid that I would see Lasse, and that he would see me. I wouldn't have managed that.

And I didn't have to wait long. When I sat on the railing down by the river a Volkswagen 1500 drove by and turned aside a bit farther on. I didn't recognize the car at first, but then I saw that it was Tomas and Börje, with whom Kicki and I have ridden sometimes before. Tomas climbed out and came up to me and lifted me up and *carried* me to the car. Börje was driving, so we sat in the back seat.

"Sweetheart!" Tomas said and hugged me. "It has been a long time. How are you these days?"

He wasn't quite sober, but he had almost no booze left, he said when I asked. But he gave me what he had. And when he was going to smoke, he took two cigarettes and lit both of them in his mouth and put one of them between my lips.

They had a transistor tape recorder in the car and on the tape there were "Save the Last Dance for Me" with The Drifters and "Twilight Time", "Only You", "The Great Pretender", and "Smoke Gets in Your Eyes" with The Platters. I can't remember the rest. Yes, they also had "Needles and Pins" and "When You Walk in the Room" with The Searchers. When I heard the music, I realized how much I have missed it.

Guys, cars, booze, cigarettes and music are all I need, I thought. I don't give a shit about Lasse! He is too formal and boring for me anyway.

Then I got sad again. I drank the rest of the Koskenkorva and pressed myself against Tomas.

"But what is it sweetheart?" he said. "You're shaking like an aspen leaf."

Börje turned around and glanced at me, and Tomas held me.

"Tell me now what it is," he said.

But I couldn't, because it seemed so exaggerated, and I didn't want him to think I was silly.

He kissed and fondled me so that he got turned on.

"Oh, I could eat you up!" he said. You're so fine! And you have beautiful legs. You really have, Eva-Lena! I think I'm about to fall in love with you."

But he talked like that just because he was randy.

Later, when I had said no and we just sat there and smoked, he asked me again why I was sad.

"No, it's nothing," I said. "Promise that you don't care about it."

"Yes, I promise," he said.

But I could see that his eyes were doubtful.

Thursday, 22 October 1964

I feel completely confused. When Jörgen and I were out driving, I happened to mention that I'm 16 years old. I thought that he had understood approximately how old I am, but when I said it he was totally taken aback. "Are you only sixteen? I thought you were eighteen." "Oh, yeah?" I said and felt a bit flattered, because it's nice if you seem older than you really are. But he couldn't accept it: "So you are only sixteen?" Yes, so what? But I didn't say that. I asked him how old he was. "Well, I'm seven years older than you." Right? That wasn't too bad, I thought, because Gert was also that age.

But Jörgen seemed so strange and drove out to the woods and held me and wanted to kiss me. And at first it was okay, but then he got demanding, *as it's called, and that was something that I wasn't at all prepared for, because he hadn't acted like that before. One of the reasons that it felt so good with him was that he wasn't in a hurry with the physical. So I didn't get it and defended myself a little. But he was so stubborn and just persisted, and that made me very disappointed.*

Yes, and at last he said that if I didn't let him lay me, it was over! I got very sad and thought that he behaved so strangely. I asked him why. Is it because I'm only sixteen? *But a couple of years here or there shouldn't make any difference, I thought. And why did he all of a sudden want to lay me? I didn't get it.*

But I said no, and he drove me home, and then we sat outside in the car and talked. I wanted to find out why it had happened, because I didn't understand it, and I was so sad that I cried. But he couldn't explain it to me, and at last he got out of the car and opened the door and waited for me to go. I found it so hard to leave because I didn't understand, but I had to climb out when he insisted on it. And he drove away, to never return (you may assume).

I don't know what it was that caused him to react so strongly. I can't make it out. I think about it a lot, but the only thing I come up with, is that I don't understand, and that I'm sad that it must be over.

I don't know what to do. Why can't I just give a shit about Lasse and go out and cruise and drink again? After all, that's what I wanted before. But now when I'm free to do it, I don't feel like it. It's so meaningless. The only thing I want is getting him back so that I won't have to be afraid.

How much longer will I have to wait before he knows what he wants? And why can't we meet in the meantime? Because I don't think he will be able to decide if we don't meet. I would like to call him and tell him that. But if I did, he would probably get angry.

I went to town again, and there I met three guys who offered Gauffin's double mix. They had the whole trunk full of liquor, they said. I knew that Gauffin's is stronger than common booze, but I drank the way I usually do all the same, because I wanted it to hit me quickly. And it was so wonderful to be drunk. I had almost forgotten how it feels.

I sat with a guy named Totte in the back seat. The two in front just kept talking about cars they wanted to have and were boring as hell. I hung on Totte and drank so much that the feeling in my lips disappeared. Then I began to feel sick and needed to get out and puke. Totte held me, and I threw up on my boots. It was so disgusting. A little got on my coat and on Totte's arm, but most of it came down on my boots.

Back inside the car again I laid my head on Totte's lap and felt ill. I was dead drunk and couldn't pull myself together even though I wanted to. It was so scary. I have never been that drunk before.

They had to stop twice. The second time I wasn't able to get out, and I puked from the car down on the road.

Then I must have fallen asleep, because I don't remember anything that happened before Totte woke me and asked me where I lived.

They gave me a lift home, and when I lay in bed, everything was spinning so I couldn't sleep. I thought that I would throw up again, but fortunately I didn't.

I will never drink so I get that damned drunk again.

I called Lasse and asked if we could meet.

"No, I'm busy this evening," he said.

"Would you have come otherwise?"

"No."

"Are you mad at me for calling?"

"Well, I'm not happy about it, anyway!"

"But I can't stand to have it like this."

"You can try!"

"But I don't understand."

"If there isn't anything else you want, perhaps we could end this now?"

"But what are you going to do tonight?"

"Picking up mother and father in town."

"Where?"

"In front of Stadsteatern. *Satisfied*?"

"No, I won't be satisfied until you come back."

"Bye-bye!" he said and hung up on me.

At first I didn't know what to do. Then I decided to go to town and wait outside the theater until he came. I'll stand where he can't sight me, but where I can observe him, I thought. I just wanted to see him again.

It would be several hours until the play ended, so I went to the movies first. Then I went back and sat on a bench in Järnvägsparken. I didn't dare go any closer. But if he came, he would have to drive by, so I would see his car and know that he was in it.

After four cigarettes he turned up. I hate his car. As soon as I see a red Cortina, there is a twinge in my stomach. He stopped at the theater entrance and hopped out. His parents came out and climbed into the back seat, and he sat behind the wheel again and drove off.

Then I went away. I was like petrified.

After a while a guy began to walk by my side. He had light, cropped hair and was in his thirty's.

"Hello, where are you going?" he said.

"I don't know."

"You don't know?"

"No, it doesn't matter."

"Then you can come home with me for a while."

"Why?"

"Why not?"

"Because I can't do anything."

"But you don't have to do anything."

"I can't even talk. You had better ask someone else."

"What are you going to do then?"

"I don't know. Walk here."

"No, it would be better if you came home with me. If you don't want to talk, you don't have to."

"What will we do then?"

"Well, we could listen to music, for instance. Do you like music?"

"Yes, but that would just be boring for you."

"I don't expect anything from you."

"Then why do you want me to come with you?"

"Just because… When I saw you walking there, I thought that you seemed so down and sad in some way."

"And then you were going to play the Good Samaritan?"

"No, not exactly…"

"But there's no point in it."

"Well, come now. I promise that you don't have to do anything."

So I walked along with him. He lived in an apartment on Smedsgränd, and he had a stereo equipment and lots of LP records at his place.

When you listen to stereo music in headphones, the sound comes from two directions and mixes in your head. I listened to Tjajkovskij's piano concerto number 1. Meanwhile he made tea and some sandwiches.

"I saw you when you were still in Järnvägsparken," he said when we sat down at the table. "And then when you went across the street."

"Where were you?"

"In front of the People's House."

"I see."

"Yes, and then it occurred to me that you were sad."

"Why?"

"I don't know exactly. Because you were like sleep walking, perhaps."

What did he think? That I had went across the street without checking for traffic because I wanted to kill myself?

"You're welcome to tell me about it," he said.

"No, I must be off now," I said.

"Okay. But if you want to talk about it some time, you are welcome back."

"Thanks, but that won't be necessary."

Then I went away from him and began to go home. He was probably just some frigging psychology student who wanted to practice on people in reality.

I walked on the road in the dark and wished that I didn't exist. If you don't exist, you can't feel, and if you can't feel, it doesn't hurt.

There wasn't very much traffic. Some guys put all their searchlights on when they saw me walking along the roadway, and some hooted. Finally, it was one that slowed down. He came from behind and stopped a bit farther on. The only things visible were the rear lights and the reflection on the asphalt in front of the car. It felt unsafe that someone sat in the dark and waited for me to come closer. I tried not to worry about it and moved on, and when I had come midway to the car, I heard a voice ask me if I wanted a lift. But I was almost home by then, so I didn't go with him.

I don't want to wait! Why do I have to wait? I want to know *now*! But I can't, because he has so many things he needs to think through. He doesn't care that I can't be without him and that I don't know what to do in the meantime. Sometimes it almost feels like I hate him because he doesn't want to see me. But I love him and want him to come back. I'm so afraid that he won't.

I could tell him that I'm pregnant, because if I were, I know that he would never dump me. If I wait until the next time I have had my period, I can tell him afterwards that I never got it, and then he'll probably start seeing me again, and I have almost a month to show him that I have changed. I have to *show* it to him, because if I just say it, he won't believe me.

I will never be disappointed if he doesn't want to see me, or if he must drive home early some evening, and I won't believe that it means that he doesn't care about me. And sometimes *I* will say that we can't meet. If I'm supposed to be pregnant I can pretend that I'm tired, because you probably are, in that state. But I would rather that he begins to believe that I'm tired of *him*, and that's why I don't want to see him so often.

Wednesday, 28 October 1964

I've been with Anita' in town looking for purses. I can't really afford something new, but I thought I could possibly be lucky and find a cheap one, because my black one, which I use in the fall and winter, isn't up to much anymore. In school I only use my brown nylon bag, but for my free time (the evenings when I go out, that is), I have my purse. In it, except for a comb, a mirror, a notebook, a pen, money, keys, cigarettes, and matches, I keep a small make-up bag with make-up things. There is an eye lining pencil, mascara, lipstick, and some other stuff. The lipstick is a Jane Helen, which is more pink than bright red, because I don't like when the lipstick is very noticeable.

I never use lipstick in school. There I just have a little chap-stick on my lips if they feel dry. E-L has a little jar of Vicks, instead of chap-stick. She always has that jar with her and takes a little out with her long finger and draws it around her lips and presses them together to spread it evenly. And on her fingernails (or cuticles, rather) she also uses it. Actually, you are supposed to smear some of it on your chest when you have a cold and lie and breathe in the vapors, but she uses it on her lips and on her cuticles.

I wasn't able to get up early and go to school today. I stayed at home and went out. On the E4 a car stopped, and the man driving it asked me if I would like to come along and have some fun. He had a car safety seat in the back seat and was rather old. It's disgusting when those who are married and have children are out running for girls, I think.

Yesterday evening I went to town. I got some booze from Kåre and Rolle, but they had only a little squirt left, so I didn't get drunk.

When they had left, I went out on the bridge on Skolgatan. It smelled of gasoline and exhaust from the cars cruising on Svartbäcksgatan, and the street lights reflected in the water. I tried to imagine how it would feel like sinking beneath the surface of the water and drown. But if I were going to commit suicide, I would use sleeping pills. Though I don't know how I could get hold of them.

Some guys came up and started talking to me. They noticed that I was sad and asked what was wrong.

"Has your guy left you?" one of them said.

And another came closer and stared at me.

"Is she sad, the sugar baby? Diddle her a little, and she'll probably be glad."

Then they went away, and I rode with two idiots who offered Eau-de-Vie.

I called Lasse though I still haven't got my period.

"Engström," his mom answered.

"May I speak to Lasse?" I said.

"Just a moment, I'll go and see about it."

Then it took a rather long time before he came.

"Lasse," he said.

"Hello, it's me."

"Hi," he said shortly.

"Were you outside?"

"Yes, I was in the garage. What do you want?"

"I just want to know if you have something special planned for tomorrow evening."

"What about it?"

"Well, if not, I thought maybe we could meet."

"Why?"

"Because I want to see you."

"Do you have difficulty getting it, or what the hell is the matter?"

"Yes, I don't understand why we can't meet and talk instead of carrying on like this."

Then it got quiet, as if he considered it, before he said:

"Yes, you may be right… Okay then, when do you want me to come?"

"At the usual time, if you can?"

"Yes, it's agreed. See you then, my little one!"

I felt so happy when he called me "little one" and he

didn't sound angry anymore, but I don't dare believe that he has changed his mind and that things will be all right between us again. He only went along with meeting me because he feels sorry for me. But I'm happy anyway. It's such a long time since I saw him.

When I sat in the car, Lasse gazed at me, drew me close and said:

"Little Star Eye, I had almost forgotten how beautiful you are!"

Why does he say things like that when it isn't true?

We didn't drive to his home, because he was going to pick up his parents from a party. We drove out to the country instead, and he stopped on a forest road. I had my tight skirt of burled cloth on, and he tried to pull it up. When it didn't work, he wanted me to take it off – and my panties as well – and he moved over to my seat and opened his fly. He already had an erection and opened a Durex packet with his teeth and rolled the rubber on. Then I placed myself over him on my knees so that he could get it in.

"If you only knew how much I have missed you!" he said as he pulled me down on him. "There isn't anyone who is as wonderful as you are!"

He lifted and pushed me up and down. Finally it was dry and almost painful, but he continued until he had come. Then he was wet with sweat, and he collapsed with his head against my shoulder.

"Are you going to kill me? he said. My heart can't cope with things like this!"

When I had climbed down from him, and he had taken off the rubber and wiped himself with a handkerchief, we smoked.

Why do you always want to smoke afterwards?

I was happy, because it felt as if everything was like it was before, and as if he didn't want to be without me.

"Why did you come tonight? I said.

"Because I don't think it's fair to you to make you wait any longer."

"So, you've made up your mind?"

"Yes."

Then I could see from his facial expression that he didn't want us to go on. I don't know what happened then. I was like stupefied and didn't want to hear him say it. But then I got angry.

"Tell me then!" I shouted.

"I think it would be best if we didn't see each other anymore," he said.

"But why did you want to fuck then? Why did you want to fuck if you mean that it should be over?"

"Yes, I know it was wrong."

"But why did you do it? And why did you say all the things you have said now?"

"I don't know. Old habits, perhaps. But it makes no difference."

"Tell me what I have done, then!"

"Don't start with that again. I have already explained the reasons."

"That we are too different?"

"Yes, and I think you're too young to commit yourself. I was myself, when I was your age."

"But there is a difference between guys and girls. Girls mature earlier."

"Yes, that's possible. But I believe that you want to be free a little longer before you commit yourself seriously to someone."

"Speak for yourself!"

"Yes, that's perhaps true for me as well. But that doesn't mean that…"

"Tell it like it is, instead of chattering around! Say that you think I'm childish and immature and that you want me to go to hell, so that you get rid of me!"

"Well, then I say so!" he said.

I was out of the car before I had time to think. At the same time as I slammed the door, I knew that he wouldn't come after me. He didn't care where I went. He didn't want to have anything more to do with me. He would be happy if I just disappeared and never came back again. If I had dared, I would have gone into the woods and stayed there until he had driven off. But I didn't have my purse and coat with me, so after a while I turned and went back.

"Forgive me," he said when I sat beside him in the car again. It was so dark that I almost couldn't see him.

"For what?"

"For everything. But sometimes I get so damn tired of everything."

"Of what?"

"The job, the studies, the economy…"

"And me! So now you get at least *one* problem less."

"You don't have to scoff me."

"I don't. I'm *glad* if it will be better for you without me."

"I admire you."

"Admire me?"

"Yes, because you're able to be so large-minded and unselfish."

"Why do you say that?"

"Because I think so."

"But that's just the way I am not! It feels like you mock me when you talk like that."

I can't remember everything we said. Finally he started the engine and turned on the headlights. "It's just as well that we set off?"

"Yes, you're supposed to pick up your parents."

"They can wait. But I don't think we'll make any progress with this."

"No, I don't think so, either."

Suddenly I felt calm and strong, as if it were I and not he who had decided that it should be over. It was so strange. When we got to town I said:

"You can drop me off here, so that you don't have to drive me home."

"No, of course I'll drive you."

"But I'm not going home yet."

Then he braked and stopped the car without a word and waited for me to climb out.

"I don't want to go," I said. "Why must it be…"

"Make up your mind now, damn it! I don't have all night."

And then I just left. I went down to the river and smoked. The only thing I could think of was that I wanted to drink myself drunk and try to forget about what had happened. But so much, that you can forget a thing like that, you can't drink without passing out.

And I couldn't give up hope that things are going to be all right again. He can change his mind. So at the same time as I was afraid, I thought that if only some time has passed, he will probably come back. If it's true that he loves me, as he has shown the entire time, he can't just stop feeling that way all of a sudden.

Anyway, I drank yesterday. There were some guys in an Opel Caravan who offered it. But they only had a little hard liquor with soda mixed in, so I didn't get drunk. I didn't say anything about Lasse to them, and I tried not to think about him. I was like petrified.

But now I believe that he will come back. He must, because otherwise I don't know what will happen.

Kicki went with me to the movies, but she didn't want to go into town and took the bus straight home. I stood in the entrance to Radiohörnan and waited for someone to come. Everything felt so meaningless. I didn't want to stand there and freeze, and I didn't want to ride with anyone but Lasse. But he doesn't want me.

Finally, an E-marked Volkswagen stopped, and the guy who sat in it stuck his head out and asked if I were going home.

"Yes, I suppose so."

"Come then, I'll give you a lift."

He was broad-shouldered and good-looking, I saw when I had got into the car. He looked like a cop, with short, brown hair and a dark overcoat. When he had asked where I lived, he said:

"What have you done tonight?"

"Well, what do you usually do on this street?"

"I don't know. I'm very seldom here."

"Where do you usually be?"

"Well, if I'm not at home in Linköping, I usually sit in my room and read."

"Are you studying?"

"Yes."

"What?"

"Law."

"At the university?"

"Yes."

"What do you usually do when you're out having fun, then?"

"Then I frequent the student's clubs. And you?"

"When I go out to have fun? Then I'm cruising and boozing."

I don't know why I answered like that, because he hadn't done anything.

"I don't think you seem to be that kind of girl," he said.

"You don't? But I am."

Then it was silent. I wondered what he was thinking and if he regretted picking me up.

"Why did you stop?" I said.

"Well, that's more than I can answer. But this isn't the kind of thing I usually do."

"That you pick up *raggarbrudar* in the street, you mean?"

Then he got a tense expression on his face and said:

"Well, you could put it that way if you like…"

I knew I was mean, but I wanted him to see reality, so that he wouldn't imagine things.

Then I felt so tired. I lit a Savoy and leaned my head against the window.

"Don't you feel well?" he said. "Should I stop?"

"No, it's nothing."

Help me, please help me! I thought.

But he couldn't read thoughts.

Friday, 6 November 1964

The last lesson E-L and I went to Café Regent (our home away from home!) and had tea with cheese sandwiches. It's so cosy to sit there and smoke and listen to music. But E-L was down and sat and scraped the palm of her hand with her comb. I don't understand why she needs to carry on like that.

And I can't really take her seriously. She sometimes implies that she wants to kill herself, but I find it so hard to believe, because I always look on the bright side of things and assume that others do so as well. And I think that those who talk about suicide, deep down still hope that things will get better, and therefore there isn't a big risk that they will put their plans into action immediately. But you shouldn't believe that those who talk about it never do it, because if nothing happens they eventually give up.

How long will this go on? Why doesn't it ever end? When I'm asleep I never want to wake up again. I want to sleep or be drunk all the time. When Lasse and I were together I drank almost nothing, and I wouldn't do it now either, if he came back. I wouldn't even *miss* booze if we were together again, because now I know that it's only him I want. But he won't come. He doesn't want to, and he will never change his mind.

I wonder what it is like to be dead. If you are aware and feel, or if everything is black, I mean.

If that guy in the E-marked Volkswagen had wanted to see me again I could maybe have fallen in love with him and finally forgotten about Lasse. But he didn't say anything. He didn't even ask my name.

Kicki didn't want to go out, so I went alone. I rode with three guys in a two-toned Ford Fairlane all evening. They had Queen Anne and something else to drink and played "In Dreams" and "Oh, Pretty Woman" with Roy Orbison.

I saw Lasse's car in town. He and Leffe were sitting in the front seat, and we happened to get behind them on Islandsbron. I got angry when I saw them and wanted them to notice us.

"Follow that bastard!" I said to the guy driving the Ford.

"In the Cortina?"

"Yes, follow him!"

Then I stared at their heads that stood out against the front window, and at those three-piece rear lights at the back of the car, until I couldn't do it any longer. When we had passed them, I turned around and held the bottle up towards Lasse in the rear window. It felt as if I won over him then.

We went to Stockholm. I don't remember everything that happened, because I was so drunk. The headlights shone on the asphalt in front of the hood. Inside the car it was almost dark. I smoked and drank. The neck of the bottle bumped against my teeth when the car wobbled. The music rumbled. "I close my eyes, then I drift away…"

The guys got into a fight with some other guys. The cops arrived. We had to wait in the car. The policeman at the entrance sang "Detroit City". I got out and laid down with my head on his shoes. He didn't care that I was drunk.

When we were on our way home the radiator water started to boil. We stopped in a field. It was dark and cold. One of the guys pissed on a hubcap so it rattled.

I met the guy from Linköping again. His name is Clas. When I saw his car slow down and stop on the other side of the street I went there and sat down beside him in the front seat without going around and talking to him first, because I knew that he had stopped for me.

"How are you doing? he said when he had begun to drive. "Are you feeling better now?"

Then I told him about Lasse, that I'm sad because he has broken up with me and that I can't forget him.

"Do you hope that things will be fine again?"

"Yes."

"Why did it end?"

"Because he thought that I was too childish and im-mature compared to him, and that I demanded too much."

"Were you together for a long time?"

"No, just for two months. But it feels like two years."

"Why?"

"Because I became so dependent on him."

"In what way?"

"In every way. Now it feels like I can't live without him."

I looked at his hands that shown white below his coat sleeves and wondered what he was thinking. He perhaps thought that I exaggerated and was silly. But I had to tell him like it was.

"I saw you in town yesterday," he said.

"You did? Why didn't you stop?"

"Because you were just about to enter another car."

"Yes, I…"

"Don't you think there is a better way?"

"Better than what?"

"To try to escape."

"But I don't know how to cope with it."

"Time heals all wounds, they say."

"Yes, but how do you stand it in the meantime?"

Then he turned his head and looked at me.

"Why do you take it so hard?"

"Because I'm stupid."

We went to his place. He had a student's room on Karlsrogatan. When we came in he helped me off with my coat and hung it up on a clothes hanger before he took off his own coat. Underneath he had a gray, V-necked sweater, white shirt, and tie.

I sat down in an easy chair in the room, and he went to fetch something to drink. Then we sat there with a bottle of Pomril each and drank and played cards. I tried to imagine that it was liquor instead of lemonade, but it didn't work.

We played vingt-e-un. When I had won three times in a row, he reached over the table and touched me on my cheek. His hand smelled of soap.

"You're good at this," he said.

"It's only luck."

"You're lucky at cards and unlucky in love?"

"Yes."

But then things changed, and he was the one who won the whole time instead.

When we had played for a while, he stood up and sat on the armrest of my easy chair and started playing with my hair. He had thought about me, he said, and wondered how I was doing.

"Why?"

"I don't know... Because you seemed so unhappy, maybe. Last night when I was out, I was actually out looking for you."

"What a pity that you didn't see me earlier, then."

"Yes, I think so too."

"Because there was a lot of booze. And the guys got into a fist fight and wound up with the police in Stockholm."

I looked at his tight pant legs and waited for him to ask me what else had happened, but he didn't. Instead he said:

"How are things at home?"

"Fine."

"What do your parents say about your way of having fun, then?"

"They don't know about it."

"But if you come home affected by alcohol they must surely notice it?"

"They don't say anything anyway."

"You don't have very good contact with them, in other words?"

"No, and that's just as well."

"It's strange," he said and looked out the window, "how people who live under the same roof and belong to the same family can be like strangers to each other."

Then he asked about their occupations, and I said that pop is a construction worker and mom a house wife. His were a doctor and a curator.

I can't remember everything we talked about. At the end he stood up and pulled me up from the easy chair and pressed his face against my hair.

"You little honey," he said.

Why can't I fall in love with him? Why can't I think that he is good enough the way he is? Why can't I stop comparing him with Lasse? Why isn't he Lasse?

I called Lasse and forced him to come. At first he said that he couldn't, but when I said that it was an important matter I needed to talk with him about, he went along with it. But he was angry when he hung up.

We were supposed to meet on the parking lot in front of YMCA, and when I arrived he was already there. I went to the car, opened the door, and sat down beside him without saying anything. I almost didn't dare to look at him because I felt that he was still angry. There was light shining from some windows at Fjellstedtska, and the water in the river glittered.

"What do you want?" he said in a cold voice.

"I can't talk with you when you sound like that."

"How the hell am I supposed to sound, then?"

"As usual."

"Come to the point now! I don't have all evening. That I even came, is because I had another errand in town at the same time."

I felt sad and didn't know how to begin, but finally I said:

"I just want to ask if we can't try one more time."

"Are you *dumb*? Haven't you grasped that it's *over*?"

"But I have changed now!"

"I sure as hell haven't seen much of that!"

"No, but let me show you then."

"If you had really changed, you would leave me alone instead of carrying on like this."

"Why are you so angry?"

"What the hell do you *think*?"

"But I can't go on like this any longer. Please! I will do anything, if you just come back!"

"Stop acting like a damn little brat and try to realize that it's *over*!

"But I love you."

"Then you have a damn strange way of showing it!"

"But what should I do? I don't know what to do!"

"That's your headache."

"I can't live any longer."

"What did you *say*?"

"I can't live any longer I said."

Then he groaned and hid his face in his hands.

"I'm so damn tired of all this that I could spew!"

"Tired of me, you mean."

"Yes, of you and of all this shit!"

"But why do you think it feels that way?"

"You're completely fucking unbelievable!"

"But it might feel better for you too if we started to be together again."

"Is that what you believe?"

"Yes, it is."

But he didn't change his mind.

"Can you tell me what I have to do to make you understand? I don't *want to*! I'm not *able to*! Why isn't that enough?"

"But it won't be the way it was before. I promise! I know that everything was my fault. I know that I was too childish and demanded too much. But I won't be that way anymore. Can't I at least get a chance to show it to you? Please! I didn't know that you thought it was bad before you wanted us to be apart."

"It's too late."

"But think of all that was good! Because you surely

didn't think that *everything* was just shit? And all that was good we can get back, if we just want to."

"But I don't want it."

"Why not?"

"Stop it now, damn it! I regret that I went along with meeting you tonight. If I had known that it would be like this, I wouldn't have come."

"Well, then I know," I said and got as hard and cold as ice inside. "But it's a pity when it comes to school."

"What do you mean by that?"

"I can't care about it anymore, so I suppose everything will go to hell."

Then he became even more upset and said:

"Fuck it all!"

"That's how it will be, anyway. But what I actually wanted to talk about was that…"

"Yes?"

That I think I'm pregnant, I wanted to say. But he knew that no rubber had come off or leaked, so how would I make him believe that?

"No, it wasn't anything," I said.

"Well, come out with it now!"

"No, but you'll perhaps get to know about it soon enough. See you!"

"What are you trying to imply?" he roared.

"Nothing."

Then I got out of the car and slammed the door.

I don't remember what I did after that. It doesn't matter. Nothing matters anymore.

Clas called and asked if he could see me, and I said yes even though I didn't know if I wanted to. I was supposed to meet him where he lives, and I took the bus there and arrived at seven o'clock.

When I came in he hugged me and said that he had missed me. He had on a white shirt and a dark blue club blazer. I had my red crimplene dress on.

He had borrowed a tape recorder, and while he was tinkering with it I went to his desk and looked at some of the books laying there. I opened one, and on the inside cover there was a name written.

"Is this yours?" I said and held up the book towards him.

"Yes, it is."

"Who is Torkel, then?"

"Torkel?"

"Yes, it says so here."

"Well, that's me."

"But didn't you say that your name was Clas?"

"I'm named Clas as well."

"But you are called Torkel?"

"Yes."

"Why did you say that your name is Clas, then?"

"I don't know. It just happened that way."

"Then maybe nothing else you have said is true, either."

"Yes, it is."

"How can I know that?"

"You just have to believe it."

He has fooled me the whole time. While I have trusted him, and talked about a lot of personal matters, he hasn't even told me his right name.

"I promise that it doesn't mean anything," he said.

"It does to me."

"But I hadn't reckoned that we would meet again."

"You mean that you tell a false name to all the girls you don't think you'll see again?"

"Don't misunderstand me. I just mean that I didn't think it made any difference at that point what I was called."

"You didn't want me to know your real name because I'm a *raggarbrud*?"

"Stop it, for God's sake. I admit that it was stupid. But there was no conscious thought behind it as you seem to think."

"No, I don't think you did it deliberately. But the unconscious reveals the truth. You were ashamed that you picked me up in town. You couldn't answer for it. You thought it was below your dignity."

"Where have you read all this?" he said and smiled.

"And when the truth comes out, you take on a superior tone and try to joke everything away," I said.

"Yes, I admit I did wrong. But as coarse and provocative as you were the first time we met, maybe it wasn't that surprising that I didn't want to tell you my real name."

"But why didn't you do it later?"

"I don't know. It just didn't come about. But now you know."

Then he got out a bottle of red wine that he had thought we should share. We sat in the easy chairs, with a glass each, and there was music coming from the tape recorder and everything was so delightful. He asked me what I am going to do during Christmas vacation.

"Nothing special," I said.

"Come with me to Austria, then."

"No, I can't."

"Why not?"

"I don't have any money."

"But I want you to come with me."

I don't know if he was serious, or if he was just talking. He perhaps knew that I wouldn't be able to. Because why would he want me to come with him?

After that he lifted me up and carried me to the bed and took my clothes off. I didn't care about anything. So while The Four Seasons were singing "Rag Doll", and I lay and watched the lights from the street that appeared in the ceiling and on the wall, I let him lay me. I tried to imagine that he was Lasse, but it didn't work, because he felt different.

Then it occurred to me that he didn't have any protection on, and I thought that if he happened to make me pregnant, I could go to Lasse later and say that it was his baby and get him back.

But when he was close to coming, he pulled out. I couldn't hold him in place, and he squirted on my stomach.

Afterwards, when I had fetched the wine bottle and lit a cigarette, I said:

"I met Lasse on Wednesday."

"You did?"

"Yes, I forced him to come."

"Why?"

"Because I couldn't stand it anymore."

"How did it go?"

"To hell."

"He didn't want to?"

"No. I pleaded on my bended knees, but he didn't change his mind."

I took a swig out of the bottle and a drag on my cigarette without showing that I noticed his gaze at me.

"Why do you humiliate yourself like that?" he said.

"I don't know."

"You do know he isn't worth it."

"No, you're the one who says that."

"What do you think yourself?"

"That he is worth everything."

The bed and the floor were spinning so I needed to press myself against the wall to keep from falling. Torkel took away my cigarette and put it out in the ash tray.

"How do you feel?" he said.

"You're just wasting your time with me," I said.

"No, I don't think so."

"Yes, because I will never forget him."

"Yes, you will."

"But it may take a very long time."

"It's okay."

"And in the meantime you will wait faithfully?"

"It probably won't take a very long time."

"But I will not forget him. I will have him back."

"Do you believe that yourself?"

"No, but it has to be that way, because otherwise…"

"Otherwise, what?"

"Why do you meet me?" I said.

"Because I'm interested in you."

"Interested?"

"Yes, and I may also want to see the end of this tragedy."

"You don't think he will change his mind, do you?"

"No, honestly I don't."

"But he must. Otherwise I won't be able to…"

"What?"

"Ah, we'll just blow it off! Time heals all wounds! There are plenty of fish in the sea! A bird in a hand is worth two in the bush!"

Why the hell did I let him fuck me?

Sunday, 15 November 1964

I haven't heard anything from Jörgen, and Lasse has broken up with E-L. But she has already met a new boy.

He belongs to a different category of boys than we usually meet, because he's studying at the university (and could perhaps be someone for her to invest in). But she isn't especially interested in him, she says. Trotz-dem she let him lay her yesterday evening. She is probably so down because Lasse has broken up that she doesn't care what she does. But shouldn't she think a little about the risks she is taking, anyway?

I walked alone in town, and a car with two boys stopped. The one driving was very good-looking, and when he asked if I wanted to come along, I hopped in. But as soon as I had got into the car he looked at his friend and said: "Now, let's go and fetch my girl!"

I was so mad at them because they had tricked me like that. But I hadn't the heart to ask them to let me out again, because the other boy (called Björn) seemed nice, even though he wasn't very handsome. Besides, he was possibly a little too young for me. You prefer to meet boys who aren't younger than 18, but he was 17. The other boy and his girl were about 20 years old, but Björn was only 17 and very childish. When he made a pass at me, he was so clumsy. I realized immediately that he was very green when it came to girls. Not that I wanted rougher stuff, but he was so childish when he talked, also. I felt superior to him, and you don't want that. But he was kind, and I noticed that he was keen on me, poor boy, so I didn't reject him.

I'm not going to see Torkel anymore. There's no point. There's no point in anything. I wish it were possible to be drunk all the time, or that it helped to smoke. I smoke twenty cigarettes a day now. Why does it hurt so much? Why does it never end? Only Lasse can make things good again. If he doesn't come back it will be this way for the rest of my life.

Last night when I was in town, I hoped that someone with booze would come. Once, when I saw a blue Volkswagen, I thought it was Torkel, but it wasn't. Two guys in a Valiant stopped twice and asked if I wanted to go with them. The second time I said no, they got angry.

"What the hell are you doing here, if you don't want to go with anybody?" one of them said.

"You can be here anyway."

"Well, hop in now, damn it!"

"But I don't want to."

"Forget it then, you fucking cunt!" he shouted and made a flying start and sped off. The next time they drove by, they pretended not to see me.

When two hours had passed, and I had said no to five offers, Chrille and Klangen, who I have ridden with once before, came and asked if I were going home. Kerstin, who Chrille is together with, was with him, so I got to sit in the back seat beside Klangen. As soon as I got in the car, he put his arm around me.

"There's no point in it," I said.

"What?"

"There's no point in putting your arm around me."

"Why not?"

"Because I can't manage being nice."

"It's okay. You don't have to do anything."

They had been to the movies and talked a little about the film, but I almost couldn't listen. After a while Klangen noticed that something was the matter and asked me if I had the blues.

"No, it's nothing," I said and leaned aside and put my head on his lap.

"But I can see that there is something," he said and began to stroke my hair.

It didn't make things better that he was kind. I just wanted Lasse to come. After a while I started to cry. I pressed my face against Klangen's thigh, so that nobody would notice it, but he felt that his pant leg became wet and said:

"Eva-Lena is crying so my pants get completely wet.

"Is she sad?" Chrille said.

"Yes, she is."

Then he tried to comfort me.

"There, there… Don't be sad… It's better now."

When the worst was over I sat up, and then I saw Chrille's eyes in the rearview mirror.

"Has something happened?" he said. "Have some guys been rotten to you?"

"No, it's nothing."

"Well, tell your uncle here! What kind of car did

they have?"

But nobody had done anything, and I didn't know how to behave. I was afraid that they would get tired of me and said that I could go out into town again.

"No, we're taking you home," Chrille said.

I didn't want to go home, but the streets were almost empty, and if I went there, I might not meet anyone who could give me a lift later.

"What are you doing on Saturday?" Klangen said and drew me closer.

"I don't know."

"I want to see you again."

"But there's no point in it."

"Why not?"

"Because I'm worthless. I only mess things up and use everyone."

"But I like you, Eva-Lena. And I want to help you."

"That's not possible."

"I want to try anyway."

Chrille remembered where I lived and drove out on the Stockholm highway. I didn't want to go home, because at home it feels even worse, but there was nowhere else to go.

"I'll call," Klangen said when I was about to get out of the car.

"There's no point."

"Yes, it is. And don't be sad now. It will be alright."

But it never will. It's going to be like this until I die. And I don't want to see Klangen again.

I went out on the E4 and thought that I would walk there and freeze and get pneumonia and die. The truck drivers hooted, and a guy in a common car blinked his headlights, but nobody stopped.

After a while I went into the woods and sat behind a boulder and smoked. When I was going to light the cigarette, I put the match in the matchbox cover so that the flame wouldn't go out, and then the whole box caught fire. I let it burn up. If I had dared I would have set fire to myself instead.

And I thought about how easy it would be to jump out in front of a car. But I've already decided how to do it. When it has become cold enough outside, I'm going to get a bottle of vodka and go out in the woods and sit in the snow and drink myself dead drunk, and then I will fall asleep and never wake up again.

Wednesday, 18 November 1964

Sometimes when E-L talks, I can get the idea that she is so down that she is thinking of committing suicide. But I find it so hard to take it seriously. I think it's mostly some sort of a game she carries on with.

When I'm down I usually sit on the shoe-rack in the wardrobe, back where it's dark, and ponder. Sometimes I think: Why does it have to be this way? But I never stop hoping that it will be better. And as soon as I can, I am moving from home. E-L and I will move in together, we have said.

I feel guilty that I'm not able to help papa to stop drinking. I know that it isn't my responsibility, but I feel guilty all the same. He should not need to do it, I think. But I never tell him what I think, because I can't make him sad. I can't talk about it, because then I get so sad myself and start to cry, and I can't stand it that I do. That's the absolute worst thing, because then it feels like I have lost.

Torkel called, and I went along with meeting him, though I had decided not to do it anymore. He offered wine this time too, and that was what I had hoped.

While drinking and listening to music we played vingt-e-un and strip poker. We sat opposite each other at the table, and after a while he looked at me and said:

"What has happened to your face?"

"I've hurt myself."

"How did it happen?"

And before I could decide if I should lie or not he said:

"Just don't tell me that you have ran into a door."

"No, I hit myself with a hair brush."

"Hit yourself? Why did you do that?"

"Because I wanted to."

"Why did you want to?"

"Because I felt like it."

"As if you wanted to punish yourself?"

"No, as if I hated myself."

I didn't dare to look at him, and I couldn't relax until he had started playing again.

"I didn't think you would call again," I said.

"You didn't? Why not?"

"Because of what I said last time about never being able to forget him."

"I see."

"Why do you meet me though you know that?"

"I may believe in my ability…"

"But it won't work."

"We'll see. Have you met him again?"

"No."

"Have you called him?"

"No."

"There, you see!" he said and smiled.

"But it makes no difference."

"No, I know," he said and turned serious again.

Then we lay on the bed with the light off. It was snowing outside, and everything was so quiet. I heard Torkel's breathing.

"Are you sleeping?" he said.

"If you never wake up from sleep, you are dead," I said.

"What did you say?"

I wish I were dead, I thought.

After a while he began to undress me, and then he laid me again.

"You don't have to pull out, because I take birth control pills," I said.

But he did it all the same. After he had been up and wiped himself off and he came back to bed I asked him why.

"I don't know."

"Did you think I lied?"

"No, I was so prepared to do it that I couldn't stop myself."

"You perhaps believed that I lied and hoped to get pregnant, so that I could go to Lasse and tell him that it was his baby and get him back," I said.

"I didn't believe anything."

"Why didn't you trust me then? Why did you pull out though it wasn't necessary?"

"It just happened. And I have explained why."

"You perhaps think that I lie as easily as you do!" I screamed and jumped up and sat in an easy chair.

Torkel remained in bed, watching me.

"Cheers!" I said and held up the wine bottle towards him.

"Why are you so unhappy?" he said.

I couldn't bear to hear his sorrowful, compassionate tone.

"I don't believe in your unlimited frigging patience," I said. "Tell me to go to hell instead, because that's how it will end, anyway!"

And then I drank until the bottle was empty.

Monday, 23 November 1964

I spent Saturday with Solan. I stayed overnight. We listened to records and did each other's hair. She set up my hair in a hair-pad, but this hairdo doesn't suit me, because it makes my face seem too square.

I did a Brigitte Bardot hairstyle for her, the same that E-L uses sometimes, with some hair hanging and some combed back above the ears and teased up and fastened with a slide in the back. It suited her quite well, though her hair isn't very long.

Then I did her make-up, and she became so unlike herself that she looked more like a raggarbrud *(that terrible race!) than a nice and well-behaved family girl. If she went into town this way she would most likely be sought after by the boys.*

But she wouldn't appreciate it, if I know her at all. She would prefer not to be considered as a sexual object. But that's bloody difficult to avoid when you're out and enjoy yourself with the opposite sex, I have to say!

Soon I'm going to make coffee before mamma comes home. When she works, I first put on the potatoes when I come home from school, and then papa or I fix dinner. Then I make coffee for mamma when she comes home at half past eight. Previously she worked at Ringbaren at Stora Torget, but now she cleans offices.

And I'm supportive and help her to shop and cook and wash dishes. While I'm washing up, she sometimes looks through the refrigerator for things that should be thrown out. They go out, and then there are lots of extra containers that need washing. But she helps with drying and it isn't completely bo ring, because sometimes we are in a good mood and have fun at the same time. We talk and sing. If there isn't anything unpleasant going on at home, both she and I can easily laugh and be happy.

I don't know how much I have told Torkel about Lasse, because I don't remember everything I have said when I've been drunk, but as of last night I'm not going to say anything else, I have decided.

We just drove around, because he was to go home early to study for an examination, and for that reason he wanted me to go home as well.

I didn't understand.

"Why would you like us to meet, if you don't have time?" I said.

"I wanted to assure myself that you feel well."

"Why?"

"Because you made me a bit uneasy last night. And honestly, I wanted to stop you from going into town."

"Why?"

"Because I don't think it will lead to anything positive."

It was cold and dark in the car, and he sat there in his overcoat and looked like a cop, again. I don't want to see him anymore. He has no warmth and no music and no atmosphere in his car, and I don't like his cock.

"Is it better for me to sit at home and stare?" I said.

"Yes, because there you can't do anything foolish any way."

"Like boozing and fucking, you mean? But that's what I do when I see you too."

Then he got at tense expression on his face.

"Do you think that's comparable?" he said.

After that, I started talking about Lasse, though I had decided not to do that, and Torkel said:

"But don't you understand that he just used you?"

"No, because in that case I used him too."

"How?"

"By letting him give me everything I wanted, but which I wouldn't have needed if I hadn't been so immature and childish."

"Don't you think you are going too far in your self-effacement attempts now?

"It's not like that! And you don't know how he is."

"No, but I can imagine! And if you are determined to cling fast to a false dream world instead of trying to accept reality as it is, you are dumber than I thought."

"Yes, I know I'm dumb. That's what he thought too. But I won't…"

"You won't what?"

"You might just as well drop me off here."

"Why would I do that?"

"So you get rid of me."

"But I can't leave you here."

"Yes, you can. You don't need to take responsibility for me. And I just use you too. You know that, and you are damned tired of it, if you'll be honest."

"I'll give you a lift home!" he said and turned round a corner so that the car skidded in the slush.

"But I'm not going home."

He either didn't hear me or didn't care what I said, because he just kept on driving. I thought he was angry, but after a while he said in a low voice:

"Why do you make it so hard for yourself?"

"Stop here!" I said.

"You just won't give up until it's confirmed, will you?"

"What?"

"That nobody wants anything to do with you."

"Have you ever considered being a psychologist instead of a lawyer?" I said.

I have written a letter to Lasse and asked if we can try again. I explained how I feel and what I have realized I did wrong, and I wrote that he can call or write and tell me what he thinks. But he will probably think it's just shit and not answer.

Torkel will probably not call or want to see me anymore, either. And that's just as well, because I only use him. I know that I can't fall in love with him and that Lasse is the only one I want, so it's not fair to Torkel to keep on seeing him. I have done it for lack of better and to avoid associating with worse, as you may have to do when you walk on Svartbäcksgatan. But it can't be especially fun for him to know that I think about and miss somebody else all the time.

The guy I rode with first yesterday evening drove out to Galgbacken almost at once. There he stopped and turned off the engine. It's always the same. It gets dark and quiet, and you hear the clicking sound from the car when the engine cools and feel the tension rise…

He wanted me to jerk him off. He opened his fly and pulled my hand to it.

"Karl-Oskar wants a greeting!" he said. "Touch him a little, then you won't have to do anything else."

I didn't want to feel that frizzy hair and the thing that was cramped up in his underwear. I didn't want to dig for it in his disgusting fly.

But he helped to get it out and put my hand on it. It wasn't as long as Lasse's but about as thick.

"Take him in your mouth," he said. "Take Karl-Oskar in your mouth!"

He was reclining on the seat with his legs apart and breathed with open mouth.

"No, I don't want to," I said.

"Yes, you do!"

But I couldn't. It would have been so disgusting. And I didn't want to jerk him off.

Finally he did it himself. It was embarrassing to sit

there and hear him pant and groan while he carried on. Wasn't he ashamed at all?

When we came to town again I said that I wanted to get out, and he dropped me off in front of Fågel Blå. I didn't feel like going with anybody else and I didn't know what to do. I'm so tired of all cold, dark cars and all ugly idiots who aren't able to talk and believe that they are going to get everything they want, though they haven't done anything to deserve it first.

A police car drove by and the cops inside stared. That's all they do – stare and drive by. And there isn't anything else they can do. There isn't anyone at all that can do something, except Lasse.

But he doesn't want to. It would have been better if I had never met him, because before I didn't know what I lacked and longed for. I only yearned for it and hoped that I would get it. At that time it didn't hurt.

Friday, 27 November 1964
E-L drinks and papa drinks and nobody cares about what I think.

But it's worse with papa anyway. I will never get used to him doing it. On Thursdays it's always tense at home (or I am tense, rather). Will he or will he not come home drunk? He usually turns up at a quarter to five, and then I am maybe standing in the window and wave and see him disappear into the cellar with his bicycle.

Or he doesn't come at that time, and then the tension

rises. Mamma and I eat, and a little later we see through the window that he is coming.

And I know immediately how things are. If he has just drunk a single beer I notice it, while mamma is more uncertain: "No, but now he can't have…?" But oh yes, I know for sure that he has, and I get very disappointed, because I don't know how he could do like that to me. I take it as a betrayal of me: How can he do this to me?

It doesn't happen every week, and sometimes he only drinks on Saturday if he and mamma visit others or have people at home, but for some periods he drinks every week. If he has gotten drunk by himself, he is always extra nice on Sunday. And then he can't put his foot down against mamma, because of his bad conscience. Then he doesn't think he is entitled to get angry, even if he has a reason for it. I think that he often, when sober, holds things back if he is irritated, and then later, when he is drunk, he explodes. He is maybe forced to drink to release his anger that he suppresses otherwise, and so it becomes as a vicious circle.

Torkel called anyway and wanted to see me. He was going to come and pick me up at seven o'clock. I snitched pop's Vat 69 and went out fifteen minutes earlier and stood behind a tree and gulped down as much as I could before he came. I don't know if he noticed, when I sat beside him in the car, that I had been drinking. He didn't say anything anyway.

"You're the only one left now," I said.

"What do you mean by that?"

"My pal also thinks I'm dumb."

"Is that so?"

"Yes, dumb and disgusting. She said so when I…"

But I didn't want him to know about the nail file.

"How did your exam go?" I said instead.

"It went well, thanks. How have you been?"

"As usual."

I want to tear off my hair and stamp and puke on myself so that I will stop hoping that he may come back.

"I've written a letter," I said.

"To him?"

"Yes."

"What was in it?"

"I explained how I feel and what I have realized that I did wrong, and then I asked if we could try start all over again."

"And?"

"I wrote that he could call or write, but he hasn't."

"But you live in hope?"

"Yes, that's what I live in."

"But don't you understand that he's never going to change his mind? There's nothing that indicates that he would."

"No, I know."

"You realize that?"

"Yes, but it makes no difference."

When we got to his place, and I found out that he hadn't bought any wine, I wanted to take out my bottle and start to drink right away. I sat down in the easy chair by the window and he sat in the other one.

"When I dropped you off on Sunday I decided to not see you anymore," he said and put one foot over his knee.

"Yes, I understood that."

"But then I realized that I don't have any right to tell you what you should or shouldn't do."

"I see."

"Yes, and it isn't true that you use me. I've known all along how it is. I can't put the responsibility for what I do myself on you."

"What are you doing then?"

"I thought I could make you forget the past."

"But now you don't believe that anymore?"

"I don't know…"

"Do you have a glass?" I said and opened my purse.

"A glass?"

"Yes, for the booze."

At the same time as I set the bottle on the table I looked at him, and I saw that he got a tense expression on his face.

"No, I don't have a glass," he said.

Then I screwed off the cap and took a gulp straight from the bottle.

"Do you want some?" I said and held up the bottle

towards him. But he just looked at me.

"What are you trying to prove?" he said.

"Nothing. Cheers!"

Then I gulped down a little more.

"I can't make you out."

"I'm a hopeless case. It's just to realize it."

"But I don't think it is as impossible as you try to make it seem."

"What?"

"That you should give up hope about him."

"Yes, it is."

"But why?"

"Because I love him."

"But he demonstrably doesn't love you!"

"You don't understand."

"No, I don't. And honestly, I think you're *dumb*."

"I'm going now," I said and put down the bottle and the cigarettes in my purse. "But you can drive me."

"No, I won't. And if you leave now, we'll never see each other again."

"But I want you to drive me."

"No, I said! If you want to go, you have to go on your own."

And I have known all along that it would end like this. I stood up and went into the hall and put on my boots and coat, and he didn't come after me.

"Bye-bye, *Clas-Torkel*!" I said and slammed the door.

Out in the stairwell I gulped down as much whiskey as I could without puking. Then I lit a cigarette and started to go. When I heard a car approach from behind, I thought it was Torkel who had changed his mind and came after me, but it wasn't.

I stopped to drink several times. Finally I sat down on a box which they have sand in during winter. I laid down on my side, and then a car slowed down and stopped by the sidewalk. I heard idling and then a door that opened and footsteps on the gravel.

At first I was scared, because I thought it was the cops, but it wasn't. It was two guys and a girl in an Opel. I got to lie down in the back seat with my head on one of the guy's lap.

While we drove, they played "I Should Have Known Better" – with a girl like you. Torkel should have sung that to me before I left. He should have known better than to believe that I would be able to change.

Nothing special happened after that. Tonight I will stay at home and go to bed early. There is no point in going out. I just want to sleep and not be aware. If it were possible to sleep to death, I would do that tonight.

Sunday, 29 November 2014

Yesterday evening when E-L was with Clas (or Torkel as he is evidently called) they fell out. She had a bottle of liquor with her in her purse and took it out and began to drink in his presence, and she said to him that she would never forget Lasse and that she wants him back. So

Torkel probably got tired of her (and you can almost understand that).

Today it's decoration Sunday, and I went with mamma and papa downtown and watched the Christmas windows-displays. On Diagonalen, at Forum, they have set up a Ferris wheel with Disney characters on board, and there were lanterns and garlands all over the place.

Yes, it was nice! Now snow is the only thing missing for us to have a real Christmas feeling.

It's fun to do things together with your parents sometimes. When I was younger I went with them to Knäpp-upp's tent varieties. I thought it was fun. Nowadays we don't go out together that often, but we sometimes have fun at home. Mamma and I can have a jocular dialogue if we feel like it. "Guben i låddan", for example, is something we often do. We have it on a record and we know it by heart. It can also be small snippets of some things that we have heard on the radio or TV and that we remember. We have a full store of expressions that come from monologues we have heard.

And we are on the same wave-length, so when mamma asks, for example: "Kicki, will you go and turn off the radio?" I say: "Yes, I'll go and close the balcony door." She says it all wrong, but mostly I still understand what she means. And if we happen to see something on TV that we especially notice, we look at each other and know exactly what the other one is thinking.

But papa doesn't get it. When we start to laugh he

perhaps looks up and says: "Uh, what?" He doesn't understand and is completely out of it.

This newspaper clipping is about an unconscious girl who was rescued by the police.

That won't happen to me.

"Police intervention" saved 16- year-old from rapist.

GÖTEBORG, TT. A 20-year-old youth from Göteborg has been taken into custody suspected of raping a 16-year-old girl. She could also have been forced to eat tablets with an abortive effect. The girl is now under care of the hospital. The girl's father contacted the police on Saturday for assistance in rescuing the girl, who he knew was in an apartment in Gamlestaden in Göteborg.

According to the so called "*raggarparagraf*" the police had no right to intervene because the girl was not suspected of any crime nor had she escaped from a juvenile detention school. However, the criminal police intervened and entered the apartment. In doing this they made themselves guilty of misconduct.

The girl was in a deplorable state. She was almost unconscious and was taken to the Sahlgrenska hospital to have her stomach pumped. According to her disposition, the 20-year-old youth had forced himself on her and thereby injured her vagina.

Afterwards, he forced her to eat tablets with abortive affects.

The girls lost consciousness.

The youth, who refused to allow the police officers entry to the apartment, has made some confessions.

The police officers made themselves guilty of misconduct when they entered the apartment, but the crimes they discovered inside clear them from any suspicion for abuse of power with all certainty, according to criminal inspector Nils-Sture Trädgårdh, who thinks that the so called *"raggarparagraf"* ought to be repealed.

I don't know what to do to make the pain disappear. Smoking, sleeping and drinking only help while I am doing it, and I can't do it all the time. The only thing that could make things better would be if Lasse came back. I feel so ugly and disgusting when I think that he doesn't want to have anything to do with me. It would be better if I were dead. Why doesn't he want me? What have I done? I love him and can't live without him. So why can't he come back? I would do anything, if only he wanted to try again.

If I died, Kicki wouldn't have anyone to be with. But it probably wouldn't be such a long time before she found a new pal. She could start being together with Solan, for instance. And she wouldn't have to listen to my harping on the same string if I didn't exist.

I don't know how mom and pop would react. They

seem so distant. But Lasse would probably be glad and feel relieved. Or would he feel guilty and think that it was his fault? I don't know. Anyway, I wouldn't do it to punish him. I would do it because I think it would be better for everyone if I disappeared.

Friday, 4 December 1964

E-L has just called. She was at the railway station and sounded very strange. She talked about her purse and said that she would pick everything out of it and go away. I didn't really get it, but I was worried and said: "Wait there, I'm coming." But she said that it wasn't needed.

Sometimes she kind of implies that she will kill herself. Mostly I don't take it seriously, but this time I became a little hesitative because she sounded so strange. All the same I find it really hard to believe that she would go so far as to commit suicide.

I went to town and hoped that I would meet someone who had booze. But I never went to Svartbäcksgatan. The guys who drive there want to have girls to talk with and have fun with and not one that just sits there, down in the dumps, and only is after to drink herself drunk. I would trick and use the one I rode with, if I went there and let someone pick me up.

And it felt wrong to go there on a Friday evening. I

just went to the railway station and bought some cigarettes, and then I walked home again. There was nowhere to go. Everyone was occupied by their own business and nobody was interested in me.

I walked on the road in the dark and felt the cars sweep by. I could easily come too far out in the lane and be run over. But what if I were just injured and didn't die? And it would be bad for the guy driving the car that hit me. So I remained on the roadside.

Sunday, 6 December 1964

Last night when E-L and I walked in town we saw Lasse with his mate with two girls in the car. E-L went completely cracked, and it wasn't possible to talk with her anymore. I don't get mad at her very often, but then I lost my temper and told her that I would leave if she didn't get hold of herself.

And there was no change, so I went away and hopped into the first car that stopped. I think it was strong of me to leave, because it's very hard for me to stand up for my feelings and thoughts when she carries on with things that I actually don't want to be a part of. But yesterday, for once, I managed to say no. I didn't care what she thought or what stupid things she might find to do when she was alone.

She called today and wondered if I were angry, but I'm not. Not in the way that I don't want to talk with her anyway. I just don't want to tolerate everything.

She had ridden with some guys that had liquor, and later one of them had laid her. (She was so drunk that she was barely aware of what happened.) How can it be enjoyable to lay someone who is completely out of it? And it couldn't have been anything for her, either. No, I really don't understand the youth of today! Booze and sex are apparently the only things they are interested in!

Kicki came along, and first we rode with a couple of guys in a very crummy Amazon. I wanted to wait for guys with booze to come, but Kicki didn't feel like drinking, and then I regretted that I hadn't gone out by myself instead.

We saw Lasse's car in town. He was the one driving, and Leffe sat beside him, and in the back seat there were two girls with blonde hair. I don't know what happened when I saw them. I was like petrified and couldn't talk. Finally, Kicki got angry with me and said that she would go home if I didn't become normal again. But I couldn't make it disappear. I just thought that I must meet some guys who had booze. So Kicki left, and when she had walked a short way, I saw that a car stopped and that she jumped into it.

I was afraid that Lasse's car would come by again, because at the same time as I wanted it to come, it felt like I didn't dare to see it more time.

After a while two guys in a Buick stopped. One of

them had a girl, but I went with them all the same, because the other one was drinking Explorer, and I hoped that he would offer it.

When we had cruised around town for a while and had played a song called "Runaround Sue" twenty times, we went home to one of the guys.

He lived in Björklinge. He and the girl disappeared somewhere, and the other guy and I sat in the kitchen and drank. I sat on his lap, and he made smoke rings that I tried to stick my finger in.

Then I don't remember what we did before we were lying on a bed and he had started to take my clothes off. It was odd light in the room, because there was only an orange Advent paper star lit in the window. He took off my pants and I was just about to say that I had my period, when he saw the string that hung out from my tampon and started to tug at it.

"What is this?" he said. "Are you on the rag?"

I didn't care what he did. I felt that he put something under me on the quilt and pulled out the tampon, and then he laid himself on top of me and started fucking.

"I have my period," I said though I knew that he already knew it.

"Yes, this is just like the Stockholm blood-bath!

"Don't you care?"

"No, it's fine anyway."

He didn't use any protection and he didn't pull out, so now I may be pregnant. But I don't think so, for this is supposed to be a safe period.

When he got up from bed I saw that he was bloody below his stomach. He wiped off most of it with a handkerchief before putting his clothes back on. Then he helped me to the bathroom.

I also had blood on me. I sat on the toilet and tried to wipe it away with wet toilet paper. Then his semen ran out. I put in a new tampon and pulled my pants on.

The soap on the washbasin was called Camé. Nine of ten film stars use LUX. A cleaner wash in an easier way with SURF. The yellow gunk, as it's known, is brushed away with PEPSODENT.

I was so ugly in the mirror. I'm always that way when I'm drunk. And I didn't feel clean, but I only washed my hands before I went out.

The others sat in the kitchen and drank coffee. The guy that had laid me pulled me down on his lap, and I leaned against his shoulder.

"Is she tired?" the other guy said and grinned. "Don't go so damn hard with the broads, Lasse!"

"Your name is Lasse?" I said and tried to fix my eyes on him.

"Yes, you've got it."

"Once I knew a guy who was called that," I said. "But he's dead now."

I wish I could sleep and sleep for all eternity. I don't want to wake up, because as soon as I remember how things are, it starts to hurt. I don't know what to do to make it go away.

I wonder where Lasse and Leffe had met those girls they had in the car last Saturday. Were they some they knew, or some they had met at a dance, or some they had picked up in town? And did Lasse fondled one of them later? It feels like I can't understand how he would be able to kiss and caress another. But of course he can. If I can lay someone else, he must be able to kiss someone else. He perhaps laid her as well.

That Lasse from Saturday wanted to see me again, but I said that there was no point in it. I don't understand why he wanted to, either. I didn't think that guys liked girls that get drunk and let the guy lay them the first evening.

Last night I was in town again. Everything felt so meaningless. I didn't want to go with anyone, so I just walked around by myself. Nobody stopped, either. I wished that Kicki had been with me, so that I would have had someone to talk with, because when I talk with her, it doesn't hurt as much and doesn't seem as hopeless as when I'm alone. But she was at home.

Finally, I let a guy in an Opel give me a lift home.

I called Lasse. His mom answered, and when I asked for him she said that he wasn't home. I don't know if it was true or if he just had told her to say that if I would call. If I had got to speak with him, I don't know what I would have said. I just wanted to hear his voice. But he is perhaps together with someone else now. He may have continued to see one of the girls he had in his car last Saturday.

Sunday, 13 December 1964

When it's Saturday you should be out and enjoy yourself when you're young, so yesterday evening I went out and danced. Solan and I were out. E-L was in town as usual and rode with some guys who offered her spirits.

I think she needs to pull herself together, because it can never be a good thing to carry on like she does. And it drives us apart, because I don't want to go out with her when liquor is the only thing she has in her head (and body). Though I don't know what to do about it.

I had rather fun and got to dance almost every dance. But there were some who had started beforehand with Lucia Day celebrations, and I don't like to dance with boys who aren't sober. I prefer sober and well-behaved boys, whose breath doesn't anesthetize you, and who have good leg and foot coordination. If they are in really bad shape, you must almost hold them up, and that's something you don't want to do.

Why is there such a shortage of pleasant boys? In all this time when I have been out, I have met at most ten boys that I could even think of seeing again. And the interest must also be mutual for it to become something.

Today it's Lucia Day, but we celebrated it in school yesterday, because we don't go to school on Sundays. (Pretty soon we won't go on Saturdays either, according to a proposal that hasn't been approved yet.)

The only time of the year I am glad to be early at school is at the Lucia celebration. I think the Lucia procession is beautiful, and it is at its best while it's still dark outside. As long as we had Söderberg it was good anyway, because she had control of the situation. I participated then and was a star boy. We came down from the art hall, where we had changed into our costumes, and we sang the entire way up the stairs to the assembly hall where everyone sat and waited. It was so atmospheric and beautiful.

We have a very nice Lucia celebration at the girls' school. Every year the procession goes out to Fyrisån and meets Fjellstedtska's Lucia procession, which consists of only boys (their Lucia is also male), and if the river is frozen and there is ice that bears, both Lucias meet in the middle, while their attendants remain on their respective waterside and sing.

And in the classrooms, we have lighted candles on our desks and drink coffee and eat ginger bread. It's bloody fine, I have to say! And everyone is sober, because we go to a first-rate and respectable school, all of us.

The pedestrian way on Kungsängsgatan between Bangårdsgatan and Stora Torget is complete now. I walked there when I got to town. Pine branch garlands were strung across the way with lanterns in them. On Svartbäcksgatan and Drottninggatan and around Stora Torget garlands have also been set out.

In front of Polyfoto I met a guy who asked me if I wanted to go dancing with him at Bälinge Community Center. He offered me a cigarette and lit it with a Consul lighter, just like the one Lasse had.

I rode with four guys in an Impala. All of them, except for the driver, were drunk. I got drunk too.

I don't remember where we went. We weren't only in town, because sometimes it got dark outside. Two of the guys got angry and went out to fight. When they came in again, one of them had blood on his face. They played "Memphis Tennessee" with Johnny Rivers and "Jailhouse Rock" with Elvis and a lot of other songs that I don't remember the names of.

Once when the car had stopped I lay on the ground. There was cold asphalt there and an empty bicycle rack that I held on to. One of the guys got angry and thought they should go and leave me behind, but then they all helped to lift me into the back seat again. They took off my boots and panties and said that they were going to fuck me. I wasn't able to care about it because I was so drunk. But they just stuck in a bottle – the neck of a bottle – and pulled it in and out.

I got home at three o'clock, and pop was up. He had

been to the toilet and entered the hall just as I came in.

"Is it about time to come home now!" he said.

He must have noticed that I was drunk, but he didn't say anything. He keeps away from it because he knows that he can't do anything about it. If he pretends that nothing is wrong, he doesn't have to deal with it, and thanks to that he can avoid admitting that he is totally incapable.

This morning I didn't want to wake up. I didn't want to remember what I had done. I got up at seven o'clock and drank water and went to the toilet. Then I fell asleep again and slept until half past two.

Now it's five o'clock. I won't drink anything tonight. Just thinking of that spiced snaps that I drank last night makes me feel sick. But it's Lucia, and if anyone offers me booze, I probably won't be able to say no.

I walked on Svartbäcksgatan in the rain and saw the lines of glistening cars sliding slowly forward in the light from the store windows and neon signs. They have hung up garlands with lamps across the street, and the light reflected in the car roofs as the cars drove by underneath.

On the square there was a line of cars. The engines were idling, and white exhaust clouds swirled out behind them. I passed a *raggarbil* with Christmas tinsel on the radio antenna, and the guy driving revved the engine and tapped with his fingers against the steering wheel while he waited for the line to start moving. It was a Chevrolet Bel Air with knee crushers on the bumpers and a jet airplane for the hood ornament. I have never cruised in a car like that.

I stood in the entrance to Pennspecialisten, because I didn't know if I wanted to go with anyone or not. Everything felt so meaningless. Lasse is gone and will never come back, and the only thing I can do is to start cruising and boozing again. But it can never again be the way it was before I met him. Everything is destroyed. The only time I don't care so much about it is when I'm drunk. Kicki thinks that I'll meet someone else who I can fall in love with, but I will be waiting for Lasse as long as I live. So it probably won't be very long.

I went with two guys and a girl in a black Chrysler. The guy in the back seat was drunk, but he didn't have anything to offer me. He wanted to fuck, and I didn't know why I should say no, so when we had stopped at a secluded place he stripped me below the waist and laid himself on top of me and did it. While he was doing it, Elvis was singing "One Night". When I heard the music, and smelled the scents of spirits and White Horse from him, my tears began to flow, but it was so dark that he didn't notice it.

Tuesday, 15 December 1964

On "Kvällstoppen" the result was like this: 1) "I Feel Fine" with The Beatles, 2) "Fröken Fräken" with Sven Ingvar's, 3) "Sleep Little Girl" with Tages.

On Sunday E-L went with two boys and a girl, and she let the boy she was with lay her though she didn't know him or even like him. Or she maybe liked him, but she didn't love him, and I think you should feel that way to lay someone. If she continues as she does now, and drinks every weekend and furthermore, begins to lay guys right and left, you never know how it will end. (It can end up in hell.) But on Sunday she wasn't drunk. The guy had drunk a little, but not she, just for once.

But I remember there was a time when we wouldn't think of going with boys who weren't sober. We watched out for those who used spirits. It was out of the question me being with a boy who drank, and I wouldn't drink myself, either. But then we started with it all the same.

Wednesday, 16 December 1964

I don't really know how it happened, but when E-L and I were at Café Regent and had coffee, we drifted on to the subject of sex (and that's a pleasant and interesting subject to drift on to!). Then E-L said (among other things), that she has never masturbated, and that surprised me a little, because I thought that all young people did that.

The first time I remember I did it myself was when I

was only nine years old. At that time, I slept in the living room with mamma, while Anita lay in the bedroom and papa slept in the kitchen in a fold-away bed. But papa came in to mamma, of course, and sometimes I woke up and heard them when they were together. I understood what it was, so I didn't dare tell them to stop, though I thought it was unpleasant. I lay there and couldn't avoid hearing, and even though I thought it was unpleasant, it awakened a desire in me, and that was when I began to masturbate. And it's probably like smoking, that you can't stop doing it when you once have started. Because later I kept on doing it when I slept alone, also.

Nowadays it's mostly in connection with me meeting some nice boy that I get sexual feelings. Sometimes when I have been turned on it has been a little problematic, because it doesn't exactly make the boys cool off when you are being responsive. But I always come to a point when it passes away and I don't want to go any further. So, you could almost say that I use the boys. But they accept it, I think (with some exceptions).

A police officer who talked with E-L on Svartbäcks-gatan once, said that if the boys in the cars don't get what they want from the girls, they are not accepted by the boys. But I don't think that is true. Almost no one has turned his back on us because we have set limits. On the contrary, there are some that have seemed to value it. And I'm in no rush to get rid of my virginity. That E-L carries on as she does right now, that she lays almost

It's eight days until Christmas Eve. I got a note from Kicki in class. "What do you want for Christmas presents?" she wrote. "I want money, clothes and spirits," I wrote back. "What do you want?" Because what I want most of all, there is no point in wishing for.

After school I bought a detective novel for 3.50 *kronor* called "Poisoned to Death". Tonight Kicki and I are going to see a Swedish film called "Susanne". It's about a car accident.

Thursday, 17 December 1964

After the movies E-L thought that we should wait for some boys who had something drinkable to offer (not soft drinks, that is), but I didn't feel like it, so I went home. And E-L neither drank nor lay anybody she said today. I think it's good that she isn't together with Lasse anymore, but I hope that she doesn't get pregnant instead or revert to alcohol abuse.

In the film we saw, the female main character got pregnant. But the thing that made the strongest impression on me was a car accident which was shown. When the film played in Stockholm, I heard that young people com-

peted to see who could stand most of the accident and operation scenes without throwing up or fainting. (The film is made by two doctors – Elsa and Kit Colfach – as propaganda against reckless driving, so you get to see a lot of things like that.) But I think I got through it rather well.

Friday, 18 December 1964

After all, I can't stop worrying about E-L. Lately she has been so quiet, and she usually isn't that way.

In a book I'm reading right now, they compare two girls who are committed to a girls' home. Both are in despair, and one of them goes around talking about it and shows her feelings, while the other one sits quietly by herself and keeps everything she feels inside. And the silent one is in the worst condition, because she has given up hope and no longer thinks that there is any way out, while the other one, who is extrovert, still hopes and believes that she will get help.

I don't exactly know which category E-L belongs to. She hasn't given any intimations of that she is thinking about killing herself for a long time now, but she isn't happy, and I know that she still hopes that Lasse will come back. Hope is probably what keeps her going.

It never gets properly cold. Today it's two degrees below zero outside, and it has been so mild and milder for a long time. Is that enough to freeze to death if you lie down in the woods and sleep? Or can you drink so much liquor that you become poisoned and die anyway?

Here is what it says in the reference book:

Alcohol's wide use as a means of inebriation is based on the often pleasant affects which follow imbibing alcoholic drinks. Small doses can produce a feeling of spiritual and bodily comfort and a favorable state of mind. After bigger doses liveliness becomes more marked, and even the shy and timid become talkative. The face reddens, and the pulse is faster than normal. Self-evaluation diminishes. Difficulties and worries disappear in intoxication's fog and with more alcohol use, judgment and coherence of thoughts are even weaker, so that the intoxicated commits unjustified and impulsive acts. Unclear and slurred speech and faltering steps are also common symptoms of marked intoxication. Further, symtoms of alcohol poisoning include onset of sleepiness, possibly partially caused by increased exertion while intoxicated. When awake once again, one often has a sense of sickness, a depressed mood, vomiting, etc. With extremely powerful alcohol consumption, the intoxicated person is unconscious with a bad pulse, slowly snoring breathing, a low body temperature and a bluish skin coloration. Death can be a result in this condition. Often, feeling unwell and vomiting occurs before this situation develops, whereby a continuing alcoholic consumption is prevented.

So it's possible, only you don't puke.

Sunday, 20 December 1964

Yesterday we had the Christmas breaking-up, and we got our semester grades. I was a little disappointed in the grade in domestic science, because I know I'm good at preparing food. I might have been a little lazy when it comes to the theoretical part, but I could have gotten a bit higher grade in the other part, I think.

E-L tends to cut her domestic science classes, but I think it's fun to prepare food. (We are fortunately in different groups, because otherwise I would probably also play hooky.) We usually prepare food and set the table, and I think it's fun, because in that situation I can show my talents without feeling nervous. There it isn't about expressing oneself verbally (which I'm actually not bad at, but which I still have difficulty with), so I think that that low grade is unjust. I would like to complain about it, but I probably won't.

Yesterday evening E-L and I rode with some guys who had spirits. Actually, I didn't want to, but when a car with two boys stopped and E-L hopped in, I did the same, even though I saw that they had a bottle. They asked if we wanted to have a grog with pure snaps and soft drink, and E-L drank of course (more than she could handle) and became drunk and disorderly. When we got out in town again, (at her initiative), I had to take care of her and try to hold her upright, and it was no plaisir, because she is bloody heavy when she relaxes like that and doesn't want to do anything herself. "I'm helping you," I said, but she didn't listen, and at last I couldn't manage any longer and I was forced to let her go.

She collapsed in front of Otto Carlsson's Furniture Store, and there it wasn't very smart to let her lie, because if some police officers came by they would see her immediately. But she struggled against me the whole time and didn't want to help when I tried to get her up. I almost got mad at her, because she really wasn't that bloody drunk. But she always does like that when she drinks, that she lies down someplace and doesn't want to get up again. Luckily, a car stopped, and I got some help to get her into the back seat. They were two guys, and one of them was very nice, I thought. He was called Janne and he was 20 years old.

First, we went up to the castle and looked at the view. E-L wanted to get out, and while she and the other guy were outside, Janne offered me a cigarette (Commerce, moderate size), and asked what I do in the daytime. He worked at Melanderska, as a hardware salesman, but he was thinking about starting studies at Hermod's and educating himself to become an engineer.

After a while we had to go out and help the other guy with E-L, who had tried to crawl under Gunillaklockan. She was so awkward and didn't want to get back into the car. At last we got her in anyway, and when she had sobered up to the extent that it was possible to talk with her, she said that she wanted to get out into town again. (It's always the same old story when she is drunk!)

And it wasn't possible to persuade her to stay in the car, so they dropped her off on Svartbäcksgatan. Then they gave me a lift home, and before I got out, Janne said that he hoped we would meet again. But that must mean in town, in that case, because he didn't ask for my phone number.

E-L went with a guy in a Ford, she said today, when she called. He gave her a lift home.

You can wonder what it is that causes me to participate in her drinking, because at the same time as I do it, I have the conviction that it isn't anything for me to be involved in. And I have such mixed feelings about going to town with her when she is drunk. On the one hand, it satisfies my need to take care of another and be the one who is the most capable and sensible, on the other hand, I don't think it's especially fun. I think that she dramatizes sometimes and becomes bothersome. When she passes a certain limit and seems drunk instead of just tipsy, I actually don't want to be involved any longer, because then we haven't fun anymore.

But it's maybe my fault too, that she lets herself go the

way she does. Because I'm the one who gives her space and the opportunity to do it by never drinking so much that I lose control myself. And in contrast to E-L, who regrets not beginning to drink earlier, this is what I think: This is something I do now, but it's not something that I want to keep doing.

And this attitude has to do with papa. It's because he drinks that I am so sure that I will never begin drinking seriously myself. When I take some liquor, it isn't at all the way it is when he *drinks, and I know it will never be that way, either. I know as sure as fate that alcohol is nothing for me, and therefore I'm not afraid.*

Tonight we will go out again. First, we are going to Fågelsången for coffee, and then we are going to do the twist. No, we are going to walk in the street, and there you are not permitted to dance. If you do it there, you will soon have the police on you. You're not permitted to attract attention in a public place. If you're happy, you must be careful about showing it when the police are around.

I hope that E-L won't be stubborn about wanting to drink again, but will consider going with some boys that don't have any spirits, because otherwise I'm not in-terested. I only want to go with guys who don't have anything, because a boy who drinks (or boozes, rather) I could never be together with. No matter how much in love I were with him, I would skip him if he drank. Besides, I could never fall in love *with someone who drinks. That's what I believe, anyway. I wouldn't allow myself to do it.*

E-L doesn't want that either, she has said, and I believe her, because she always wants to be the center of attention and play the leading part, and that doesn't work with a boy who also wants that role. That's probably why she fell for Lasse. He didn't like to drink, and he was the care giving type, whom I believe she prefers.

Why does it feel so unpleasant when you wake up after having been drunk? You just want to disappear and not remember what has happened. Do you regret that you have drunk, or do you regret what you have said and done when you have been drunk? I don't know.

We rode with two guys in a Dodge. Nothing special happened. They had spirits and we drank some, and then we got out into town again. Kicki was mad at me because I couldn't walk properly. She arranged for us to go with two other guys. When they were going to give her a lift home, I got out into town again. I stood in the entry to Wolrath's and smoked. All the lights were off in the store windows and almost no cars were out anymore. Down by the traffic lights a taxi had stopped for a red light, but otherwise the street was empty.

I didn't know what to do. It was cold, and nobody stopped. There wasn't any place to go and warm up, either, because all the stores were closed. It felt so unfair and unnecessary that it was warm inside the stores when there was no one there.

It's exaggerated and ridiculous to remain in town when almost everyone has gone home. It feels degrading. The guys who drive by look down on you, and no one thinks that you are worth picking up.

I don't know how long I had been standing there when I saw a police car come sliding on the other side of street. I became uptight, and my heart started beating faster, when I noticed that the cops were watching me.

Then the car slowed down and stopped. What did they want? What would they do? I didn't dare to look, but I saw out of the corner of my eye that one of the cops got out of the car and started walking towards me across the street. I could almost not breathe when he came nearer.

"How are you doing?" he said and stood in front of me.

He was rather young and had a black leather jacket on.

"I'm doing fine," I said and hoped that he wouldn't notice that I had been drinking.

"Why are you standing here?"

"Isn't it allowed?"

"Yes, of course it is. But wouldn't it be better if you went home?"

The police car was a black Opel with a search light

on the roof, and the other cop sat behind the wheel and glared in our direction.

"Do you possibly have an identity card with you?" the cop in front of me said.

"No."

"What's your name?"

"It doesn't matter."

"Well, I think it does."

"Why?"

"There are so many young girls that disappear…"

"But I haven't disappeared."

"Where do you live?"

"In Vilan."

"I see. How do you get there at this time, then?

"I don't know."

What should I do if they wanted to give me a lift home? I got scared just thinking of it.

But I hadn't needed to worry.

"Yes, we thought it looked like you didn't feel quite well and thought it would be best to stop and check that everything was all right," he said.

"I see."

My throat ached so much that I almost couldn't swallow.

"But don't stand here and freeze any longer now. Try to get home instead."

Then I almost screamed. What would he have done if I had started screaming? But I never dare to do as I feel. I'm so cowardly.

And that was all.

"Excuse us for disturbing you and bye-bye," he said and saluted and left.

I went with a guy in a Ford. He played "Baby Love" and offered Sticks chewing gum and smokes. I was freezing even though I was hot, and my head and throat ached, but I still let him do what he wanted. He pulled up my sweater and took out my breasts and fondled them. I don't mind very much when they carry on with my breasts, but I don't want them to kiss my mouth, because some of them have such disgusting lips and tongues. I didn't even like Lasse's kisses.

I don't think it will ever feel again like it did before to walk on Svartbäcksgatan. At least not when I am sober. And I don't feel the same Christmas atmosphere that I did when I was little. Everything just changes and disappears. Now Christmas is just a wait for the holidays to end, so that I can go to town again. Because on Christmas Eve nobody is out. That's when every-one is home with their families and watches "Donald Duck" on TV and drinks mulled wine and eats the Christmas ham. Very funny, I must say! If you could at least get drunk. But that's impossible. You just have to wait.

Monday, 21 December 1964
When E-L and I were out we met two boys in a VW, and they were rather pleasant. But E-L wanted to get out

again and was so disorderly. (I can't help wishing that she would be the way she was before she started drinking and before she met Lasse. I wish that she would come back.)

But I didn't allow myself to be persuaded to go with her (I knew that she just wanted to get out to hunt for spirits), but I was on the contrary successful in getting her to stay, and then we went with them all evening.

My boy was called Inge, and he was a bus conductor. He asked me if I wanted to come with him to the movies on Wednesday and said that he would call. A Swedish film called "Dear John" has started now, and we could possibly go to see it. It's based on a book by Olle Länsberg, about whom there was a lot of writing a while ago.

Yes, he who lives will se! (If he calls me, I mean).

Friday, 25 December 1964

"Now we have lights here in our house, Christmas has come, hopp tralalala!" Father, he drinks in days before Christmas, but on Christmas Eve he is sober and kind. This is how it has been in all the years before, and this is how it was this year, also. Things are a little tense before, but it has always sorted itself out for Christmas. I can't remember him ever being drunk on any Christmas Eve.

Papa is the one who gets the Christmas tree, and the evening before Christmas Eve we bring it in. Then he and I decorate it. We join hands with it, while mamma cooks the ham and things like that. When we are finished, we eat ham sandwiches, and mamma wraps Christmas presents and writes some rhymes for the labels and seals the packets.

For Christmas Eve grandma always is with us, and sometimes Stig, Anita and Anders as well, bringing Christmas presents with them. We put all the parcels under the Christmas tree, and then I'm the one who hands them out after "Donald Duck" is over on TV.

After opening presents, we eat. We have way too much food in my opinion. There are meatballs and pickled herring and ham and liverwurst and sausages and brawn and whatnot. And boiled ling. I like that. And mamma and grandma want rice pudding, but that they have to eat themselves, because nobody else wants it. The leftover rice we usually remake into orange rice pudding.

And this year it was the same as usual. In the evening we lit live candles in the window and ate fruit and cracked nuts. And grandma drank mulled wine, even though it's alcoholic. She is a Pentecostal and isn't really allowed to drink such, but she thinks mulled wine tastes good, so she drinks it anyway. And it's good for the blood stream, because it stimulates blood circulation, and she needs that for her angina.

I got a fancy nightgown from papa for a Christmas present. It's light blue with white laces. He had gone out and bought it on his own. Mamma and I are the ones who mostly go shopping, but this year he got a whim and went out to buy this nightgown for me.

From Stig and Anita I got jewelry (a gold chain with a four-leaf clover), from mamma I got a pair of gloves and money, and from grandma a book.

I usually save money the entire year, and then shop for Christmas presents with what I have managed to save up. It isn't very much money, because I don't have so much to save, but I buy something for everyone, and I'm careful to choose something that I hope they will like. This year papa got a cigarette lighter (that was way too expensive), mamma a little bottle of perfume, Anita a book, Stig a smoking pipe rack, Anders a puzzle, and grandma a manicure case.

Sunday, 27 December 1964

Yesterday we went up to Toje and asked if he had any spirits to sell (but he hadn't), and then we went out into town. We stood in front of Wolrath's, where warm air blows up, and then Staffan (Anita's ex) and one of his mates came along.

Yes, and we went with them, and they offered us spirits at his mate's apartment. Each of us got a so called busgrogg, and it was a strong drink, it really was, and then things became a little foggy, so to speak. And E-L became so awkward and fussed about everything.

But at first it was rather pleasant, because we sat by lighted candles at the table and ate figs and nuts while we smoked, drank and played cards. It was pleasant until E-L got drunk and started talking about something she had read in the newspaper about a 16-year-old girl who had been raped and drugged by pills by a 20-year-old guy. I don't know why she kept on talking about it. Because something similar could happen to us, perhaps. We could be unlucky and come up against some real lunatics. You don't think it will happen, even though you know that the risk exists. You think you will manage to avoid it. And until now, we have.

Pop was mad as hell when he realized that I was going out. But if he thinks that I will sit at home and stare any longer just because I have been sick, he has got it wrong. What I do is none of his business, and it feels disgusting when he interferes.

Kicki and I went to a guy we know and asked if he had any spirits for sale, but he said that he needed it all for himself. He was supposed to go to a Christmas ball in Funbo IOGT and was changing clothes when we came. So we went out into town again, and there we met two guys in a blue Zephyr who said that they had liquor at home. Kicki knew one of the guys, and we went with them.

At first, we drank and played cards. Then the guys fell out, and the one I was with threw an empty liquor bottle into the TV, so the screen cracked.

The guy Kicki knew was a lot older than we are, and

he had been together with her sister once. When Kicki went home he accompanied her, and I went out into town, because the other guy was also too drunk to drive. I went across St Olofsbron, which they have opened now, and up to Svartbäcksgatan.

I was stupefied and didn't know what to do. Everything was so bright. The lighted garlands which hang over the street glittered and were reflected in the asphalt. In every second garland there is a star in the center, and in the others there are two by the sides, and it's so magnificent when you see them in a row. They light up the whole street. Though in some windows the lights were off, and it was dark.

I stopped in a gateway and lit a cigarette. There was no point in walking around anymore. When a car, in which they were playing "You'll Never Walk Alone", drove by and I heard Gerry and The Pacemakers sing, it felt like I wanted to lie down on the ground and never get up again.

"When you walk through a storm, hold your head up high and don't be afraid of the dark," he sang.

On New Year's Eve, Lasse is going to Rune Ek's variety. If I go there as well, I may see him one last time. But there is no point in doing it. There is no point in doing anything at all.

When the cigarette was finished, I walked on all the same.

"Walk on, walk on, with hope in your heart, and you'll never walk alone."

They only lie.

Torkel is probably in Austria now, if he isn't at home with his parents in Linköping. I said that he could send me a postcard from Austria, but he never got my address, and he probably wouldn't have sent me anything anyway. He is also gone. Everyone is gone.

It was almost empty in the street. A black and white police car drove by, and when I saw the cops sitting there, staring out the window without seeing anything, it felt as if I hated them.

Then a black Mercedes stopped, and the guy who drove rolled down the window and said:

"Are you going home?"

"Yes, I suppose so."

"Hop in then!"

And I did.

Monday, 28 December 1964

Wieviel Uhr ist es? (Quelle heure est-il?) *It's half past three. I wonder why E-L still hasn't called, as she said she would. She was going out again yesterday evening, but I didn't see her, even though I went out for a little stroll myself. I had decided not to go out, but later I regretted my decision and took the bus downtown and hoped that I would find her there.*

And then, when I was walking there thinking about whether I should go home again, a car stopped, and who was sitting in it if not – yes, Lasse! He came there driving, and when he stopped and asked me where I was going, I said like it was, that I was going home, and then he offered to give me a lift. I was a little doubtful, considering E-L, but after all, it's over between them, and he could give me a lift home anyway, I thought.

And I have always been a little curious about him. Already the first time we met, I realized that he and I had the same attitude. I felt that we were in agreement on that E-L must come in the car and be taken care of. That mate of his was drunk and nobody to count on, and E-L was drunk and gone from this world, so I knew it was Lasse and I who were in possession of the common sense and had to see to it that E-L came off the street and into the car before she got herself into trouble.

So now, when he stopped and started talking to me, it was like getting a chance to find out about what that similarity feeling included. When I climbed into the car I understood that it could be more than his only giving me a lift home. Not that I would have let him go as far as ever, but I was not negatively disposed to the possibility that it could be more than just talking.

And he didn't take me directly home. First, we went for a drive in town, and I didn't mind, because then I could look for E-L at the same time. Then he drove to Gamla Uppsala, and there he stopped and embraced me. We also kissed a little, and then he began to stroke my back, and he unbuttoned my bra. That I didn't object, I think was because of what I felt the first time we met, *that it could just as well have been he and I. I was curious about how it would have been if he had chosen me instead. And after all, it's over between them.*

But if the truth is to be known (and it is), I regret it a little and think that I perhaps shouldn't have done it, because I feel that I must tell E-L, and that isn't going to be easy. I understand that she will be sad when she finds out that I have ridden with him. In any case, she won't be happily surprised and say: "You don't say! How fun! You must tell me about it! What did you think of him?" That isn't what she is going to say! She could do that about someone else, but not about him. So I am a little uneasy, because I don't want us to come apart. After all, she is the one who means the most to me.

Why doesn't she call then? When she phoned yesterday, she said she would. I hope that she hasn't come up against something bad. But in her case, the risk is probably higher that she has done something to harm herself. Drunk too much or tried to kill herself, or…

Oh my God, just think if she saw us yesterday, and that was the straw that broke the camel's back! What if she were in town somewhere and saw me sitting there with Lasse in his car!

But if she were in town, I think I would have seen her. Though she could also have been sitting in a car. And then she saw me and Lasse and thought that all was going to pieces and went away and killed herself!

No, it can't be! But I must get to know if she is at home.

I must call. But how will that be? I ring and ask for her, and her papa says: "No, she isn't home. Do you possibly know where she is? Because she hasn't been home since yesterday afternoon."

In that case, what do I do? Go to town tonight and look for her? Go to the police and report her missing? (But that ought to be up to her parents and not to me, I think.)

Or should I sit at home and wait and become crazy not knowing? No, I'll probably go to town and ask if there is someone who has seen her. I can call Lasse and ask him to come and help me, ha, ha! And then we can sit there in his car and be worried and concerned about what may have happened to her.

What makes me the most uneasy, is that I no longer feel quite certain of that she couldn't do something to herself. Why in the name of heaven don't I? Is it she or I who have undergone a change? Why don't I know, all of a sudden?

On Saturday night she was talking about not going home... But I took it just as the usual drunken talk. I didn't listen very carefully. And she hung herself out the window. I thought that that was also such a thing she usually does when she is drunk and wants to attract attention. I didn't take it seriously.

But what if it were? What if it were an attempt to expose what she had decided to do? And then yesterday, when she saw me in the car with Lasse, that became the triggering factor!

But if she hadn't come home, I think her parents would have called me and asked if I know where she is. So she is certainly at home. That she hasn't called, doesn't have to mean that she has gone away and killed herself. I don't know why I suddenly got that idea.

Ulla Bolinder is a Swedish author, born in Uppsala but today living in Knivsta, not far from Stockholm. She has been working at advertising agency, restaurant, hospital, archives and publishing house. Her first book was published in 1997. In her novels she often deals with social issues with emphasis on the individual.

http://www.ullabolinder.jimdo.com